"So full of twists and turns, it keeps you guessing until the very end. An amazing story of suspense and grace."

—Tracey Bumpus
Managing Editor, FaithTalk

~ ~ ~

"Enough hair-raising action, savvy laughs, and flat-out pulp punch to make me want to come back again and again. Stunning!"

—Matt Bronleewe
music producer for Natalie Imbruglia
and Michael W. Smith

~ ~ ~

"Here's a novel with the feel of real life—fast-paced and thought-provoking."

—Sigmund Brouwer
Bestselling author and coauthor of *The Last Disciple,*
The Weeping Chamber, and the Mars Diaries

~ ~ ~

"If this is what people mean by 'faith-based fiction,' then count me in. *Forgiving Solomon Long* is immediate (though richly layered), refreshingly adventurous, and informed by eternal truths.

"And just when you think you might know where author Chris Well is heading, he throws you a curveball—one that, while altogether surprising, is somehow more realistic than what you might have expected. And, truth be told, far more gratifying."

—Jay Swartzendruber
Editor, *CCM* magazine

"Packed with colorful characters, smart dialogue, and a powerful message...Chris Well masterfully weaves together literary and pop-culture references, Mafia culture, and smatterings of Scripture into a fascinating modern-day parable without sounding preachy or trite. Sure to be a hit."

—Janet Chismar
Senior Editor, Crosswalk.com

CHRIS WELL

Forgiving Solomon Long

HARVEST HOUSE PUBLISHERS

EUGENE, OREGON

Unless otherwise indicated, all Scripture quotations are taken from the New American Standard Bible ®, © 1960, 1962, 1963, 1968, 1971, 1972, 1973, 1975, 1977, 1995 by The Lockman Foundation. Used by permission. (www.Lockman.org)

Verses marked KJV are taken from the King James Version of the Bible.

Cover by Terry Dugan Design, Minneapolis, Minnesota

Cover photo © ImageState/Alamy Images

The hymn chorus on page 281 is from "Turn Your Eyes Upon Jesus" by Helen H. Lemmel, 1922.

This is a work of fiction. Names, characters, places, and incidents are products of the author's imagination or are used fictitiously. Any resemblance to actual persons, living or dead, or to events or locales, is entirely coincidental.

FORGIVING SOLOMON LONG
Copyright © 2005 by Chris Well
Published by Harvest House Publishers
Eugene, Oregon 97402
www.harvesthousepublishers.com

Library of Congress Cataloging-in-Publication Data
Well, Chris, 1966-
   Forgiving Solomon Long / Chris Well.
      p. cm.
   ISBN 0-7369-1405-6 (pbk.)
1. Police—Missouri—Kansas City—Fiction. 2. Crime prevention—Citizen participation—Fiction. 3. Kansas City (Mo.)—Fiction. 4. Organized crime—Fiction. 5. Murder for hire—Fiction. I. Title.
   PS3623.E4657F67 2005
   813'.6—dc22   2004015872

Printed in the United States of America

05 06 07 08 09 10 11 12 13 / BC-KB / 10 9 8 7 6 5 4 3 2 1

For my loving wife, Erica

~ **Part One** ~

"The belief in a supernatural source of evil is
not necessary; men alone are quite capable
of every wickedness."

—JOSEPH CONRAD (1857–1924)

~ ~ ~

"There is an appointed time for everything."

—ECCLESIASTES 3:1

– 1 –

Monday afternoon. On the last day of his life, Father Nathan McNally ran his finger along the back of the pew and found dust. It wasn't that much, really, but the young priest thought he might mention it to the maintenance man—better to hear it from him than from the grumpy senior priest, Father Summers. It was cold out, even for November, and the frigid blast off the streets burst right through the sanctuary every time someone opened the big front doors of the church.

There had been relatively few confessions today; only a little time was left before the session was over. Mrs. Johnson and old Miss Lawry were up front by the altar. Father Mac, as he was popularly known among parishioners, had found out in his brief (but not quite brief enough) conversation with Mrs. Johnson (bless her heart) that, among other family news, her nephew had won some sort of writing award at his school. Old Miss Lawry had little to say—she seemed barely aware of where she was. Too bad. After this stop, the ladies were attending a birthday party for a young niece who had just turned two.

A couple visitors were sitting toward the middle of the sanctuary, here to admire the church design or, perhaps, to simply come in out of the cold. They tried to chat quietly but, of course, the acoustics of the big open room meant the sound still echoed. Father Mac had wondered whether he should offer to speak with them (he did, after all, have a growing reputation as "the people's priest") but decided they would rather be left to their visiting.

As the new priest in the Kansas City–area church, he was also generally considered the most accessible. And chose to be so. He was a modestly handsome young man with soft brown hair and black-rimmed glasses that made him look more well-read than he sometimes was.

As Father Mac waited for last-minute confessions, he began a mental checklist for the week ahead: The local high school had some sporting event coming up. The kids from church would be glad to see him come show his support. They weren't the best players on the court, generally, but they worked hard.

There was another meeting scheduled for the Urban Church Coalition, too, later in the week. He was still waiting to hear where it would be held. The group, made up of local church leaders and prominent residents, hoped to finally break the grip of organized crime on the neighborhood. Father Summers had told him to leave things be, that it was not the place of "the new priest" to meddle in local politics.

But Father Mac knew these people needed to be free. Free from the tyranny of the local despot. Free from the shadow of fear hanging over the neighborhood.

Besides, as he explained to Father Summers, if the local merchants weren't bleeding all their money on a "protection" racket, that meant more money left for the church. That wasn't the young priest's priority, of course, but it seemed like a good point to make.

Father Mac was pulled from his thoughts by the snap of the confessional door. Turning toward the aisle, he made his way to the booth. Stepping inside, the silence was thick. He waited for the person to speak.

Finally: "I'm not too good at this." A man's voice.

"Well, it's not that hard, really," Father Mac replied gently. "As the cliché goes, 'Confession is good for the soul.' And clichés are generally true. Just tell me what's on your mind."

Father Mac could hear the faint noises of the others out in the sanctuary. Someone coughed.

Then the man said, "I should probably tell you I don't have much faith in God."

"I see," Father Mac replied. "Do you mean you feel He let you down at an important time in your life? Like He was too distant?"

"Actually, I have a hard time believing there is a real person called 'God.' And even if there is, he has more important things to do than worry about our little lives. You live, you suffer, you die. Death is a gift."

Father Mac furrowed his brow. "This really is not the proper place for such a discussion," he replied slowly, calmly. "If you would like to schedule an appointment with my office, we could discuss this topic at length. I could share with you some of the resources available on this topic. However, the real purpose of 'confession' is to admit to the sins you have committed."

"I've done a lot of bad things."

Father Mac couldn't place it, but there was something off about this man's voice. Something out of place. "Could you be more specific?"

"You mean, like, you want me to tell you about my childhood or my relationship with my dad or something like that?"

"If you feel the need to," the priest replied. "But I'm not an analyst. This is not about what others have done to you. It's about what you have done. We can go in any direction you like—the important thing is getting your sins out in the open so the Lord can deal with them."

Another lengthy pause. Father Mac pulled off his glasses and wiped them with his robe, his attention wandering. He could hear Mrs. Johnson finish murmuring her prayers at the altar and then try to convince feeble Miss Lawry it was time to go.

The man on the other side of the screen spoke again. "I kill."

"I...I'm sorry," the priest stammered, replacing his glasses on his nose, dimly aware he had only smeared sweat on the lenses. "What did you say?"

"I kill people."

Father Mac couldn't help thinking of a recent news program about a priest caught between his vows and becoming a federal witness. "Do you mean that you killed someone by accident?"

"No." Another pause. Waiting. "For money."

Father Mac mentally sorted through any articles he'd read and movies he'd seen that might prove relevant. He'd read that *The Sopranos* was not as true-to-life as many assumed, but it certainly left a vivid impression. "Why would you do such a thing?" Somewhere in the back of his mind, Father Mac noted the sound of heels clacking out the door, Mrs. Johnson and Miss Lawry headed for the niece's birthday party. He couldn't hear the other visitors; they must have already left.

"Why not?"

The stiffness of the answer shocked the young priest. His mouth went dry. *He's been stalling.*

Father Mac tried to speak, his words catching on sandpaper. The room was silent—he was alone with this man. "Wh-what do you want?" he finally coughed.

"Fat Cat had a good thing going. You church types should have left well enough alone."

As the first bullets splintered through the wooden confessional wall, Father Mac didn't recognize what was happening. What were those popping noises? Then he saw blood. His blood. As he fell against the confessional door and out onto the floor, he felt numb.

A tall man in a tan overcoat stepped out of the other door. Holding his gun with a steady black-gloved hand, he fired two bullets into Father Mac's head. The priest's last thoughts in this world were about apologizing to maintenance for the blood pooling on the floor.

The man grimaced. "You're welcome." Shoving the .45 Taurus and the silencer in separate pockets, Solomon Long walked briskly toward the big doors and pushed confidently out into the sun. As he reached the street corner and checked his watch, he pulled his collar up against the wind. He removed his gloves and pulled an antibacterial towelette out of his pocket, wiped his hands, then crumpled and tossed it. Pulled a wrapped sandwich from one pocket and, munching on tomato and bacon on whole wheat, headed to the bus stop.

With a stiff face, he glanced at the gray sky. Looked like snow.

– 2 –

Wednesday afternoon. Detective Tom Griggs fidgeted, staring out the counselor's office window. He was dimly aware of his wife, Carla, and the counselor making chit-chat. From this vantage point, he could see the top of the Kansas City Power and Light building on Baltimore and 14th.

There had been a rash of muggings on Market lately. He heard that Booker and Croteau were on the job, but—

"Detective Griggs?"

Jarred from his thoughts, Griggs turned to see Carla and the counselor staring. Carla cold. Angry. "Sorry. Just noticing your view."

The counselor smiled calmly—*he should be calm,* Griggs thought as he considered the man's pig face, *he gets paid whether I listen or not*—and got up from his chair. "Actually," the counselor said, walking across to the window, "I was asking what you feel the problem is." He drew the blinds and popped on a lamp. "There. That should help us focus."

"What do I feel the problem is?" Griggs worded it like he thought it was a trick question.

"You see? This is what he does," Carla accused. "He's always somewhere else."

"Please, Mrs. Griggs," the counselor broke in gently, back in his chair, holding up hands in surrender. "Everyone gets their say." Turning to Griggs: "Now, Tom, what were you saying?"

"I'm not sure. Most times, I don't know what I feel about something until I'm told what to feel."

Carla sighed.

The counselor put fingers together in a thoughtful steeple. *Did they teach that in shrink school?* "You feel emotionally smothered," he said to Griggs, taking the comment more seriously than Griggs intended. "You don't feel allowed to create your own emotional identity."

"It was a joke."

"Sometimes a joke is a manifestation of some deeply held feeling. When one doesn't feel comfortable admitting something openly, one might blurt it out as a joke. A sort of test balloon, to see how the idea will be received."

"And sometimes a joke is a joke."

"Sometimes." Calm, letting silence hang in the air.

"I don't know if I feel anything," Griggs shrugged, feeling his teeth with his tongue. Something from lunch stuck there. "I work hard. Sometimes I have a problem leaving the job at work."

The rest of the session was a wash. Some yackety about not blaming each other for everything. Griggs wanted to say, "But you don't know what I have to put up with," but kept his peace in hopes the session would wrap up faster. It didn't. More blah–blah about communication and togetherness and whatever else.

He didn't hear much of it, his head full of developments at the joint task force as his people and the FBI cooperated to clean up Kansas City from the remnants of organized crime. They had indicted dozens of key figures through blood and sweat and hard work. But with each success, somehow Fat Cat—Frank Catalano—swooped in and filled the vacuum.

Griggs casually checked his watch, thinking of the man they had cooling for him back at headquarters. One of Fat Cat's little people, someone the boys in blue hoped would squeal on his boss. Griggs was sure it would only take a little—

"Do you think you can do that, Tom?"

Griggs was startled from his thoughts. Without knowing the question, Griggs nodded at the counselor and grinned. "Sure." Checked his watch. Another five or six minutes, then he could get back to the job.

— 3 —

Earl "Dr. Bones" Havoc paced the garage floor. Derby in hand, the middle-aged man wheezed and again lamented the damage smoking had done to him. Pulling another cigar from his coat pocket, he lit it and continued listening to the Asian man speak.

"It's excellent product," Alan Chin said in smooth English, which still surprised Bones. Shouldn't this kid have a thicker accent? "Top of the line. And we're offering you a good price."

"Oh, I don't doubt that," Bones replied in a scratchy voice, winking at his stoic soldiers stationed across the garage. "But Mr. Catalano has a strict policy against the drug trade. It's bad for business." Took a puff and exhaled dramatically.

Chin looked bored. "Perhaps if we were to speak with Mr. Catalano directly."

Bones' men bristled. The men in the Chinese delegation felt the temperature in the room jump and reached for their weapons.

Bones waved his hands. "Easy, boys," he said, taking another puff. He studied Chin, who still looked bored. "When I speak, you're hearing the voice of Mr. Catalano. I don't know how you do things overseas, but over here I am what you call an underboss. One heartbeat away from owning this city."

Another puff, another exhaled cloud. None of the soldiers had relaxed yet. "But I am all about racial harmony, so we can overlook it this time."

Bones went up to Chin and put an arm around his shoulders. "Tell you what I'm gonna do," he said. "I will take this matter back to Mr. Catalano and we'll see if he has a change of heart."

"And we talk again?" Chin spoke with a soft, measured voice. Bones had a hard time reading this guy.

"Sure, friend," Bones replied, patting the man on the back. He walked away, took one last puff of his cigar, dropped it to the cement and crushed it with his heel. He turned back to Chin and made eye contact. *We're all friends here.* "Sure. We're here to serve you."

After the Chinese hit the road for the evening—why they wanted to meet so early made no sense to Bones—his boys finally relaxed and let out a collective sigh of relief.

"Hey, Dr. Bones," one of them said, "you really gonna go back to Fat Cat with this?"

Bones spit on the cement and winced. "What are you, kidding?"

– 4 –

Detective/Third Grade Charlie Pasch checked his watch and scooted his chair closer to the screen. Behind him, two guys from the Bureau dug poorly wrapped sandwiches out of a wrinkled, brown sack. They were on a "stake-and-bake" (as one of them liked to call it) in an unmarked van on Cotton. The "bake" part of the term referred, of course, to the discomforts of a stakeout during the sweltering summer months. But today—partly sunny with flurries, Charlie had seen online, high 37, low 29—they had been freezing out the evening as the dinner crowd picked up.

On loan from the homicide division, Charlie was the youngest detective working organized crime. And sometimes he felt it. Of course, he had only been on the force a few years, had started out in college with hopes of becoming a screenwriter, before pressure from his dad to get a "real job" led to his present career path.

Through his bank of TV screens, Charlie's focus was on the glass storefront of the Poignard, two blocks away. A fancy steak-and-lobster joint he would have to save up for a month for before even considering taking a date there. It also served as one of the key bases of operations for Frank "Fat Cat" Catalano, with the mobster's businesses occupying most of the building, and his own offices located at the top.

"Charlie," one of the agents chomped, "do that thing."

Charlie pulled at his headphones to hear, still staring at the screens and sipping on stale coffee. At least it was warm. "What thing?"

"That thing with *Star Trek*."

The other agent stopped chewing. "You have a *Star Trek* thing? What, like a stupid pet trick or something?"

Charlie set down the headphones, sighed to himself and turned to the others. "No, I was telling Danny here that one out of every three episodes of *Star Trek* is a remake of *Heart of Darkness*."

"*Heart of Darkness*?"

"By Joseph Conrad."

No response. "The novel."

"Oh." The man frowned, mayonnaise on his lip. "One out of every three episodes, you say?"

"Give or take," Charlie replied. "You know, Kirk and Spock on their ship out in deep, dark space. They get to some remote planet where a Federation captain has disappeared, and the natives have made this guy like their god and reshaped their whole culture around him."

"Really?"

"Sure. The Nazi episode, the one with the Prohibition gangsters—each time, Kirk and Spock find the guy, he dies at the end, and on his deathbed says some variation of 'the horror...the horror.'"

"Ohhh," the man nodded, eyes lighting up. Big grin. "*Apocalypse Now.*"

"Sure." Charlie fought not to roll his eyes. "*Apocalypse Now.*"

"Hey," the first cut in, "I saw Cap'n Picard the other night in some Western. Had a big ranch. Split it up among his daughters."

"That would be *King of Texas*," Charlie said. "A remake of *King Lear.*"

The two men blinked.

"It's a play."

The awkward silence was peppered by street sounds bleeding in from outside the van. The agents both grunted "huh" and went back to their sandwiches. Charlie grabbed a small bag of potato chips, put the headphones back on, and returned to the surveillance.

For three months now, the joint task force had been keeping tabs on the comings and goings at Fat Cat's various holdings. Charlie was newer to the game than some of the others, of course, but it seemed to him that most crime bosses would stick to something more out of the way. But that wasn't Catalano's style. According to the man's file, Catalano had built a million-dollar empire with roots deep into about everything in the city, from the legit (media, construction, trucking) to the illegal (loan sharking, racketeering).

Charlie impatiently checked his watch again. Soon it would be dark. He leaned closer to the screen and waited for something to report.

– 5 –

Across town, Kansas City PD on Locust Street. Griggs paced as Tony "Six-Pack" Danielson squirmed under the hot light. The room reeked of sweat and failure. Griggs glanced over at his partner, fellow detective Michael Jurgens, nonchalantly leaning against the wall, arms folded.

Six-Pack finally said, "I can't."

"Look, Half-Pint—"

"It's 'Six-Pack.' 'Half Pint' was the girl on *Little House on the*—"

Griggs slammed his palm on the table, silencing the man. He traded glances with Jurgens. After five years, this was routine. The two men could finish each other's sentences when it came to grilling these fish. Jurgens once commented it was like he was still married, only it cost less.

Softening, Griggs added, "It doesn't really matter, Tony." Smiled thoughtfully. "If you don't give us Fat Cat, we have no reason to protect you."

Six-Pack's face fell. "Wait..."

"In fact, Tony, we have no reason to hold you at all."

"But—but," Six-Pack protested, "you caught me breaking the law, fair and square. You gotta take me in!"

"I'm sorry, Tony," Griggs offered, noting his partner's cracked grin. "We just don't have enough evidence to hold you." Griggs checked his watch. He and Jurgens hoped to hit the batting cage that afternoon.

"I can tell you stuff." Six-Pack looked down at the table, eyes bugged, breathing heavily through his nose. Desperate. "I want to confess."

Griggs sat back down in the chair across the table. He set his elbows on the sticky table top. "Tell me what you got."

"You know that warehouse gig last month? I did that."

Griggs paid close attention to Six-Pack's body language. Hugging his arms close, usually an indicator of deception.

Griggs also watched the eyes. When a person remembers something, the eyes typically point up and left. When making something up, the eyes go up and to the right.

"I planned the whole thing. Did the research, called the guys—"

"Who did you call?"

"Freddie Carbone. Hadley Smith." Eyes up and right. "We jacked the truck from a rental lot. Cut the fence, took the truck to the warehouse, grabbed all the computer crap we could—"

Griggs cut him off with a dramatic sigh. "You're lying." He leaned forward and murmured icily, "If people weren't watching us right now, I'd kick your lying teeth in." Threats. Power. That was all this kind understood.

"But..." Six-Pack trailed off. He was looking desperate. "Manelli will kill me."

"Nothing we can do. Unless, of course, you turn over Fat Cat. Small price for your life."

Six-Pack's head hung low. "I can't do that," he whispered hoarsely, on the verge of tears. "You don't mess with Fat Cat."

Jurgens grumbled, "You don't have a lot of options."

The detectives let silence fill the room for several painful minutes, nothing but the rhythmic hum of overhead lights and the tortured breathing of Six-Pack. But, squirm as he might, he was not going to talk.

Fine. Griggs went to the door and opened it. "Cut him loose," he told the uniformed officer outside, loud enough for Six-Pack to hear. "We don't need him."

It was a cruel gamble. For reasons surveillance hadn't yet figured out, Tony Six-Pack had done something to incur the wrath of a crime lord in St. Louis. Normally, the weasel was protected under the graces of Fat Cat, but apparently that relationship had gone south. Considering Tony's nickname—they started calling him "half-dozen" after he got a reputation of only getting half a job done, and somewhere along the way it morphed into "six-pack"—it was a good bet he'd halved the wrong job this time.

As Six-Pack was escorted out by the KC police, Griggs snatched his suit coat off the back of a chair and headed for the door. Jurgens followed. "I didn't think you would really unload him," Jurgens grimaced. "Are you sure about this?"

Griggs tried to smile; it was more a frown. "If he's useless to Fat Cat, he might as well turn snitch. If he's not talking to us, he's useless to us, too. And without real protective custody, he's dead." They continued down the hall. "Dead on the street, dead in the clink, dead in the shower—he's dead, call the florist and toss some dirt on him."

Griggs stopped and turned to Jurgens. "But if we throw him out to the dogs," he said in a low and distinct tone, "he might be frightened into making the right choice."

They neared the exit, blinding sunlight bursting through big glass. "Besides," Jurgens commented, "even if Six-Pack dies, what have we really lost?"

Griggs didn't answer.

~ 6 ~

Later that night, two of Catalano's men nervously stood by the little door outside the Poignard, unaware that federal agents were videotaping from two blocks away.

"So, he's in this Broadway show version of *Sweet Smell of Success*," said the gaunt Albert Holland, scuffing one of his shoes nervously on the sidewalk.

"What," asked the plumper Todd Sallis, rubbing hands to fight the cold, "with people singing and stuff?"

"I think so."

Just back from dropping off a corpse at the construction site outside town, now they had to make their report to Fat Cat— *Mister* Catalano. Always a scary thing, ever since what happened to Lenny "The Heap" Conway after he whacked a guy by mistake who was still useful to the boss (confusion over multiple meanings of the word "bought"—who knew this was the one time the boss actually meant a cash transaction?) You didn't want what happened to The Heap.

"*Sweet Smell of Success*? With Burt Lancaster and Tony Curtis?"

"That's the one." Knowing the boss wouldn't like them jim-dawdling, Holland finally pulled open the nondescript door to the stairwell, entered, and pressed for the elevator, followed closely by Sallis.

"Now a musical comedy."

The elevator doors opened and Holland went in first. "You know what else I liked Tony Curtis in? That movie with Marilyn Monroe." He pressed for the top floor. The doors closed.

The elevator hummed as it rose, floor by floor, lighted buttons flickering. "You know," Sallis said, "somebody made a musical outta that, too."

"Really? Now that makes a kinda sense."

"Yup," Sallis said. "Played a couple of summers back at the Starlight. Tony Curtis was in it, but instead'a the young guy, this time he played the geezer millionaire."

As they neared their floor, he turned to Holland. "You think Tony Curtis is connected?"

The doors whooshed open and the conversation abruptly stopped. The lights were on in the hall, but the offices were dark. If it weren't for the glow of the boss' cigar reflecting on the window, they might have thought the place empty.

They reverently pushed through glass doors. Behind the desk, Mister Catalano—no one called him *Fat Cat* to his face—had his exec chair swiveled toward big, tinted windows, facing the city below.

Holland cleared his throat politely. Neither he nor Sallis dared speak first. When the boss said, "Tell me," Holland replied with false casualness, "Ronald Newman is no longer a problem."

Catalano brought a lit cigar to his knobby lips and puffed. "Brilliant."

Holland cleared his throat. "I also got a call from Zimmy," he said. "Six-Pack is out."

Clouds swirled as the boss chuckled. "Leave him alone."

"But boss," Sallis blurted, "they'll kill him."

The chair whipped around. Catalano's eyes glowed dull red—must have a been a trick of the light. "Don't be brilliant," he bristled.

Holland and Sallis froze. Catalano relaxed and tossed a gentle smile, exhaled another cloud, and swiveled back to the window. "Is that it?"

"Yes, sir," replied Holland. Meek.

"Leave us."

Holland and Sallis quickly exited, relieved, assuming "us" was meant in the royal sense. After the two were gone, a voice cut the blackness. "What was that all about?"

Catalano turned toward where the man was sitting in darkness, on a couch against the far wall. The man lit a menthol, the flicker illuminating crags in his face.

"Just some quote–unquote business," Catalano replied, voice raspy. "A former associate has run into some trouble."

"You're hanging him out?"

"My quote–unquote compassion got limits." Another puff from the cigar. "Besides, if Tommy Manelli kills one of my people inside my own territory, I gotta protect my interests."

"Ahhh," the man caught on. "Then you have an excuse to move in on St. Louis."

"Exactly." Catalano poured more dark liqueur into his tumbler, hand trembling slightly. "All the more reason for me to need a judge in my...circle of friends." He held the cigar high in a salute. "A man needs all the friends he can get."

Catalano burst into a fit of coughing. After he composed himself, he said, "Especially with the changes I have in mind."

"How are your sons, Mr. Catalano?"

"They're good, they're good," the old man replied. "It's always a thrill when your sons follow you into the family business." Another puff on his cigar. "These last few years, they've really proven themselves. Gino is a real operator. Ritchie has the muscle. And Frankie has the heart."

Catalano took another puff. Watched the cloud of smoke float and dissipate. "Thank you, by the way, for throwing your influence and helping with Frankie's...situation."

"It was the least I could do," the other man said. "It would have been a shame if he had been tied up in jail and had to miss the party Sunday night. Still planning to make your big announcement?"

Catalano coughed, wiping a tear from his left eye. "I can't think of a better time. All the necessary players will be in the room." Smoke rings. "Once I pass on the day-to-day operations, I'll be free to devote my attention to the big picture."

The guest took a long drag from his cigarette, ash falling to the floor. "It's gonna be some birthday party."

— 7 —

Pastor Fresno Jones of Mercy Street World Mission Church finished his final points from the pulpit, like rounding third base and heading for home. He had to shout above the whirring of the fans. Of course, when you're feelin' the Holy Ghost on you, ain't nobody preachin' quiet.

"This is a *no drugs* zone! This is a *no lust* zone!" The congregation urged him on with "uh-huhs" and "hm-hmms" and claps of their own.

"This is a *no pornography* zone! This is a *no gambling* zone!" He pushed his glasses back up the bridge of his nose. "Jesus said, *If I be lifted up, I will draw all men unto me!* He didn't say *I will draw all enemies*—He said *I will draw* all *men!* When we lift Jesus high, it's like putting our banner high, telling the enemy, *You're not welcome here!*" More shouts of approval.

He stopped a moment. It got quiet, except for the steady buzz of the fans. "But it's not enough to simply forbid the enemy from coming here," he rasped. "Jesus told us to go."

Building steam again. "Jesus told us in Acts 1 to take Jerusalem"—[*Yep!*]—"and Judah"—[*That's right!*]—"and Samaria" —[*uh-huh!*]—"and the ends of the Earth!" Shouts. Clapping.

"He says in Matthew 16 that the very gates of *hell* cannot prevail against us!" [*Amen!*] "Now, have you ever heard'a anyone bein' attacked by a gate?" [*Preach it!*] "No one was ever sitting quietly at home, watching their *Monday Night Football* or their *Everybody Loves Raymond* or their *Law & Order,* and suddenly there was a crash outside and it was a gate come to attack them!" [*Yep!*] "Nobody was ever just minding their own business and suddenly, *Hey! This is the gate! We've come to rob you!*" [*You got that right!*]

"We got to storm the gates! We got to influence and change this culture! We got to stop watching from the outside and tsk-tsking and pointing our fingers and raising our eyebrows and we got to roll up our sleeves and get in there and change the world!"

As he built momentum, the pews started to roar. "It's not enough to send missionaries *out* to the bushes and *out* to the jungles and *out* to the rice fields!" [*Yes!*] "We have got to start sending missionaries *into* the world of sports!" [*That's good!*]

"And *into* entertainment!" [*Amen!*] "And *medicine* and *literature* and *politics!*" [*That's right!*]

"Until it's about Monday Night *Revival!* And Everybody Loves *Jesus!* And *God's* Law & Order!"

The crowd thundered shouts and applause. Pastor Fresno pulled out a kerchief and wiped sweat off his face. He pointed upward. "That's right, give Him praise!"

After the service, the pastor stepped down from behind the pulpit and joined the ministry team on the floor. A woman in her early twenties pressed through the crowd. "Pastor Fresno, I don't know what to do," she sniffled.

His face held a look of gentle concern. "What is it?"

"I think my dad's in trouble. Some men were in the store this afternoon."

It took him a second to place her: This was Abbey, Tyler Smart's daughter. Tyler owned the small hardware store three blocks over.

"They went to the back to talk to my dad and...I don't know, something just felt wrong. I think they threatened my dad. When they passed me on the way out, I got this strange feeling off them."

"I see." It sounded like Fat Cat's men had paid a little visit to check on their "insurance." Times were tough in the neighborhood—some local store owners were having trouble keeping up payments. Of course, the recent death of Father Mac had sent the expected shock waves of fear through the locals.

Pastor Jones mentally kicked himself again for letting the problem go on as long as he had. But ever since he had the revelation of reclaiming the culture for the Kingdom, he knew this was part of it. People needed to be free of tyranny, especially from despots like Fat Cat.

But sending this girl to the police was tricky, too. You never quite knew who was on the payroll.

"Abbey," he said gently, "let me look into this, okay? I'll talk to your father. Maybe we can discuss this problem at the next Coalition meeting."

She sniffled again. "Okay." She hugged him, he patted her on the back, and she walked away. Pastor Jones met with the remaining members of his flock, huddled around the front of the pulpit. He only half-listened, his thoughts divided between his present duty here and his duty toward the community group. In light of Father Mac's death, they needed to be doubly sure their next meeting place was safe.

He never noticed the eyes watching from the street.

～ 8 ～

As Solo left the church service, he turned his collar up against the rising wind and glanced up at the nearing clouds. Under his breath, he cursed the pastor and God.

The wind sounded shrill in his ears, reminding him of his mother. "The Lord sees you," he heard in his mother's unforgiving screech. "He knows how worthless you are."

Solo navigated his way through the pedestrians and litter on the sidewalk, randomly thinking back to his childhood. His dad drinking earlier and earlier in the day. His mother charged up by an all-day evangelist marathon of Professor Joe Butcher ("Bless Your Heart!") and Angel Mosley and *The Stone River Hour*. She never focused her righteous anger on her soggy husband, but always on the boy. "The Good Book says if you spare the beating you ruin the child," she would say in justification.

One of the kids at school had told him the Bible also said not to provoke your children to wrath, but Solo could never find the spot for himself.

Fighting off memories of the rhythmic beatings as she wailed "Onward, Christian Soldiers," Solo walked the several blocks to Zoo Girls, where he had parked his nondescript Dodge. Feeling the need to de-church, he went inside.

Eyes adjusting to darkness, Solo nodded a subtle greeting to Joey, the thick-necked bouncer, and headed to the bar to order something with a kick. While in town working for Fat Cat, Solo got free drinks.

"Hey, Solo! You workin'?"

Solo turned to see Saul "Turk" Bendetti take the bar stool next to him. In addition to being one of Fat Cat's key men, Turk also owned the club. Even in the dim lighting, the short man's leathered face showed the wear and tear he had seen as a made man. Nobody messed with Turk.

Solo took a sip. "I was." Another sip, slowly. "But I got enough religion for one night and came here."

"Say it ain't so." Turk motioned to the barkeep to bring him the usual. As Turk waved, Solo noticed the nub on his left hand, the fourth finger missing at the knuckle.

"Naw, it ain't like that." Solo glanced around the bar to make sure nobody was paying attention. He considered the possibility of listening devices, but decided the throbbing music shielded them. The writhing bodies he ignored. "I got a job to take care of certain...elements."

"Oh, so you hadda go to church."

"Righhht." Solo forced a grin.

Turk took a swig and whirled around to see what else was going on at the Zoo. He turned back to Solo, who was still dully staring at the bar and sipping. Thinking. "So, what's the story with these people, anyways?"

Solo was abruptly pulled from his drink. "What?"

"The picketers, what's with that?"

Solo shrugged. "Does it matter?"

"No, I'm just sayin'," Turk went on, "business was cruising along fine, the neighborhood was what it was, and people got along. Now suddenly they get it in themselves to turn over the orange cart."

"Apple cart."

"What?"

"The phrase is 'turn over the apple cart.'"

"Apple cart, canoe, I don't care how you say it, why are they causing trouble now?"

Solo made a *hmm* face. "Sometimes the Feds make trouble. Sometimes the cops make trouble. How is this different?"

"Ahhh," Turk said in an *aha* voice, "but Feds and cops see that stuff on TV all the time. They see Gene Hackman and get it in their heads." Turk leaned in close, which made Solo uncomfortable. "But these churchies and these store owners— where did *they* get the idea to cause trouble? Gene Hackman ain't never played no reverend I know of."

Solo didn't feel like correcting him, so he sipped his glass dry and changed the subject. "Heard you had some excitement last month." He motioned to the bartender for a refill.

Turk pulled back to his own space and laughed. "Oh, you mean those Russkies?"

"Yeah, that was somethin'," the bartender butted in, grinning stupidly, leaning forward on the counter.

"Shut up, Vito, I'm talking here," Turk warned gruffly, then turned back toward Solo with an easy smile. Solo had heard the story already, but he wasn't going to mention it *now*. Turk's sudden bursts of anger were legendary. Solo was sure he could take him if it came to it, but there was no paycheck in it, so he slurped and listened.

"So," Turk continued, a hand on Solo's shoulder, "these guys in these black coats and beards and dark glasses come around the club here, don't hardly know the language, ya know?" He chuckled. "Come in here and talk to one a' tha girls with that Commie accent so thick she don't know what the pig he's talking about."

What the pig? "Uh-huh." Slurp.

"So they come back a coupla days later and catch Vito here behind the bar and he eventually figgers out they're trying to muscle him with some kinda protection racket." Turk started laughing harder, wheezing a bit at the man's naiveté. Or nerve. Solo didn't really care which.

"So Vito tells them, 'Look, you gotta talk to the boss,' so then the loser comes back again that afternoon and this time I'm around, ya know? And Vito finds me back in the office and says, 'Boss, I think you better talk to this guy.' "

"Uh-huh," Solo agreed, slurping again from his glass. "So the guy came back alone?"

"Yeah," Turk agreed, then caught himself. "I mean, the other o'his guys are outside waiting in the car, I guess they had the car warming outside or whatever.

"And then this long-haired Commie trash explains that I hafta pay him for 'protection.' So I start laughing in his piggin' face right there, I'm wiping a tear outta my eye and I tells him, 'I don't think I have to worry about no "protection," ' you know? Like, he still don't know who I am."

Solo nodded, set his glass down. It was empty, but he didn't really want another drink. "I guess that made you pretty mad."

"Oh, that wasn't even the kisser!" Turk grabbed Solo's arm to emphasize that the good part was coming: "So, this guy pulls out this Polaroid of the club—you know, those instant deals where you click, and then this picture slides out, and you flap it around like a piggin' seagull until the picture appears?"

"Yeah."

"Like, I didn't even know they made those cameras anymore—I thought everyone had disposables or digital or whatever."

"Sure, sure," Solo said with forced casualness.

"And then this loser pulls out a lighter and torches the Polaroid right in front'a me," Turk cackled, "and he's looking at me with this stupid grin and these crooked teeth and I realize he's threatening me! *Me!*"

"Really?" Pretend surprise. Pretend indignation.

"Yeah," Turk continued, oblivious to the condescension in Solo's voice. "I'm all, 'Who do you think you are, coming here in my club and threatening me?' And I kick him in the shins or whatever and, like, elbow his neck and then I'm seeing red, right?"

"Sure," Solo said, as Turk howled with laughter.

"So the next thing I know, we're out back in the alley, and he's in the dumpster and his friends have all scat off in their old Dodge," Turk howled, "and then poor Vito here has to find someplace to dump the body!"

Turk wheezed another laugh, then took a victorious gulp of his beer and wiped his mouth on his sleeve. "True story."

"Sounds like a real Kodak moment."

Turk looked down at the counter and glowered. "Nobody comes into my bar and treats me like that," he grumbled to no one in particular. "Nobody."

~ 9 ~

Back at the station. Griggs at his desk, thinking. Time to call it a night and go home; but these days, going home for dinner meant another fight, trading blame again for the death of their daughter—or another night of chilly silence. He hadn't decided which he disliked more.

He looked again at the police report on the priest shooting. Clearly a professional hit. Fat Cat had to have ordered it. But so far nobody in the surveillance team had heard or seen anything useful to connect the dots.

On the wall across from him was a chart he had meticulously pieced together over the last few months. Photos, mug shots, surveillance pics of known members of Catalano's criminal network. Griggs looked over the faces of some of the key players.

Earl "Dr. Bones" Havoc, Catalano's underboss. One of the smarter men in the system, a dark streak percolating under his smooth and intelligent exterior. Barring any surprises, next man in line behind Fat Cat to run the show. Whatever else may happen, Bones was the man to watch.

Saul "Turk" Bendetti, probably the oldest friend Fat Cat had in the world, all the way back to parochial school. There were stories about how he lost his finger; Griggs wondered who knew the real story anymore.

Gino Catalano, Fat Cat's oldest son. Under that thick charm was some mean blood. As the son of the boss, he had been shielded from the consequences of some of his childhood shenanigans. As he got older, his criminal activity became more sophisticated.

Ritchie Catalano, Fat Cat's middle child. Probably started causing trouble right out of the cradle. This one had no charm —just a penchant for grabbing what he wanted. Thanks to anger management issues, had been in and out of jail several times in just the past couple years, but none of the major stuff had stuck.

Frankie Catalano, Fat Cat's youngest. By all accounts, sweeter disposition than his gene pool deserved. Not that he didn't have a rap sheet, too, of course.

An assortment of other photos along the chart. Most of the known associates. In the center a flabby and hostile Frank Catalano, caught in an unflattering mood. Griggs stared at the photograph.

He found himself fiddling with his wedding ring and debating again whether to go home.

– 10 –

Solo excused himself from the company of Turk at the Zoo Girls club and walked outside into the brisk chill of the day. He knew better than to take the direct route back to the hotel. Clutching a flyer hailing Kansas City as the "city of fountains" and a set of directions printed off the Internet, he took I-29 SOUTH/US-71 SOUTH—he wondered what the locals called it—and, a few exits later, found himself on CHOUTEAU TRAFFICWAY, exit #9. Sitting at 3815 N CHOTEAU TRFY, KANSAS CITY was the "Children's Fountain," erected 1995, one of several city fountains located north of the Missouri River.

Parking and walking, he saw six sculptures of children playing. He didn't quite understand a couple of the figures, although he could make out a ballerina and a soccer player.

Checking his watch, Solo decided it was time to check in with Gus. He began looking for a safe pay phone.

Solo hated cell phones. Hated the idea of people being able to reach you anywhere, anytime. You can't be alone with your thoughts when every telemarketer or wrong number is a phone call away.

Besides, he'd heard about one contractor, Mack the Hammer, who was in the middle of a gig and forgot to turn off his cell. It went off at the worst time, and now he was serving twenty-to-life.

A man in Solo's line of work needed to be able to run silent at a moment's notice. He didn't need to fiddle-foo around with some gadget every time he was stalking a target.

It drove Gus nuts. "Solo," he'd say, "you gotta be reachable."

"But a cell phone means my name on another database."

"So's a lottery ticket, but that don't mean the cops are gonna come banging on your door every time you make a call."

Solo wasn't too sure about that last point. Surveillance seemed to make a new leap every day. "Invisible" was getting hard to come by.

Gus would sigh and throw up his hands. "Fine! You don't wanna join the rest of us in the twenty-first century? Fine!" Then he would point and use a lecture voice. "But you gotta be reachable. You check in, you hear me? I don't wanna get an update from a client—like, say, they change their minds—and then I can't reach you because you're offing some target for gratis."

"Gus, the cops are a half-step away from hacking your calls to listen in, then using your cell as a tracking device."

"The cops don't do any of that stuff. You're paranoid, Solo."

The conversation generally ended with Solo promising to make regular calls from the road—always from a pay phone, in a secluded place, after Solo determined it was safe.

Like now, for instance. Solo had already passed up two pay phones because there was somebody nearby or because he didn't like the lay of the land. He kept walking 'til he found one to his liking. Deciding it was safe, he checked for the dial tone and started plunking coins in the slot.

— 11 —

Thursday. Dinner at the Griggses' house. The incessant ticking of the grandfather clock. The stench of lavender poms. The occasional shriek of silverware scraping ceramic. Griggs cut his gray steak (he would have preferred dull pink), jabbed a square piece with the fork, and stuck it in his mouth. He chewed, avoiding eye contact with Carla. The third place setting was empty, as it was every night. Kayla Rae was never coming back.

Most nights, Griggs had to work at keeping his mind occupied during dinner. Tonight wasn't a problem. Following their little talk with Six-Pack, Griggs and Jurgens had gone to check on the boys in the surveillance van. Keeping tabs on Fat Cat's business wasn't easy, considering the many enterprises he held in his stubby fingers. Their case was hindered by a judge who refused to let them set all the necessary taps. They gathered bits and pieces watching from the outside, but this could take years.

Griggs' suspicion—that someone must be feeding Fat Cat information—was just a hunch. The "facts"—a chip from a questionable source, a vague reference on a tap—were not legally admissible. Worse, they were unconvincing to others in the department. In time, Griggs eventually learned to keep his suspicions to himself.

Carla broke the silence. "You remember we have another session Monday, don't you?"

Griggs stopped chewing. Looked up. "What?"

"Monday," she repeated. "Counseling." She paused and acted as if she were speaking to a child. "Remember?"

He sighed through his nose and started chewing again. "Yes, I remember."

"I hope you can be there in mind as well as body."

"Yes, dear."

"If you decide to come at all."

"Carla, I *told* you, that other time was something I couldn't help." He tried to focus again on steak and peas. His mind was swirling. "I wish you would try to understand what's going on at work right now," he said, staring at the place setting. "This Fat Cat case is a big deal. If we break this, it could mean a promotion."

He motioned around with his knife at the large, immaculate dining room. "We could get a bigger house, move to a nicer neighborhood—"

"A bigger house? We're barely together in the one we have," she accused. Her elbows jutted as she cut her steak with dramatic flair. "And this is a *great* neighborhood."

Griggs slammed his fork and knife down on the table. The glasses and plates rattled. Carla looked at him. Startled. His fury passed in a moment and his face relaxed. He pushed back his chair and stood up. Transferred the cloth napkin from his lap to atop his partially eaten dinner. He glanced at Carla and their eyes locked. "You can invent reasons to be upset, but I'm not going to invent reasons to apologize," he said, struggling to keep his voice steady. "You're mad because you choose to be mad."

As he turned to leave the table, she said softly, "I love you, Thomas."

He stood a moment, his back to the table. "Actions speak louder than words," he grumbled as he left the dining room.

In the living room, he plopped into the big fluffy lounge chair. *Actions speak louder than words,* he repeated mentally. It was a stupid thing to say.

He pulled the paper out from under himself and searched for the TV remote. After all, she still took care of him, took care of the house. The remote wasn't in the drawer. They had simply lost the ability to communicate, and he always seemed to fumble with the words and make it worse. He searched the coffee table and the magazine bucket and finally found the remote in the seat cushion under him.

Throughout the search, he had tossed aside several of Carla's half-knitted projects—scarves, ear warmers, he wasn't sure what they were supposed to be. All he knew was that, ever since the death of their daughter, she had taken up the nervous habit of knitting every free moment, then abandoning each project halfway through to start the next.

Flipping channels, he barely watched images as they flickered past. He couldn't stop thinking about Judge Reynolds, who had refused them the legal access they needed to build their case against Fat Cat. Claimed they didn't have "just cause."

Griggs hoped that was really it. The alternative—that Reynolds was one more name on the payroll—was not pleasant. Reynolds had a gruff manner, but he'd always seemed like a straight arrow.

Of course, there was that time Griggs almost decked His Honor. "Why do we care about the Mafia?" Reynolds had asked. "It's just a bunch of lowlifes shooting other lowlifes."

Now, Griggs and company were trying to circumvent the good judge, but that was tricky—and political. Once you got a judge mad at you, it always came back to bite you.

It was important to make sure every shred of evidence was obtained legally or it wouldn't stick. And Griggs wanted it to stick.

As soon as Six-Pack regained his senses and came in off the street, Griggs knew it would make a great lead. Not that Fat Cat would have trusted Six-Pack with a lot of sensitive information, but Tony would have picked up enough to point them to the next set of leads. Follow the trail of dead mice and sooner or later you're bound to find the cat.

As Griggs idly flipped through the paper, he vaguely noticed the phone ringing. He turned up the TV, though he wasn't really watching this infomercial either.

"Tom!" Carla was in the doorway, holding out the receiver. How long had she been there?

"Okay, okay," he muttered, fumbling for the mute button.

"It's Michael," she said.

He crawled out of the chair and reached for the phone. "This is Griggs."

"Hey, Griggs," he heard Jurgens say in a tinny voice. "They found Six-Pack."

"Yeah?"

"He was in a dumpster by the mission on Woodward."

– 12 –

Still chewing, Frank Catalano wiped the alfredo sauce from his mouth with a cloth napkin and motioned to the waiter for more wine. At either side were Turk and Dr. Bones.

The greasy kid across the table, Howie Jay, continued. "All I'm sayin' is that the boss had an agreement with you folks," he grunted, between gnaws on his chicken and gulps of beer and the occasional coming up for air.

Catalano considered the little man as they dined in the large, private room in the back of the Poignard. This five-star establishment was a jewel in his empire, one that actually turned an honest profit. He wiped his mouth again and regally set the napkin atop the table.

"I appreciate your visit," Catalano said in a low, no-nonsense tone, "but I don't think it would be in my best quote–unquote interest to continue the arrangement my predecessor had with your organization."

"But—"

Catalano cut him short with a look. "Don't be brilliant with me. I made a point of listening to you as a favor to our friends in Chicago. But now, you'll have to excuse us." He motioned to Turk and Bones. "We have real business."

Howie's face reddened. "But I don't think you understan' what I'm talkin' about, Fat Cat..."

Catalano's men stiffened. *He had just called the boss "Fat Cat."*

One of the FBI agents listening from the van outside mumbled to himself, "Ooh, that was a mistake."

Catalano's eyes flashed for a second. An eternity.

Realizing his error, blood drained from Howie's face as his fork clattered to his plate. "I-I'm sorry, Mister Catalano— honest!" He pushed back from the table, his chair clunking to the floor. "I din't meanta—"

Catalano dully glanced at the blond thug by the door. "Please escort this gentleman out." The leather-jacketed man and a darker man who had been sitting by the bar each grabbed Howie by an elbow and dragged him toward the back exit.

"No, please," Howie whined, digging heels in carpet, "you gotta understand how sorry I am!"

As the man was pushed through the back hall, wailing, Catalano didn't bother turning around. "I'm sure you are," he grumbled softly.

"You'd think they'd learn," Turk said, taking a swig of his bottle of beer.

The waiter appeared, removing all evidence of Howie from the table. No eye contact with any of the men. "Is that all, sirs?"

Catalano thought for a moment. "You know, Marcel, I do believe I would like some tiramisu."

"Very good, sir."

In the van outside, one of the special agents turned the infrared cam toward the alley behind the Poignard, as Howie was kicked senseless by the thugs. "Do we help the poor guy?"

The other flipped to the next page of his magazine. "Call for a black-and-white." He glanced up at the screens a moment, then flicked eyes back to the magazine. "And an ambulance."

Inside, the waiter presented the boss with his dessert and quickly exited, bumping into a thick man in a dark jacket. When the man reached Catalano's table, the boss was sipping wine, eyes closed, deep in thought. The man stood silently, arms respectfully crossed in front of him, waiting. After a moment, Catalano acknowledged him. "Tell me."

"There's been a development, Mr. Catalano," the man leaned in and whispered. "They found Six-Pack."

– 13 –

At the homeless shelter on Woodward, the Lifehouse, Pastor Fresno Jones stuck the big spoon into the oversized pot of stew and glopped it onto the next tin plate. He looked up at the homeless man and smiled. The pastor made a point to make eye contact and share a smile with each and every person who came through the line. To some of these people, it was the best thing he could offer—all the preaching in the world could not reach a man if you didn't first treat him *like* a man.

He felt a rumble in his stomach. He and his family had decided to fast one dinner a week and spend an hour at the mission serving others. His wife, Sheila, was back in the kitchen cooking. His daughter, Amelia, was helping scrub plates in the big metal sink.

He turned his eyes and smiles back to the line and recognized the next man. "Well, hello there, Homer," the pastor greeted cheerily. "I'm surprised to see you this far back in line. I was starting to worry."

"Hi, Reverend," Homer answered sheepishly, grinning. "I hadda talk with the cops earlier."

"Oh?" Pastor Fresno raised both eyebrows in a friendly face. "I hope you didn't get into trouble?"

"Nothing like that, Reverend. I jes' found a body in the dumpster out back and hadda tell somebody about it."

The pastor wasn't sure how to react. First Father Mac, and now this. Then he noticed the uniformed officers who had entered, gently inquiring of the mission's patrons if they had seen anything. He turned back to Homer. "Well, I'm glad you're okay."

Homer, plate of glop and bread in hands, moved to the next station, and now Pastor Fresno was digging up a new smile for the next person in line.

If he'd paid closer attention to the room, Pastor Fresno might've noticed the man in the back corner, the lapels of his overcoat turned up to shield his face. As the officers continued to move from table to table, nobody saw Solo quietly head for the back door.

— 14 —

Flurries pelted the dark streets. Solo, still feeling the stranger in this town, tentatively dodged through passersby on the sidewalk, seeking shelter. He had to get inside somewhere and look inconspicuous. He didn't know who had whacked this guy they were talking about back at the mission, but the last thing a pro needed was to be near the scene of someone else's job.

He would need to go to another name on the list and come back to preacher man.

As snow fell, he ducked into Lost And Found, a collectibles store—used LPs, used books, all sorts of stuff. As the door banged shut with a ring, Solo smiled at the shelves overflowing with worn paperbacks.

But first he went to the LPs. It was a relief to hear the sounds of Fleetwood Mac crackling overhead in full vinyl glory. None of that nu metal or gangsta trash. It was a matter of quality, Solo told himself, and the new "thangs" weren't as good as the classics. Rolling Stones. KISS. AC/DC.

As he flipped through raggedy album covers, he stumbled across an old Kansas album and flipped it over. Great—"Dust in the Wind." *You live, you suffer, you die.* It was the mantra Solo chanted to himself whenever he doubted his calling. He wasn't killing these people—he was rescuing them.

He spent some time in the used books, too, but didn't see much worth getting excited about. After pocketing a copy of *Les Misérables*—it wasn't his first choice, but the kid at the register was unusually attentive—Solo got to his car and drove out to his ratty motel. It was cheap, and everybody kept to themselves. After circling a couple of times, he parked in back.

Solo shuffled toward the flicker of the tiny motel office. Inside, a pimply kid named Wally hunched behind the front desk, watching a tiny TV and trying to read the funny pages from the *Star*. The kid looked up and grinned stupidly. "H'yuh."

"Any messages?"

"Nope."

Solo pulled out his money clip, peeled off a fiver, and handed it to the kid. "Let me know."

"Sure thing."

Solo turned and strode out to the parking lot toward his room. The kid was an idiot, but he knew the score.

Inside his room, Solo flicked on the lights and the TV. He considered the greasy, half-eaten drive-thru meal lying on the unmade bed, then reached for the open bag of jelly beans on the nightstand and started picking out the green ones. Each one made a dull *ping* as it connected with the metal trash can.

～ 15 ～

Friday. Outside the station, cold and cloudy. Inside, the squad of six only a little less so. Four cops and a couple of Feds, trafficking leads. It was good to bond—often it felt like them against the world. They knew there were others in the system competing for the same collar, clomping all over what could have been legitimate evidence.

Griggs, sitting on the edge of his desk, nodded to Charlie. "What have you got?"

The kid jolted in his chair, caught stealing a glance at Detective Jordan Hall, a cute redhead in her late twenties. Trying to play it casual, Charlie shrugged.

"Nothing special. As far as we could tell, only regular folks went through the front doors at the Poignard."

Special Agent Martin O'Malley, one of the Feds, cut in. "Actually, at least one mob guy visited last night." To Charlie's confused look, he added, "After you took off, sport. It was a weasel from out of town. Sounded like he worked for Joey Pratt."

Griggs perked up. "Pratt?"

"Yep," O'Malley said. "We got him on tape making some business talk with Fat Cat."

Charlie squeaked, "Who was this guy?"

"Nobody you would have made," O'Malley encouraged. "This kid was in from Chicago to discuss some business. We'll have the transcript by lunch."

"Good," Griggs said, turning back to Charlie. "Bring the video in and we'll get a look at this guy. Either going in or coming out."

"Oh, you got footage of him coming out." O'Malley turned and nodded toward Jackson. "Jacks and I are developing some pictures of him leaving via the back exit. Not pretty."

Jacks snickered. "Apparently, the kid called Catalano 'Fat Cat' to his face."

The room winced collectively. Griggs chuckled grimly, "I can imagine the pictures now." He looked up. "Is he still alive?"

"As far as we know," O'Malley said. "We called 9-1-1, so there should be a police report. Not that he would have pressed charges."

"Of course not," Griggs agreed, stretching for a file folder. It wasn't the one he wanted, so he flipped through a stack until he found another one, yanking it out and opening it. "Speaking of police reports," he said, "any updates on this priest situation?"

Detective Hall—Charlie was right, she was cute, but also sharp—spoke up. "What do you mean 'updates'?"

"We know this is part of the picture," Griggs answered matter-of-factly. "We just don't know where it fits."

Charlie turned to Hall and asked her, "The priest started that neighborhood watch or whatever, right?"

"Sure," she replied, "but there's nothing physical to link it to Fat Cat. For that matter, there's nothing to link it to anybody. No gun recovered, no witnesses—"

"In broad daylight, in a public place," Griggs sighed.

"Yes," Hall agreed. "But this time I think when people say they didn't see anything, they really mean it. This guy was pro."

"All the more reason to think Fat Cat was involved," Griggs said. "Even if he didn't place the order himself."

"He made his point," Charlie said. "What happens next?"

Griggs closed the file and placed it on the stack on his desk. He shrugged. "I don't know." He let the room stay silent a moment. "Any thoughts?"

"I think this is it for now," O'Malley suggested. "Fat Cat is going to pull back to see who got rattled."

"Besides," Jacks added, "if he pushes again so soon, he risks his guy getting caught."

"Maybe," Griggs said, thinking.

"I think the contractor is still here," Hall nearly whispered. "I think he might go for another one."

Griggs regarded her. "Why do you think that?"

Hall's eyes flickered and she shrugged. "A hunch."

"Oh," Charlie teased, "woman's intuition?" His grin faltered as she shot him a look.

Griggs thought a moment. "Hall—put together a list of all the members of this 'community group.' We should keep track of them."

Jurgens, who'd been quiet till now, spoke up. "So what then, Tom? We try and tail all of 'em?"

"Let's start with getting that list." He stood up. "Let's keep our eyes and ears open." As he paced, he made a point to make eye contact with each of them as he spoke. "The first thing that even smells like another hit coming, we hawk on that." He smiled awkwardly. "All right?"

The others nodded silently. They were with him all the way. One way or the other, they would bring Fat Cat down.

— 16 —

Eight-thirty A.M. Saturday. Across the street from Zoo Girls, Deacon W.O. "Skillet" Wilson had his digital camera pointed at the parking lot, adjusting his camera so each license plate was in focus. Gotcha!

Breathing out cold air, he smiled to himself, imagining the faces of the car owners when they got the postcard in the mail.

"Good morning, Deacon Wilson," he heard from behind. Whirling around, he saw Pastor Fresno, on his morning walk to church, another couple blocks away. "Snapping some photos?"

"Sure thing, Pastor," the old man grinned proudly. "Heard about that church in Texas?"

Pastor Jones folded his arms. Skillet was always up to something. "Enlighten me."

"This church in Texas," Skillet replied breathlessly, "the minister there takes pictures of the nearby adult store parking lot. They use the license numbers to get the home addresses, and they send a little postcard. On the front, there's a photo of their car caught in the adult store parking lot. On the back, a note says, 'Saw you in the neighborhood. Stop by church next time you come through. We'd love to have you visit.'"

"I see," Pastor Fresno replied. "And do a lot of people take them up on their invitation to church?"

Wilson frowned. "I don't know." Grin again. "But the card should embarrass them enough to stop coming here."

"But, Skillet, they'll just go somewhere else."

"And what's wrong about that?"

Pastor Fresno smiled. "Is this an invitation or is it intimidation?"

Wilson shrugged. "I want these people to know someone sees them."

"So how does this work, Skillet?" The pastor raised an eyebrow. "You take your picture and what happens next?"

"We get someone to trace these plate numbers to the owners of the cars," Wilson replied.

"Have you checked on the legality of this?"

"Well, for the church in Texas, they use an online service that searches a database for a fee. In Texas, license information is a matter of public record. They've sent three hundred postcards."

"I see," the pastor replied. "Have you checked into whether this information is legal in Missouri? Or how much it's going to cost?"

"Well, not really. But Pastor, din't you tell us to 'storm the gates of hell'?"

"That I did, that I did." The pastor smiled and put a hand on Deacon Wilson's shoulder, gently leading him across the lot toward the church. "But we're also supposed to count the cost before we do a thing. This doesn't mean we don't go in, but we need to be shrewd about it."

"So what do we do?"

"Well, I would bring this up with church leadership through official channels. After all, if your card is telling them to come to our church, then you're representing all of us. We need to be in this together. Then, we need to find out whether this is legal, determine the cost, then find where the money is going to come from."

"The church in Texas said the program costs about 15,000 a year," Wilson said.

"Well, see, that's some kinda money to just jump in there," the pastor said. "But if we do come up with an official church strategy, maybe we can get funding from local businesses and private individuals with a similar passion to clean up the neighborhood."

He stopped and winked at Skillet. "Besides, that store is part of Frank Catalano's holdings."

"Sure."

"We got some things planned for Mr. Catalano. Who knows what all might come of it?"

— 17 —

Stake-and-bake again. Charlie, chomping loudly on a stale piece of Juicy Fruit gum, had shot a lot of footage and would soon need a new tape. He was now looking at the screen dedicated to the Lonely Pony, a rundown club six blocks from Fat Cat's tower. At 4:24 P.M., the camera caught a couple of out-of-towners entering the club. Horst Donovan, one of Smart Tommy's men, and Evil Duke Cumbee.

After only six minutes inside, the two left the club with Dr. Bones. As the three began to walk up Cotton, Charlie reached for the walkie-talkie on the windowsill. "Well," he announced, "the boys are going for a 'walk-talk.'"

～ 18 ～

Another too-quiet Saturday afternoon in Tyler Smart's hardware store. With one lone customer milling around toward the back, Tyler was up front reorganizing one of the displays, shuffling around hooks on pegboards to space out the tools. Since that chain store had opened a couple months back, his sales were dropping week by week. Maybe spreading the tools out would make it seem less like he couldn't afford any new stock.

"Hot enough out there for ya, Tyler?" It was Pastor Fresno, just in off the sidewalk.

"Hello there, Reverend." Tyler paused briefly before turning back to the pegboard. "What can I do for you?"

"I was checking to see how you've been. Didn't see you at the last meeting."

Tyler paused again. "I got busy. Tough competing with that chain down the road, y'know?"

In the back of the store, watching the two men talking up front, Solo briefly considered this opportunity. Killing the hardware man in his own store would check one more name off the list—but a twofer would be even sweeter.

His car was parked two blocks down, there for an emergency; the plan was to finish the job, casually catch the bus, and double back for his car later. The cops would expect a pro to have a ride—the bus got Solo out under the radar.

Solo glanced toward the front, where hardware man leaned toward preacher man and spoke in low tones. "I'm not so sure about the coalition thing anymore, Reverend," the man said. "I don't want to make trouble."

"But Tyler, the only way to break the yoke—"

"You weren't here when those men came in." Tyler's voice shook with fear and anger. "It was a fright. I was sure I was gonna die. Got me a family to think of."

Solo glanced toward the sidewalk to make sure no one would interrupt. He needed to time this just right.

He saw preacher man put a reassuring hand on the hardware man's shoulder. "Don't be afraid," he said in a gentle voice. "The Lord has us all in His hands." He smiled. "Please come to our meeting tomorrow night. It'll be secret. I promise."

Hardware man looked down, like he was ashamed. "We'll see, Reverend."

Preacher man was turning to leave. Solo felt the moment come like a sugar rush. He took a step toward the front, hand on his .45, when another player entered the field, passing the preacher in the doorway. Solo paused and preacher man was gone.

"Mr. Smart?" Solo saw Smart turn toward a young lady in a dark business outfit, hair pulled back to reveal a cute, freckly face. "Sir, I'm Detective Jordan Hall," she said, flashing a badge. "I wanted to ask you a few questions. May I do that?"

"Um, I suppose, miss." The man sounded nervous. Having a cop in the store made Solo nervous, too. He folded his overcoat over one arm.

The cop asked, "Is it possible we could speak privately?"

"I'm the only one here to watch the store," Smart replied. "Besides, I'm not sure I could be much help to you, ma'am. I don't want any trouble."

"Mr. Smart, I need to speak with you regarding a local community group. We are trying to assemble a list—"

"Please!" Smart glanced nervously toward a passerby on the sidewalk. "Can I contact you later?"

"Of course, Mr. Smart." The cop handed him a card. "You can call me at this number. If you're afraid, we can protect you."

"Uh-huh," he replied, pocketing the card. "I'll be in touch, Miss"—pausing, looking down at the card—"Hall."

"Thank you, sir," the cop said, exiting. "You have a nice afternoon."

"You, too," Smart replied, turning toward the front counter. He didn't watch her leave.

In the back of the store, Solo decided the hit couldn't happen here. With a cop nearby, his timing was all off. He needed to improvise.

Solo walked up to the counter where the target was fiddling around. "Excuse me," he said, flashing his best smile, "what is the longest screwdriver you got?"

⁓ 19 ⁓

It was going down tonight. Instead of the posh Poignard, the gang was all in the back of the Lonely Pony, where Dr. Bones, the underboss, had made final arrangements. It was a trash heap, where the gun monkeys spent their days. But apparently it had sentimental value for some of the older boys.

Holland and Sallis stood in the back of the dank club, in smoke and flickering fluorescent, hoping not to catch anyone's attention unnecessarily. Holland, humming something from *Singin' in the Rain,* nodded toward the arriving guests. "What's up for the boss's birthday?"

"Something about a big announcement." Sallis wiped his mouth on his sleeve. "Some big announcement."

"About what?"

"Dunno."

The two fell silent, eyes darting nervously around the room at all the people filing in. Gangsters, soldiers, reps from other territories. Whatever the boss was planning, the mafiosos were certainly turning out to pay their respects.

Holland turned to Sallis. "You know what I was thinking about?"

"What?"

"Sheriff Lobo."

Sallis squinted. "Sheriff Lobo?"

Holland set his jaw and nodded. "Sheriff Lobo."

"The guy on the television show?"

"Sure, sure."

"Why were you thinkin'a Sheriff Lobo?"

"What," Holland demanded, "I need a reason? This is a—whaddaya call it?—free country."

Sallis shrugged. "Okay."

The two eyed the growing crowd. At different corners of the room, the boss's three sons—Gino, Ritchie, and Frankie—were whooping it up with others. Ritchie was drunk already.

Holland, arms folded, turned and announced to Sallis, "See, I was thinking how Sheriff Lobo contradicted his source material."

"Source material?"

"You know, the parent show. Lobo was a spin-off of another television show—"

"Oh, I know this, I know this—*B.J. and the Bandit.*"

"*Bear.*"

"What bear?"

"The show was called *B.J. and the Bear.*"

"With Burt Reynolds?"

Holland sighed. "No, no, with the truck driver and the monkey. And the monkey was named 'Bear.'"

"Righhht." Sallis whistled. "It's been forever since I watched that."

"And in that show, Sheriff Lobo was the bad guy, see?"

"Uh-huh."

"But when he had his own show, he was a *good* guy. You know, fightin' crime and stuff."

"You sure?"

"Pretty sure."

Sallis scrunched his nose. "I don't get it."

"Get what?"

"If he was a bad guy on one show, why would he be a good guy on the other?"

"That's what I'm sayin'," Holland answered, nodding, excited, "the spin-off is contradicting the source material." He glanced around at the crowd still filling the ugly room. Harsh light bounced off gray walls. "Like with *Enos*."

"*Enos?*"

"Yeah," Holland replied, "the spin-off from *Dukes of Hazzard*."

"What, he was a bad guy and then a good guy?"

"No, he was some idiot hick, and then he moves to the city and becomes a cop with all these special talents, like someone you call a *idiot savant*."

"You'd think people'd pay better attention."

"You'd think."

Holland sighed. "Good thing life ain't like that."

Sallis squinted. "How you mean?"

The room hushed as Catalano entered, a king to his throne room, Dr. Bones at his side. Turk went up and put a beefy arm around the boss and squeezed. "Happy birthday, Frank!" The room echoed with shouts of approval and best wishes.

"Thanks, thanks." Catalano waved to the crowd as he took his chair at the rickety table in the center of the room. The two other chairs remained empty.

After a show of lighting his cigar—Dr. Bones dutifully offering a lighter—Catalano tried to speak, made an ugly cough, started again. "I wanna thank you alls for coming out tonight. It means a lot."

Amid smiles and chuckles of encouragement, he continued. "And I thought, with friends in the house, this was a good opportunity to make an announcement. When a man reaches my age, he starts to think about life. Where he's been. Where he's going."

The various well-wishers tried not to frown, wondering what was coming next. "I'm old, and I got plans," Catalano said. Another puff on his cigar. "In order to move onto the next phase of my life, I'm passing the day-to-day stuff to my sons." It was said that simply, no words minced.

The room was never more silent. Catalano reached toward Dr. Bones, who was visibly surprised at where this seemed to be going. "Show the map." The underboss silently unfurled a document on the table for Catalano, who tapped on it. "I am cutting the territory three ways."

Holland glanced around for Catalano's three sons, standing in different parts of the room. Did they know about this?

"Before we hand over the reins," Catalano said, "I want my sons to tell me—in front of alla yas—who loves me most? I'll give that son the largest cut of all." He turned toward his eldest; all eyes in the room followed suit. "Whaddaya say, Gino?"

Gino smiled slyly, pushing back his hair. "Pa, I love you more than words can say, y'know? More than anything I see, more than anything I got." He shrugged. "I love you like money, Pa." He shrugged again and leaned against the wall. The room approved with shouts and applause.

The Catalano patriarch smiled widely, holding his arms wide. "Good boy!" As applause faded, all eyes turned toward his second son, Ritchie. "Ritchie? What you got?"

The room encouraged Ritchie as he swaggered toward the center, blinking. "Pops," he said finally, flashing pearly whites, "everything Gino says goes for me, too. But he din't go far enough. I love you so much, Pops, it's like I hate everything else. Compared to you, all the good stuff makes me wanna puke!"

The room roared with laughter. Holland watched Turk sinking into his corner of the room. The man clearly didn't like this.

Holland didn't know what to make of it, either. Catalano's demand of his sons wasn't about "love" or "respect." It showed an insecure old man who needed reassurance.

"You're a good boy, Ritchie," Catalano beamed. "I'm proud to give you as much territory as I give Gino." He turned to his youngest. "Now, Frankie, whattaya say?"

The room grew quiet as Frankie pushed away from the wall. His eyes dropped as he whispered. "I got nothing to say, Papa."

Catalano sputtered. "What? Try again."

Frankie looked up, barely made eye contact with his glowering father before he was looking at the floor again. Turk coughed nervously.

"I can't just shove my heart through my mouth," Frankie said at last. "I love you, Papa. But if I haven't done enough to show you that by now, nothing I say now is gonna make up for it."

Silence. Everyone holding their breath.

"Fine," Catalano groused at last. "But 'nothing' gets you nothing."

Turk spoke up, lurching across the room, "C'mon, Frank, this is a crazy way to—"

"Shaddup, Turk," Catalano warned. "I loved little Frankie most, and he embarrasses me in front of the whole family?" He turned to the underboss, gesturing toward the map. "Split up his share between the other two." Dr. Bones, pale, nodded.

"Frank," Turk pleaded, "stop and think about this a sec."

"Are you gonna shaddup?" Holland saw several of Catalano's people put their hands near their weapons.

Turk held out his hands in a conciliatory gesture. "Look, Frank—you can shoot the doctor, but that don't fix the disease." He leaned forward and spoke in gentle tones. "Fix this. Take it back, before you regret it."

Catalano, shivering with rage, stood and pointed a finger at Turk. "Lissen, you traitor! Who do you think you are?" He huffed and coughed. "You come in here to my birthday party and make a scene in front of the family? You dare to question me? *Me?*"

Catalano coughed again. Turk instinctively reached out to his boyhood friend and was rebuffed. "I want you out of my sight," Catalano said in a hoarse whisper.

Turk shrank as Catalano continued. "I see you again, I kill you." Catalano leaned forward and narrowed his eyes. "You are no longer part of me."

Turk, close to tears, whispered, "Sure, Frank." Headed for the door, past a mix of blank and hostile stares. Stopped in front of Frankie, who was still in a daze. Turk put a hand on Frankie's shoulder and leaned in. "Luck be with you, son."

And then Turk was gone.

— 20 —

It was a few minutes after ten P.M. when Griggs finally found his wife in the family room on the couch, head bowed over a tattered Dr. Phil paperback, knitting needle and yet another abandoned project at her side.

"What do I do for dinner?"

She looked up wearily, pretending she wasn't annoyed. "What?"

"What about dinner?"

"You can have some chili from the fridge." Setting the book on her lap, holding her place with a thumb. Closed eyes, hand on forehead. "Put it in the microwave a couple minutes. If it's still not hot enough, put it in another one or two minutes."

"Thank you." He gave her an awkward smile and headed down the hall. Jordan—*Detective Hall,* he chided himself, stay professional, stay professional—had turned up few leads so far regarding that community group. The few members they did know of were all playing it close to the vest, not that he could blame them. Griggs, mentally cataloging the few bits of info Hall had reported, suddenly found himself thinking about her hair.

In the kitchen, Griggs pulled open the freezer door and grabbed a plastic container with a frosted red brick. Held the container under running tap water until the frozen brick plopped out onto a microwave-safe, floral-patterned plate. Put the plate in the microwave, punched up two minutes.

Found himself thinking about Detective Jordan Hall again. She had tinted her hair earlier in the week. Nice. He couldn't describe the exact color—had a reddish tint when the light hit a certain way.

The microwave beeped and he pulled the plate out. Still a brick. He chipped at thawed edges with a spoon, stuck it back in the microwave and punched up two more minutes. Watched the bowl spin through the window, thought back to lunch a few days ago. Jordan had—

The oven beeped. As he stirred the meaty soup, he realized it wasn't chili. It was spaghetti sauce.

"How's it coming?" His wife. Sudden. There.

"I guess I wasn't paying attention," he said in measured words, not making eye contact. Was his face flushed? "I guess I've been thawing spaghetti sauce." Could she read his mind?

"I said the chili was in the *refrigerator*," she lectured, opening the larger door and pulling out a clear container that obviously held chili. She always made it with chick peas.

She threw the container back in the fridge and slammed the door. "I needed that spaghetti to take with us tomorrow night."

"I'm sorry," he whined, stirring the lukewarm sauce. "I didn't do it on purpose."

He stopped and looked up. "What's tomorrow night?"

"Don't tell me you forgot about Carol and Ted, too," she said.

"It's late and my mind was on the job," he whined defiantly. "Some of us are doing important things with our days," he added, immediately wincing when he heard his words.

Carla stalked out of the kitchen, leaving him with his thawed spaghetti sauce.

– 21 –

At 12:01 A.M. a black-and-white unit called in to report a homicide. Tyler Smart, 56, dead at the scene. Stabbed on the steps in front of his apartment building. A business card pinned to his chest by a long screwdriver.

— 22 —

It was after one A.M. when Solo got back to his room. The stale air reminded him of the basement of his boyhood home.

Flipped on the TV. Infomercial. Something about thinning hair and spray paint. He threw his overcoat on the wooden chair and emptied pockets on the little table. Except for the .22; that went on the nightstand. Not enough to stop a bull elephant, but at arm's length it would put a bullet in a person's skull.

Solo wrinkled his nose at the smell of his socks as he dropped them to the stained carpet by the pile of clothes and shoes. Shivering in boxers and sleeveless t-shirt, he turned on the heater before collapsing into bed, without bothering to shut off the lamp.

In the flicker of the TV, his thoughts drifted back to the black preacher. This would be his third consecutive hit in town. Normally, Solo would finish a job and move on—do the gig, drop the weapon, skip out. That was the routine. But this "package deal" of Fat Cat's was too good to pass up. This was more dinero than Solo would normally see in a year.

Catalano knew the Feds were keeping tabs on his regulars, so he had called in some out-of-town talent. And Solo came with brutal recommendations. The only stipulation here was that each hit had to look deliberate. There were five names on the list; all five needed to die in a conspicuous manner to send the message.

The death of the hardware man—stabbed with a tool lifted from his own store—certainly kept to the theme. Adding the cop's calling card to the mix was frosting.

Solo pulled the list off the nightstand and focused again on Fresno Jones. The priest hadn't been much of a problem for Solo; the pageantry of the Catholic Church was foreign to him. But this preacher man, with his yelling and thumping on the pulpit, that struck a nerve.

Solo leaned back in the bed, arm crooked behind his head to prop him up. Much like his father used to do. That is, before he disappeared when Solomon was ten.

"My husband has gone out like Enoch," Solomon's mother had boasted to the neighbors, explaining how a man could seem to disappear into thin air. "The good Lord took Elijah in a fiery chariot and he knew not death," she would explain to anyone who would listen—the mailman, the kid bagging her groceries, whomever. They would nod politely and go back to whatever activity had been interrupted. "But he took Enoch in thin air. Just like my John, praise be, just like my John." And then the neighbor or whomever would nod again, certain the old religious freak had simply driven her husband away.

After that, whenever his mother would lock Solo up for "quiet time with Jesus" in the basement—he remembered the loose dirt floor, random rose petals strewn about, skittering roaches, and the odor of dozens of rancid fruit pies—she would rattle on about his father's miraculous disappearance. "Solomon," she would say through the door from the kitchen, between stanzas of "Bringing in the Sheaves" and applying the rolling pin to yet more raw dough, "why can't you be more like your dear father?"

What? A drunk? A deadbeat? A deserter?

"The good Lord counted him worthy and saw fit to rescue him from this tainted world of sin and iniquity."

Solomon could smell the baking fruit pies through the door between him and the kitchen. *Sharing in the act of creation,* she would call it. Then she would bring the fresh pies down to the stale basement for storage. In all his life, Solomon had never seen one of these pies eaten in their house—to actually eat them would be an act of *carnal pleasure,* she would say. But you couldn't throw them away, because that would be a sin, too, what with all those children starving in Kenya.

Once, at age six, Solo wondered aloud why they didn't simply mail the pies to Kenya. He was given "quiet time" for close to a week. His school barely missed him.

By the time he was eight, the taunt of all those uneaten pies—apple, blackberry, cherry, all manner of fruit—no longer bothered him. By the time his father was gone, the smell of baking pies merely sickened him.

"Enoch walked with God," he could hear her say through the musty door, followed by the scraping of the oven door and the stench of fresh fruit pie. "He walked with God and then the good Lord took him away from this world."

Huddling in the corner of the damp basement, arms tight around locked knees, Solomon tried not to listen to the constant chatter. If she would just shut up for a moment, he could think or breathe.

But then she would stop. For tense moments, Solomon would hold his breath, straining his ears. Worried a moment that she, too, might have been taken away by the good Lord, leaving Solo locked up in the basement till the devil came knocking 'round. Then he heard voices floating from the living room, eventually making out the distinctive accent of evangelists on TV.

Solomon was alone with the smell of pies.

Solo jumped out of his vision, alone in his motel room in a small town on the edge of Kansas City. He looked at the crumpled list in his hand again and decided the preacher man had to go next. His manner poked at all sorts of bad memories. Solo leaned over to the lamp on the nightstand and shut the light out.

He fell asleep to the flicker of the television.

- 23 -

Frankie Catalano lost his inheritance around eleven P.M. Three hours later, he was at Angie's rat-bait apartment at the Manton Arms, looking for comfort. But she wouldn't have any of that.

"What are you, a *moron?*" She pushed him hard like a roller-derby queen, smacking gum angrily. Oh, how he hated that noise. "All you had to say was a few simple words to your old man to make him happy. All you had to say was 'I love you, Papa.' Kids say it all the time!"

Frankie nervously felt his jacket for cigarettes. Remembered how much he hated this fabric. "In front of all those people?"

"*Yes!*" Shrieking, pacing, flailing arms wildly. Her shoes flapped as she pattered back and forth across the chipped hardwood. "*Especially* in front of all those people! It's your old man's birthday and you embarrass him in front of *them?*"

Frankie was confused. She was making a kind of sense, but everything was still so hazy. His world had suddenly been pulled out from under him—he was just trying to grab on to something for balance. "I love my Pa."

"Don't tell me—tell *him!*" She slapped her hands on her legs in a huff. A dog was yapping in one of the neighbor's apartments. "All he wanted was to hear that his sons loved him. Your brothers were smart enough to say it."

"No!" Frankie yelled, barely aware of the pounding on the wall from next door. "All he wanted was a show! Gino and Ritchie gave him the show!" He was pacing furiously now, in front of the ugly hand-me-down couch with the fraying orange and brown pattern. "They don't love him! They spent years planning the best way to use him, to use the family, how they'd run things after the old man kicked off! They been practicing talking honey to his face for years!"

He plopped down on the couch, rubbing his head. Trying to make the room stop spinning. "I guess they don't got to imagine no more. He's just handed it over to them."

"And you got *nuthin'*."

"Neither does he, Angie." Frankie looked up. Sad. "He thinks they'll take care of him, take care of his business. But he's just a shriveled old man to them now. I gotta take care of him."

"Are you *crazy?*" Angie's eyes bugged now. "If he sees you now, he might have you popped."

He jumped to his feet. "He won't pop his own flesh and blood." He looked at her with pleading eyes. "Will he?" Frankie frowned. "I hafta find Turk."

"Turk? He's as good as dead!"

"He's the only one who really knows the score."

"What good is a man who knows the score when he's dead?"

"I knowed Turk since I was in snot and diapers. He's like an uncle."

"He turned on your father."

"He was just lookin' out for Pa."

"And he's as good as whacked for his trouble."

"Pa let him go," Frankie said, "and Turk is gonna lay low a while. I need to talk to him. Maybe we could let him stay here. Till things cool off."

Suddenly, Frankie was pelted with a face full of laundry. He sputtered, "What are you doing?"

"You are *not* bringing him *here!*" She was shrieking to wake the neighbors. "You are *not* coming *back!*"

"Angie, what are you—"

"I don't need a loser like you around! There are enough losers in this building already!"

"But, baby—"

"And you think you can bring a marked man *here?* Might as well paint a big bull's-eye on the building! If a man like you ain't smart enough to stay in your own family, you're certainly not smart enough to stay here!"

Frankie smacked her with the back of his hand, sending her flying across the room. She landed on the rickety coffee table, both crashing to the floor. She looked up with hatred, blood trickling off her lip.

A pounding at the door. "What's going on in there?" An old lady. Frankie heard a dog yapping through the apartment wall. "Do I gotta call the cops? It's the middle of the night!"

Frankie felt his family blood rising, but shoved it aside. Disoriented, cut off from his family, this was not the time to bring the law down.

He turned to Angie with cold eyes. Her face finally showed fear. "Fine," he said in a low, clipped tone. He whirled and stomped to the door. As he threw it open savagely, the old lady was taken aback and pulled her robe more tightly around her neck.

Wordlessly, Frankie pushed past her and down the stairs. Reaching the exit, he pushed into the night.

— 24 —

Monday morning. Crisp. At police headquarters, Griggs blinked at the sun beaming through the windows. He was stirring powdered creamer in his coffee when he noticed Charlie sipping from what looked like a cup of cereal. "What's that?"

Charlie slurped and wiped his mouth on his sleeve. "Fruit Loops."

Griggs raised an eyebrow. "In your coffee? That's disgusting."

"I have a theory," Charlie replied amiably. The two began down the hall for their morning meeting. "For many, 'coffee' is not actually the end consumable, but simply a *vehicle* for the end consumable."

Griggs smiled at the younger detective, tasting his own coffee. It was terrible, but at least it didn't have cereal in it. "Let's pretend I have no idea what that means."

"If people *really* like the taste of coffee, why mask it with all that other stuff? Some people dump sugar or cream in their coffee. For a while, I used Swiss Miss with the little marshmallows. One day, I ran out of Swiss Miss and all I could find in the apartment was Fruit Loops. I tried it"—a proud slurp—"and a new taste sensation was born."

They had reached Griggs' office, where the others were waiting. "What's the geek going on about now?" It was Jurgens.

Griggs smiled and sipped before answering. "Just telling me what he puts in his coffee." He sipped again and set the mug beside him as he sat on the edge of the desk. "Actually, it explains a lot."

He glanced toward the clock on the wall and saw it was past nine. "So what do we know about this latest one?"

"Latest what?" Jordan—Detective Hall—didn't know yet.

"There was another hit last night." Jurgens, flipping through the folder he'd brought to the meeting.

She turned to Griggs. "Are we sure it's a hit?"

Griggs pursed his lips. He didn't want to be the one to tell her. "Spill the details, Jurgens."

The officer looked up from his file. "Clearly a deliberate act. Nothing stolen or lifted from the victim. Stabbed in the chest with a screwdriver—which, given he's a *tool* man, seemed like a message."

"That doesn't mean anything," Hall said, rolling her eyes. "Crime of passion, maybe. The screwdriver might have just been handy. It could have been..."

Her eyes clicked. *There it is,* Griggs thought.

"Wait—did you say *tool* man?"

"Yep," Jurgens answered, smiling cruelly, chomping gum. "Had your card pinned to his chest, Detective Hall. With the screwdriver."

She ran out of the room, holding a hand over her mouth.

The room was left in silence. Jurgens grinned stupidly. Griggs had half a mind to deck him for it. Instead, he turned to the others. "Same guy, you think?"

"Hard to say," Charlie spoke up. "Local killers tend to favor a method or weapon of choice. A knife or a certain kind of gun. But we should have all of Catalano's boys cataloged. If this is somebody from out of town," he sipped again from his cup of Fruit Loops, "he's probably using a variety of methods."

"Maybe. Sounds kinda far-fetched," Jurgens said. "What does Catalano care about these guys, anyway? Some little store owner? He's gonna call in some hotshot from L.A. or Chicago to whack some guy who owns a hardware store?"

Griggs picked up his coffee and sipped. "Depends on how much of a threat Catalano thinks this little community group is.

If they get support from enough store owners, a lot of protection money could dry up."

There was a knock at the office door, and everyone turned to see Special Agent O'Malley enter, bringing yet another file. "And the story just keeps getting more complicated," he announced. "Did you hear what happened at the birthday party over the weekend?"

Griggs set his cup back down. Something about the Feds made him nervous. "Do tell."

"Ain't seen nothing like this before," O'Malley said, handing the folder to Griggs. "And I've been on organized crime for ten years." As Griggs flipped open the file and skimmed, the agent continued. "Fat Cat has been threading together the whole city for, what, a couple years? Every time one more boss goes down, Fat Cat adds the territory to his pile. As crime lords go, he's all about mergers."

Jurgens smirked. "Tell us something we don't know."

"How about this: Fat Cat is no longer in charge."

Charlie nearly jumped out of his chair. "Somebody whack him?"

O'Malley motioned him to relax. "No, he handed off his territory. Voluntarily."

"So who's in charge now? Dr. Bones?"

"Near as surveillance can tell, his two older sons have split the territory between them. For some reason, the third son was cut out."

"Why?"

"You wouldn't believe me if I told you," O'Malley said. "This circus is getting too freaky for me."

Charlie mused out loud, "Catalano has been so shrewd until now. And he suddenly splits up the territory like this?" He looked up at Griggs. "How long does he expect that to last before it becomes a blood war?"

Griggs looked at O'Malley, who had no answer.

— 25 —

It was eleven A.M. when Turk rolled off the couch, knocking over the ashtray. He rubbed his eyes and squinted as he stretched. His missing finger throbbed, reminding him of the time he and Frank had robbed the pawn shop. Back when they were punk kids who thought they would live forever.

Why? The question had kept him tossing all night. It plagued him still, as he donned a wrinkled checkered shirt, beer-stained pants, and bejeweled cowboy boots. *Why would Frank turn on me?* All they'd been through together. The years. The pranks. The jobs.

Stumbling toward the front door, he felt old as he limped onto the front steps of his building. The door man sniffed at him. What had he heard?

Turk clutched the man's jacket and pulled him close. "Whaddaya sniffin' at?" Pushed the man hard against brick.

As he headed toward the market a couple blocks over, Turk was walking straighter. Some juice would do him good. And something with a kick. Yeah, he grinned. It was a new day—everything would be okay.

As he reached the curb, his thoughts drifted back to the old man with the sausage cart who used to sell on this corner. One winter, back when he and Frank were kids, they and the guys demanded free sausages from the man every time they passed by on the way to ditching class. The man gave in first, afraid. But after a few times, he refused. So Frank would pester the man, and the rest would follow his lead, once even turning over the man's cart, sausages spilling all over the sidewalk.

Eventually, the man began to move his cart for business from one block to the next, day to day, hoping to get outside Frank's reach. That final day, they had iced up some snowballs real good and pelted the sausage man until there was blood all over the snow and concrete.

Turk was jolted out of his reverie by the sudden appearance of some punks who started swirling around him like vultures. "Hey," one taunted, "look who it ain't!"

"Yeah," another answered, jawing on tobacco, spitting, "if it ain't old Turk."

Turk grunted. "Watch yourself, punks."

One guy lunged from behind, tapping Turk on the back. Turk swatted his arm around and continued tentatively toward the market. *Juice and a kick,* he thought, *all I need is to get me a juice and a kick.*

Out of the corner of his eye, Turk saw the kid making another move and he whirled. As he turned, a couple others jumped in and kicked. Turk fell to the sidewalk and they pounced, kicking him in the ribs and legs and head. He tasted blood just before it appeared on concrete. He thought of the sausage man.

Through blurring eyes, Turk looked up and saw other people passing, trying not to get involved. A man with a brief-case, sissy suit and sissy tie, heading for his sissy job. A woman with a scarf on her head and an ugly mole on her chin, lugging a bag of laundry. The stupid kid clerk from the pharmacy with the pizza face. Occasionally, someone would sneak a glimpse with wide, sad eyes, but turn and rush past.

The kids, bored, scattered, leaving Turk on the ground. He started to crawl a bit, yeah, that's it, stretching toward the hydrant at the curb to pull himself up. If he could reach the hydrant, everything would be okay. He would stand up, straighten himself out, and head to the market down the street for a juice and a kick. A juice and a kick. Everything would be okay. If he could just reach the hydrant.

Pulling himself up, he decided he would rather go to his club, where he could feel strong again. In charge. Fumbling for keys, he ignored the stares from the street as he got in his car and sped off.

It took him only twelve minutes to reach Zoo Girls. He was surprised to see so many cars in the parking lot so early. Stumbling through the door into the dark—it took his eyes a second to adjust—he was surprised to see a bunch of the guys hanging around the bar. Dr. Bones, Gino, some of the boys. Jawing it up with Vito, tending bar.

Everyone stopped and looked at Turk, standing awkwardly in the door, an uncertain grin on his face. Like a man who couldn't decide whether the surprise party was for him or not.

Dr. Bones broke from the group and came toward Turk, wide arms. "Turk, pally, good to see you!" The underboss pressed a twenty into Turk's hand, a tacky gesture. "Make yourself scarce, we got business."

Turk's mouth was dry. "But it's my club," he rasped.

"Not anymore."

– 26 –

Solo parked his car in a pay lot, folded a couple bills, and stuck them in the slot. Strolled casually toward his post on Market Street. He was running a little late, but wasn't worried. The target walked this stretch every Monday morning—and took his time, chatting and visiting with passersby and regulars all the way between Market and his church a few blocks over.

Solo went into the drugstore, grabbed a Batman comic and newspaper, took them to the counter. Paying the clerk, he headed back to the street to set up his stakeout. In his years of watching people, he had learned that the thing about a comic book is you can glance up and then back down without losing your place. With a book or magazine, the up-and-down means you read the same passage five or six times—Solo got bored too easily for that.

He glanced up from his comic. No Reverend Jones; preacher man would not have passed yet. Solo was leaning against brick in front of the drugstore—to his left, a vendor sold novelty neckties; to his right, a cart offered flowers. Seeing the roses, Solo thought of the basement in his childhood home.

He concentrated on his comic again, missing the days of ads for Sea Monkeys and X-ray specs. Bruce Wayne was lamenting the deaths of his parents again, the driving force behind his vigilante neurosis. Solo didn't know why they always made such a big deal over it—after all, he had lost *his* parents (after his father had disappeared, they took his mother away, following the discovery of the unmarked grave in the basement—the rose petals had been the clue), and he had come out all right.

Disgusted, he tossed the comic to the pavement and pulled the newspaper from under his arm. He glanced up and saw the target across the street.

"Hey!" A voice to his left. "Pick that up!" Solo was abruptly aware of the flower vendor, pointing to the splayed comic on the sidewalk. An older, heavy-set man with a hook nose and an attitude. Lucky that Solo didn't plug him then and there. "This ain't your living room, man! Pick that up!"

Solo, hoping not to make the scene worse—when following a target, the last thing you do is call attention to yourself—stepped to where the wind had blown the comic and bent to pick it up. Glanced again across the street. Preacher man was jawing it up with a fella in front of the little grocery store.

Solo rolled up the comic and shoved it in his coat pocket. Turned toward the tie vendor, who smiled awkwardly. Solo smiled awkwardly back.

"That's better then," the buzzard at the flower stand proclaimed. Solo conspicuously ignored him, fumbling through an assortment of novelty ties dedicated to forgotten movie stars and cartoon characters. Felt the fabric on a black necktie with a picture of Iron Man; pretty sharp, but would hardly help you disappear in a crowd.

"Cold enough for ya?" The tie vendor, a heroin survivor with straggly black hair, chatting it up, trying to break the tension. Solo glanced casually across the street, saw preacher man moving down the sidewalk past the grocery. Solo turned back and let go of the Iron Man tie. "Too flashy for my blood," he said clumsily, walking on.

Solo casually matched the speed of the target across the street. When preacher man stopped again, Solo stopped and found himself in front of the camera store. A card table on the sidewalk displayed used books and CDs. Solo, out of antibacterial wipes, kept hands in pockets. Back at the motel, he had tried to read the book from the used-book store; all those germs and words kept him from getting into it. He had shoved the book in the drawer, replacing the Gideons Bible he had thrown out.

Glancing across the street again. The target was now in conversation with some guy at the cleaners. Solo studied the second man with a killer's eye: curly red hair, out-of-season striped tank top. Khaki shorts.

Solo ducked into the camera store, grabbed a telephoto lens. As the clerk watched, Solo made a great show of looking in all different directions out the big plate glass window—before resting eyes on the heated exchange across the street. From Solo's vantage point, he could see the man in the tank top agitated, gesturing wildly. Preacher man trying to reason with him.

Solo smiled inwardly, certain this was a result of his own handiwork—the message from Fat Cat was surely making the rounds, making locals nervous about joining preacher man's righteous parade.

Behind him, Solo heard someone striking up with the clerk. "Hey, what's the deal with the hardware store?"

Solo squelched the urge to turn around. He heard the clerk reply, "The old guy got hisself killed."

"Someone rob his store?"

"Nah," the clerk said, "on the way home. Probably a mugger or something."

Solo fought the urge to correct him. Setting the telephoto lens on the counter without making eye contact, he exited to the sidewalk and snapped open his newspaper. The locals had to know it was a hit—deliberate, intentional.

That was the contract.

After some searching, Solo found the small item at the bottom of the front page. A black-and-white photo of the man, an uncomfortable smile on his face. Scant details of the death. "Still under investigation." "Suspected mugging." No mention of the weapon, no mention of the cause of death.

Solo crumpled the paper. The cops were hiding information, hoping to avoid false confessions or copycats. But it also meant there was a big question mark over the man's death.

Solo fumed. It had been a mistake to kill hardware man so close to his home. Solo had counted on somebody stumbling across the corpse and yelling to the neighbors. But whoever found the body must have called the cops without looking too closely.

The screwdriver and business card sent the message to the *cops,* but if the info didn't spread through the neighborhood, it was useless. Solo might as well not have killed the guy at all.

This development meant that killing preacher man at home was out. Not that he was home all that much. Always visiting the sick and imprisoned. Getting clothes or food for somebody.

Solo calculated the distance from here to the target's church. During the day was no good, Solo's surveillance had found— there were witnesses coming and going at sudden and irregular intervals.

Preacher man was moving down the sidewalk again; Solo followed suit, here across the street. Was so focused on the target, he had lost track of where they were. Then he saw a familiar steeple in the distance. The Catholic church from before.

He must have gotten turned around somewhere—he had no idea they were this close—until he realized it was a different steeple altogether.

As he stepped from one block to the next, Solo tried to regain his bearings. Then he hit his second surprise, this one no mistake—preacher man was at the hardware store. Some girl was there, distraught, talking to a couple of cops. Plainclothes. One was the girl cop from before.

Solo pulled back into a doorway, pulling up the newspaper, covering his face. He began calculating the bus schedule, self-consciously glancing at people around him.

Most targets weren't so mobile. Most targets, you figure out point A and point B, then sit and watch. Your target shows up at point A at X time of day, you meet him there, BAM, end of job. Your target goes to point B X times a week, you intersect at a convenient moment, BAM, end of job.

But this do-gooder, with all his walking and talking and handing out coats and cans—this was not normal.

Solo had seen enough for today. The presence of the cops, him being this close to the hardware store so soon, it made him nervous. Besides, Solo had decided his plan of attack. He had decided the circumstances of the target's death.

Solo dropped the rumpled comic and magazine into a wire trash can and headed back for his car.

— 27 —

Across the street at the hardware store, Abbey Smart was berating Pastor Jones. "You *knew* he was threatened!" Tears streaming, she pushed him, but he barely budged. "We came to you for help!" Sobbing. Jordan and Charlie watching in awkward silence.

"I'm very sorry for your loss, Abbey. And God is—"

She cursed and spat on the floor. "Where was *God* when those men came to the store? When they killed my father? Your *God* is long on big speeches, but comes up short when it's important."

"God knows how you feel, Abbey," Pastor Jones said, calming. "He's not some distant force. Why, when they murdered His own Son—"

"Excuse me," Jordan interrupted, "did you say some men came into the store and threatened your father? Did you see them?"

Abbey sniffled. "Yeah."

Jordan exchanged a look with Charlie, then turned back to Abbey. "Can you give us a description?"

Abbey sobbed and buried her face in the chest of Pastor Jones, who put a gentle arm around her. He spoke to Jordan in low tones. "She's had a rough few days, detective. But she told me about the incident; she believes they were pressing him as part of their protection scheme."

"You think they followed him home last night and killed him? For not paying?"

"No," the girl said, sniffling, "not about money." She gritted her teeth. "Because of that group. That coalition. My daddy was afraid, but the pastor here begged him to sign up."

"So he was part of the neighborhood group," Jordan replied, thoughtfully. "Sir, are you part of this group?"

The pastor looked back and forth between the two detectives. Weighing the risk of trusting them. Finally, he said, "Yes. I started the Urban Church Coalition with Father Mac."

"That's why they killed him," Abbey murmured.

"We're still a small group," the pastor said, "which is why we've kept our membership secret. But once we rally the whole neighborhood? Fat Cat might burn down one of us, but if we all went on strike at the same time that would be something else."

"I see," Jordan nodded. "Reverend, if you could trust us with a list of who's in that coalition, we could press for police protection. In fact, I think we should get you off the streets."

The pastor stared at the two detectives, still unsure. Finally, he sent up a silent prayer and decided he had to trust somebody. "I have too much of the Lord's work to stop now," he said. "But if you want to protect the others, I can tell you who they are." He told them three names, which Charlie scribbled in his notebook.

Charlie pocketed the notebook, then got a sort of faraway look in his eyes. "How would Fat Cat know who's in the coalition?"

Jordan wrinkled her nose in a cute, unself-conscious way. "Maybe there's a traitor."

"A Judas?" The pastor had a shocked expression.

"I don't know what that is," Jordan admitted.

Charlie spoke up. "Judas is the man who betrayed Christ," he said in his lecture voice. "The authorities paid Judas thirty pieces of silver to betray Jesus, who they then arrested and executed."

Jordan winced. "That's horrible."

Charlie grinned. "He came back."

"Judas?"

The preacher chuckled. "No, child, our Lord Jesus came back. Even death couldn't stop Him from doing the Lord's work." He paused. "And I can't stop, either."

— 28 —

Thanking the reverend and young lady for their time, the detectives took their leave. Heading back to the car, they stopped at the drugstore so Jordan could get some aspirin. Charlie was thrilled to find a wire spinner rack with comic books. "This is awesome. You can't find these spinner racks anymore!"

Inspecting a few of the bent comics, he noted, "Of course, they don't keep the comics in the best condition."

Aspirin bottle in hand, Jordan scanned the rack as Charlie ogled it. Seeing a familiar cowl-and-cape, she remarked, "Hey, they still make Batman comics."

"Yep," he said, spinning the rack again. "About four or five different titles." He looked up, slipping into his lecture voice again. "Batman is one of the classic archetypes. A boy loses his parents—murdered in front of his eyes—and he's driven to avenge their deaths every night for the rest of his life."

"Ew," she said, "I didn't realize it was so dark."

"The real Batman is pretty dark," he said. "You know, I have a theory that every story, at its root, is about a father and son. Batman, *Citizen Kane, Hamlet*—"

"What about *The Joy Luck Club*?"

"I haven't read that, so I wouldn't know."

"*Steel Magnolias?*"

"Okay, okay," he repositioned, "maybe I meant that every story is about *parents* and their *children*."

"Every story?"

"Okay, maybe not every story," he caved, thrilled with the banter. "But many stories. The presence—or absence—of someone's parents has a lot to do with how they turn out."

He began casually flipping through one of the comics. "You know, one of my favorite runs on Batman was Larry Hama writing and Scott McDaniel penciling."

She feigned interest. "I don't know, I thought George Clooney did okay."

He smiled. "I meant the comic book. McDaniel has a real kinetic style, so his pencils are best when the figures are jumping and moving. So, Hama wrote these great stories with people jumping from helicopters and motorcycles and stuff. They only did a few issues together, but it was great."

"Sure." She blinked. "I just thought George Clooney was cute."

At the counter, the clerk rang up the aspirin. Jordan counted out her change and they headed for the exit. Hitting the sidewalk, she asked, " 'Pencils'—what is that?"

"What do you mean?"

"What does it mean when a guy 'pencils'?"

"You know, he...*draws*. Uses a pencil. Another guy inks it, someone else colors it in. Scott McDaniel was the guy with the pencil. He's penciled some of my favorites—Spider-Man, Superman, Daredevil—"

"Has he drawn Wonder Woman?"

"You know, I don't know that he has."

"When he draws Lynda Carter, get back to me."

Charlie was grinning like an idiot when they reached the car. This was the longest he'd ever discussed comics with a woman. There was hope for her yet.

～ 29 ～

Ritchie Catalano woke with the taste of bile in his mouth. He blearily looked around the bedroom, sunlight through curtained windows burning his brain. Through the door to the living room, he could see several of his friends strewn about, sleeping on furniture and carpet. The woman in bed next to him stirred. She looked as bad as he felt. Ritchie eased off the bed, walking on bare feet across the carpet to the kitchen. The carpet was warm where the sun hit it.

In the kitchen, he searched the cabinet for instant coffee. Something flavored, like "Swiss" or "French" maybe. His head throbbed—but then, Pops' surprise announcement was big. Ritchie had suddenly gotten half the family business—it was more than he could ever have hoped.

Of course, he deserved it all. While Gino had that smarmy way of dealing with people, Ritchie always cut to the edge. You never had to wonder what Ritchie was thinking.

He smiled as he found the canister. Tilted the tin, began to tap powder into a ceramic mug. Tap, tap, tap. As the powder drifted into the mug, he thought again of Gino and frowned. His older brother always got the privileges. The best clothes, the best car—Ritchie's whole life, Gino got first dibs, Ritchie got the leftovers. Always with the hand-me-downs.

Even last night's arrangement. Gino got first cut. Ritchie got what was left.

Noticing the mug had too much powder, he smashed it on the counter, shards of ceramic flying, clacking off the wall.

Fuming, he grabbed a towel and wiped blood off his hand. Recalled the Big Wheel he got when he was six. His older brother had grabbed that and taken it. Young Ritchie had felt so helpless.

"Yo, Ritchie," came a voice from the living room. One of his soldiers, eyes drooping, hair flailing, leaned in the doorway. "What's up, man? Break something?"

Ritchie wrapped the soaked towel tightly around his left hand. "Just thinking."

The other man stumbled to the small kitchen table and fell into the metal folding chair. He rubbed his head, making the hair worse. "About what?"

Ritchie grimaced. "We gotta take over the family business."

"Whattaya talking about? The old man handed you and your brother—"

"All of it." Ritchie kicked a ceramic fragment on the kitchen floor. "Gino won't be happy unless he has it all. Sooner or later, he's gonna come after it." His friend squinted, not following. "So we take it first."

The man nodded silently while Ritchie searched the cabinet for another mug. His hand throbbed, but that didn't matter. The territory was rightfully his.

Ritchie wasn't six anymore. And this wasn't about a Big Wheel.

— 30 —

Griggs was staring out the counselor's window again at the Power and Light Building. Thinking about the Kansas City Chiefs. They weren't having the best season so far, but as long as—

"Detective Griggs?"

The counselor and Carla staring at him again. "I was just thinking about work."

"That's interesting." The counselor smiled thinly. "Because Carla was explaining that you spend a great deal of time at the office."

"You're never at home, Tom."

"What do you mean never at home, I was—"

The counselor held up his hands. "Please, Tom, she is merely expressing how she feels." He pulled off his glasses, folded them, and held them thoughtfully in one hand. "While you may feel you actually are home a great deal, a lot of that time might be tied up with getting ready for work or, after you're back, sort of downshifting from the office. The end result being that, even when you're home, you're not actually home."

"A man has to work."

"Yes, of course."

Griggs felt his blood rising. "And I got to earn a living if I'm going to make money for the wife."

"I work, too," she said.

"Yeah," he shot back, jumping to his feet and pacing nervously. "But a part-time teacher's salary isn't going to—"

The counselor made like a ref again, gesturing for Griggs to sit. "Tom," he said in a calming voice, "what it sounds like is happening here is that how you say *I love you* and how Carla hears *I love you* are different things." He cocked his head. "Have either of you ever heard of Dr. Chapman's concept of love languages?"

Neither had.

"We each have inside of us our own special way that we feel loved," he continued. "For example, perhaps one spouse needs to be touched. Now, her husband loves her very much, and he buys her gifts, he buys her flowers, he buys her candy—but he rarely touches her, rarely caresses her, so she still doesn't really feel loved."

Griggs was checking his watch. "Sure." Still trying to wrap his head around this Fat Cat development.

Earl "Dr. Bones" Havoc was underboss. In most organized crime structures, that would put him next in line. But skipping him for, not one, but two underqualified candidates? Even in a system as unstable as the modern Mafia, that could only lead to more fractures in the organization. More blood.

Why would the boss suddenly hand off the reins like that? In most cases, the captain's chair would only be vacated by death or prison. There were those rare cases where someone decided to retire—but Fat Cat claimed he wasn't heading to Florida yet. He had declared he was passing off day-to-day operations so he could focus on the big picture.

As Griggs mulled over the statement, something about Fat Cat's mysterious intent made him nervous. *What do you have planned, Fat Cat?* And how could the scenario play out, except with bodies in the street?

"In the same way, Tom, you do a lot of great things for your wife, but—"

He was interrupted by the chirp of a cell phone. Ignoring Carla's eyes, Griggs pulled the cell from his pocket and checked the ID. "I gotta get this." Flipping it open, he said, "Jurgens, hold on." Heading for the door, he turned back to the counselor and Carla. "I gotta go." Rolled his eyes. "I'm sure I'll hear about this later."

– 31 –

Bones paced the length of the garage, ignoring the thick smell of oil. "Turk out on the street!" Neatly threading a path through patches of grime and sawdust on the cement floor. "Smart Tommy's soldiers stompin' back to St. Louis in a huff!"

It was chilly in the garage, so he kept his overcoat on. "And Frank just gives away his power!" Two of his soldiers watched, arms folded, mouths grim.

Bones, fiddling with the brim of his hat, stopped short and threw his arms out. "Here I am, next in line, and he gives it to those two no-good bums! Spur a' the moment!"

Bones sighed and leaned against the black car with its hood up. There was the clang of a bell at the back entrance. His men stiffened and reached into their jackets.

There were footsteps approaching, and then Ritchie stepped out of the shadows, a couple of his soldiers following. Bones' own men still had their hands in their jackets, waiting to see where the conversation might go. Ritchie smiled and nodded at the underboss. "Hey, Bones."

"Hey, Ritchie!" Bones grinned widely and held his arms out warmly. "How's the new boss?"

"Good, man, good," Ritchie replied, wrinkling his nose at the smell. Glanced around, noting the men standing guard. "What's news?"

"We was waiting to see what you think, Ritchie." The older man leaned in, spoke in a low tone. "You talk to Gino?"

Ritchie shrugged. "Not since the party."

"How did he seem?" Bones shrugged. "Good mood, bad mood, what? He seem cheesed off?"

Ritchie exchanged a glance with one of his soldiers, then answered warily, "No."

Bones looked down with a soft face. "I saw him at Turk's club. I think you may have offended him."

Ritchie exploded. "Where does he get the nerve?"

Bones paced the filthy garage slowly, choosing his steps and words carefully. Making sure his voice carried the right amount of tender concern. "For the time being, you need to stay out of his way." Bones held out his arms. "Until he calms down."

"Someone must'a said somethin' outta turn." Ritchie spat. "Some creep must be makin' trouble!"

"That's what I'm afraid of," Bones said. "Go to my house—chill there, be safe." He pulled a key from his pocket and pressed it into Ritchie's palm. "Until I smooth it out."

The young Catalano made a dark face. "Will I hear from you soon?"

Bones grinned like the snake in Eden. "We're here to serve you."

— 32 —

Solo stayed in his room on Tuesday. He knew he wouldn't move on his next target until tomorrow; no sense calling attention to himself between now and then. He spent the bulk of his day nibbling on day-old pizza and jelly beans and flipping television channels with the remote—infomercials, Oprah, cartoons—his mind drifting the whole time.

Around mid-afternoon he pulled the newspaper clipping out of his wallet again and unfolded it, absently trying to fix the creases and wrinkles in the smudged paper.

"GOD TOLD ME TO JUDGE THEM,"
WOMAN TESTIFIES
(PRIEST POINTE, KS)—Martha Proud prayed before hitting small children with a thick wooden rod—and God would tell her how many times to hit them. Proud, 67, principal at the God Loves Children private school, lectured on disciplining children

during testimony in Priest Pointe, Kan., where she faces eight charges of assaulting children at a rural commune between 1975 and 1977.

"I didn't enjoy it, but God said to do it," Ms. Proud said.

Proud was also said to have sung the chorus from the hymn "Onward Christian Soldiers" as she beat the children, often beating them in rhythm as she sang.

She would also lock them in the shed behind the barn for "quiet time with Jesus," where they would spend hours during the hottest part of the day.

Ms. Proud said the children had to grow up to be good citizens and eventually get into heaven. "God sees them," she said. "He knows how worthless they are."

Solo finished reading the story again, then gingerly folded the clipping and slipped it back into his wallet. The woman in the story had the wrong last name, but sounded awfully like his mother. He hoped to someday find the truth. But today he napped away the afternoon, dreaming of stale blueberry pies.

~ 33 ~

Jurgens fiddled with his coat button while he watched Griggs pace. "You're gonna wear a hole in the tile there."

Griggs stopped and gave a sideways smile. "Funny," he said. "And you're gonna end up losing that button, you keep yanking on it like that."

"Hey, you keep your nervous habit," Jurgens said, chomping gum, "and I'll keep mine."

They were waiting for an audience with Judge Reynolds, one of the names on the list Charlie had gotten from the preacher. Griggs didn't like waiting. He sighed and went to the wall next to Jurgens and leaned. Jurgens was eyeing a leggy blonde by the elevator. Griggs asked, "How's the big smoke-out going?"

Jurgens didn't hear him. Griggs puckered and blew a spike of breath into Jurgens' ear. Jurgens jolted, turned. "What?"

"The smoke-out, how's that going?"

"What are you talking about?"

"You know, the *smoking quitting*," Griggs said, searching for the phrase, "the act of no longer smoking cigarettes. You still off 'em, right?" He gave a nod. "That's what the noisy gum is about, right?"

"Oh," Jurgens nodded, now chomping for show. "Right. Still a work in progress. Smoke-free for"—he looked at his watch dramatically—"what time is it now?" He chortled, that snort that drove Griggs nuts.

They were finally welcomed into the chambers as Judge Reynolds was wrapping up for the day. Jurgens announced, "We need to speak with you a moment, Your Honor." He had left his gum stuck under the register outside the office. Griggs wondered if some poor sap would find it the hard way.

Reynolds looked up from the blotter on his desk, wrinkles around tired eyes. He unhappily pushed wire-rimmed glasses up the bridge of his nose. "What can I do for you boys?"

Griggs tentatively moved toward the judge's desk. "Judge Reynolds, we have reason to believe your life is in some danger."

The older man turned to the stacks of books collecting dust. "I think that comes with the territory." Adjusting his glasses, he picked up the first couple of books and headed for the book-case. Shelving them, he turned back. "Don't you?"

"Yes, Your Honor," Griggs replied, watching him sort through more unshelved books. "But we are referring to a specific and immediate threat."

The judge sighed. "And did you arrive at this conclusion based on information from one of your wiretaps?"

Jurgens stood against the far wall, arms folded. "Actually, the taps have been no help."

"I see," the older man said, picking through another volume. Flipping pages, he seemed to find what he was looking for, then snapped the book shut and headed for the shelf. Without turning back he said, "And yet you people hound me all hours of the day and night to sign warrants for more."

Griggs jumped in. "It's not that the taps are useless," he said, making an annoyed face at Jurgens, "but they are one component of an ongoing investigation."

"I see."

"Which brings us to—"

"Detective, perhaps you should get to the purpose of your visit."

"Of course, Your Honor, I would—"

"I am not a young man, and I would at some point like to enjoy my twilight years."

Containing his frustration, Griggs gritted his teeth. "I'm getting to that, Your Honor. There have been two murders in the past ten days, which we have reason to believe are linked." He nodded toward Jurgens and then locked eyes with Judge Reynolds. "That link is what brings us here."

The judge casually grabbed a volume off the table. "A first edition of Robert Browning," he said, gingerly flipping open the book. He pointed at a passage. *"Hand grasps at hand, eye lights eye in good friendship, / And great hearts expand / And grow one in the sense of this world's life."*

He closed the book and set it down on the desk and stared vaguely into the distance. "This is about Tyler and Father Mac, isn't it?"

"Yes, Your Honor," Griggs replied. "It is."

Judge Reynolds was misting up. "I didn't mean for anything to happen to them."

"Sir?"

The older man looked up at Griggs. "How did you find out about the coalition?"

"Mr. Jones—I mean, Reverend Jones—gave us the list. We need to take you into protective custody, Your Honor."

"No."

Griggs was taken aback. "Sir?"

"N-O."

"But why?"

"Because I said so!"

"Sir, you are an important public figure," Griggs said. "We're going to have to insist—"

The judge stood. "I've been a civil servant for a great many years," he said. "I have an office to maintain, I have a duty to perform, and I will not run out on my obligations because some pantywaist cop said *boo*. Do you understand?"

"But—"

The judge repeated, "Do you understand?"

Griggs fumbled for words. "Y-yes, Your Honor."

There was a tense moment before the judge finally said, in a gruff but submissive voice, "All right then." He pulled a suit jacket off the back of his desk chair and flung it around his shoulders to put it on. "Do what you have to do." He went for his briefcase and snapped it shut. "But do not interfere with my civil liberties or with the execution of my duties."

"Yes, sir."

Reynolds took his briefcase and headed for the door. Jurgens unfolded his arms and stepped aside. "Good day, gentlemen," the judge said as he exited. "Please shut off the lights when you leave."

~ 34 ~

After spending the day inside, Solo decided to stretch his legs and go out for the paper. He pulled on yesterday's pants, put on his coat and shoes, and made across the parking lot for the front office.

"Howdy," said the unshaven goober behind the desk. Bald man with Coke-bottle glasses, watching *SpongeBob* on a little television behind the counter.

Solo croaked, "Paper?"

The goober nodded toward the corner, where a lone paper sat forlorn in the rack. Solo went over, grabbed the paper, and headed back for the desk, handed over a couple bucks. "I need change for the pay phone, too."

As the man was getting Solo's change, he sneezed into his hand—which he then used to grab the quarters out of the drawer. He held the germy coins out. "Here ya go."

Solo hesitated, staring at the man's hand. The goober frowned, impatient. "You want your quarters?"

"All right." Solo, disgusted, took the quarters and shoved them into his coat pocket. "Where's a pay phone?"

"Right outside the door there."

Solo glanced at the sidewalk pay phone. "Where's the next one?"

The goober blinked. "Um," he stammered, "I guess about two blocks down." He pointed out the window.

Solo took his paper and pushed out toward the sidewalk. Hiking the two blocks, he got to the phone and shoveled some change in. Punching in numbers, he was relieved to hear Gus pick up. "It's me," Solo announced. "Hold on." Pulling the pouch of antibacterial wipes out of his coat pocket, he grabbed a towelette and wiped off the receiver.

"Hey, Solo, you wiping the phone again?"

Solo returned the receiver to his ear. "Maybe."

"What is it with you, man, you got a complex or something?"

"I like being clean," Solo grumped.

"I ain't complainin', man, I just think it's an interesting thing, you in your line of work, always washing your hands."

"Whatever," Solo said. "Anyway, the preacher man goes next. Unless, of course, you got any of your updates."

"Haven't heard a peep. Heard through the vine there was some rigmarole the other night. You hear anything?"

"Just some birthday party," Solo said. "Been keepin' to myself last coupla days, low profile."

"Okay, well, thanks for checking in."

"Sure, Gus. See ya." Solo hung up the phone and walked the two blocks back to the motel. In his room, he doffed his coat and pants, pulled the change out of his pocket, and set it on the table. He placed the coins in a neat, sequential order, then went to the sink and washed his hands thoroughly.

Passing the table again, he stopped and stared at the coins. He went back to the coat, got another antibacterial wipe, and wiped each coin before setting it back in place.

He returned to the sink and washed his hands thoroughly.

～ 35 ～

Dr. Bones and his men pushed into the darkness of Zoo Girls. It took a while for their eyes to adjust from the blinding snow outside to the slimy, flashing lights of the club. Electronic music pulsed from the speakers as Bones strode across the floor toward Gino's table.

"Hey, boss," Bones said, noticing some notebooks on the table among the bottles and half-filled glasses. Gino's own men were standing to the side.

Gino smiled, motioning for Bones to sit. "Welcome!"

Bones, hat in hand, pushed into the circular booth. He stopped a few places over from Gino, who sat in the middle. His soldiers remained standing.

Bones motioned to the club around him. "How's the new digs?" He had to yell over the music.

"Pretty good, pretty good." Gino nodded to the stack of loose folders on the table. "Been checking the books, making the rounds, meeting the locals." He leaned back and cupped hands behind his head. "Got a sense some a' them are feeling the pinch."

Bones didn't know where this was going. "Yeah?"

"Some wondering if I could lower the cost of tribute," Gino said, shrugging, "if only for the time being."

"Lower the *what?*"

"I thought it might be a nice gesture," Gino said. "What do you think?"

Bones leaned forward and pointed. "You know what I think? I think they're testing you. Trying to see if you're as strong as your father."

"But they seemed supportive, they're just—"

Bones held up his hands in surrender. "All due respect—you are, after all, the new boss," he said, "these people are looking for a sign of weakness. This is your time to be strong."

Gino leaned forward. Elbows on the table. "You think so?"

"Gino, I been around this neighborhood a long time, and I know how these people think. They think your father was tough? You gotta be tougher. Frank Catalano was a stick? Then Gino Catalano has gotta be a club to the head."

"You sure about this?"

"Gino," Bones said, snake grin, "we're here to serve you." He leaned forward and said in a low voice, "By the way, you seen Ritchie lately?"

– 36 –

"I love you, man." If Griggs wasn't drunk, he was sure on his way. Leaning precariously on one elbow, he pointed shakily at Jurgens across the table.

Jurgens, of course, was craning his neck to see whether they could get their turn at the dartboard. "What?"

Griggs took another swig out of his glass. "I'm just sayin' you're great."

Jurgens turned and looked at him. "What are you talking about?"

"You always keep cool." Griggs sat up against the back of the chair, rotating his neck to pop it, trying to clear his thoughts. "No matter how much trouble we have fighting bad guys, you always seem like you got your act together."

Jurgens gave a goofy smile. "Don't tell me you're drunk?"

Griggs shook his head, leaning elbows on the table. "Here we are, trying to make the streets safe from organized crime," he said, "and we're caught up in departmental politics, we're getting heat from the other guys at the station, and every time we punch a hole in the evil empire, someone else pops up. They're like the hydra or something."

"A hydrant?"

"No," Griggs said, taking up his glass of beer, finishing it, clomping it back down on the table. "The hydra is that thing where every time you cut off a head, it grows two more to replace it."

Jurgens nodded, craned his neck again to see whether the dartboard was free yet. "And don't forget, we don't get any love from the judge."

Griggs looked in his empty glass, deciding whether to pour more out of the pitcher. Finally, he pushed the glass away and leaned back in the chair. "There's a traitor in the system."

"Aw, you're nuts, Tom," Jurgens pooh-poohed loudly.

"No, I mean it, Mike," Griggs replied in a low voice, leaning forward, looking to see if anyone was listening. "Think about it—Judge Reynolds drags his heels authorizing the tools we need for surveillance. His reasoning is that organized crime is not a pervasive influence in this community."

"All right," Jurgens yawned. "So?"

"Yet, here he is a charter member of a group whose sole purpose is to strategize against said pervasive influence."

Jurgens pulled a cigarette from his pocket and lit it. "Fine, let's say His Honor has the odor of fish on him," he said, taking a drag. "What do we do now?"

"We follow him and see where he leads."

"Where he leads, we will follow?"

Griggs smiled slyly. "Exactly."

Jurgens looked over. The board was free. "C'mon, we're up."

"You're smoking again."

– 37 –

Wednesday. Solo following preacher man. Same side of the street as the target this time, cutting closer than usual. Solo was bored and eager to advance the game. A light snow was falling. He stuck out his tongue to taste snowflakes.

Preacher man stopped by the newsstand to talk to someone. Solo, three doors back, looked in the window of a pawnshop. The sight of a saxophone in the window triggered unfortunate childhood memories.

"Good morning, Homer," he heard preacher man say to the disheveled bum whom Solo saw reflected in the window. Recognized him from the shelter the other night.

Solo shivered and noticed his breath. Pulled his coat tighter. The wind bit into him, cutting to the bone.

"Good morning, Rev," the homeless guy said. "Funny, seeing you out here like this. I'm use'ta seeing you behind the counter dishing out grub."

"Sure, sure."

Solo heard an awkward silence between the men before homeless guy said, "Well, guess I'll catch you next time."

"Wait a second," preacher man said, clutching homeless guy's arm.

Solo inched closer to hear—and was surprised by an ugly ape inside the pawnshop, frozen in attack posture. Solo gave a rude gesture and stepped to the next store window on his right, a butcher shop. Through the glass, he saw dead meat.

Turning his ear back to preacher man and homeless guy, he had missed where the conversation had turned. He heard the homeless guy say, "So, I can get it tonight?"

"Sure," preacher man replied, "just come to service."

"Oh, I don't know about that," homeless guy said. "Ain't been inside church a long time. Don't got me the clothes."

"Aw, don't you worry none about that," preacher man pshawed. "It's not what a man wears that saves him, it's what Jesus does on the inside."

Homeless guy thought a second. "Maybe."

"I'll look for you there, Homer," preacher man replied. "We can talk afterward."

As the two men parted, Solo made a mental note. Still staring in the butcher shop window, he lit a cigarette, if only to make himself more inconspicuous. As he turned left to throw the match in the snow, he noticed two cops—blue uniforms—walking up the sidewalk in his direction.

He flinched and turned to follow preacher man—and walked smack into him. *Where did he come from?* Preacher man was looking right at Solo with deep eyes, gentle pools surrounded by wrinkles. In smooth, honey tones, the man said, "You seem troubled, friend."

"We all got troubles," Solo replied nervously, eyes darting for the uniforms. This was the closest he'd ever been to a target without pulling a knife.

"The Lord told me I should talk to you."

Solo forgot the uniforms for a moment. "Yeah, well, he says lots of things. He and my mom had all sorts of talks together. Anytime she shared his thoughts, it was bad news for me."

"I can't help those who've abused the phrase," preacher man said. "Not everyone who claims to be a prophet is one. A person could just as easily say they were speakin' for aliens or for the ghost of Abraham Lincoln—but sayin' a thing don't make it so."

Solo thought of the clipping in his wallet. "How'm I supposed to know the difference?"

"Well, son, we find in the Bible—"

Solo cut him off, spitting on the sidewalk. "Don't talk to me about the Bible." Took another drag from his cigarette. "It's full of contradictions."

Preacher man smiled slyly. "Oh, really?" He pulled a book out of his pocket, covered in worn leather. "Why don't you show me one?"

Solo stepped back. Not counting the copy he'd thrown away back at the motel, this was the closest he'd been to the business end of a Bible in decades. And last time, it had been the perfect size for his mom to club a little boy in the head. "I..." he faltered. Collected himself. "Too many contradictions in there for me to know where to start."

"Good," preacher man said amiably, holding the Bible out farther. "It should make it easy for you to find one."

Solo stared at the small book, licking his lips nervously. Said nothing.

"Actually, you're right," preacher man said at last, pulling the Bible back, to Solo's relief. "It is full of contradictions." He flipped the little leather book open. "It contradicts everything you do," he said, flipping the pages, "it contradicts everything you stand for."

Preacher man stopped and looked a little puzzled. "I don't know why the Lord is telling me to say this, but He wants you to know that just because someone has ruined fruit pies for you, that doesn't mean there's anything wrong with fruit pies."

The world stopped for Solo. "What did you say?"

The pastor put a gentle hand on his shoulder. "Remember, we are not defined by what's been done to us. We are defined by what we do."

Solo struggled for an answer, then heard the blue uniforms behind him striking up a conversation a few doors down. He made a stone face and pushed past the pastor. "I gotta go, Reverend."

~ 38 ~

"I don't know if we should be here."

"What do you mean?"

"Here. I don't know that we should be here." Griggs turned from Jurgens, gripping the bat more firmly, watching for the ball. "Don't you think?"

Jurgens, outside the cage, spit his gum into the trash can, unwrapped the foil on a hot dog. "What, because it's so cold out here?"

Griggs narrowed his eyes. The baseball popped out of the machine, shot toward him at what, eighty-five, ninety miles per hour? Griggs swung and hit, the ball shot wide into the net and was credited as a foul. "No, man," Griggs leaned in, positioned the bat a little higher over his shoulder, "playing hooky like this."

The machine shot the next ball. Griggs connected hard with the sweet spot of the bat. Griggs was sure it would have been a home run. He turned and grinned at Jurgens, then got back in position.

Jurgens shook his head, chomped on the hot dog. "You've been wound tighter than, well, I don't know." He chewed and, half-done swallowing, added, "Besides, you're working tonight. *We're* working tonight. We gotta go watch Preacher Jones work the pulpit."

"I know, but still—" The machine shot another, Griggs connected again. Then he rolled the bat to loosen his wrist, jumped back into the stance. It felt good. "I just don't feel right."

"It's no big deal," Jurgens said. "Relax."

Griggs had his eye on the machine. Another ball rocketed toward him. A swing. A miss.

— 39 —

At the Lonely Pony, the gunmen were in the back room killing time with a game of chess. Dr. Bones didn't like the boys playing cards, thought it fostered a reckless attitude. Holland meticulously set up black pieces on his side of the checkered board. Terry the Weasel—named so for his face, not his disposition—setting up white pieces. The other guys around the table, money in hand, choosing sides.

His eyes on the board, Holland's mind raced. It was all strategy. Chess, life, the job. This new direction in Fat Cat's biz was creating friction among the gangsters, with nobody knowing who answered to whom anymore.

Weasel made the first move, jumping his knight over the row of pawns and out onto the playing field. Holland moved a black pawn forward. Weasel pushed out one of his pawns and said, "So what happened with Six-Pack?"

A guy named Joe Fix, popping Sudafeds like candy, blinked. "Why, what happened?"

Sallis, looking on, was sucking on a Jolly Rancher. "He got whacked."

Holland and Weasel traded a couple more moves before Weasel said. "Who did it?"

"Nobody knows for sure," Holland said, taking first blood. The men watching set money down on the table. "Probably somebody from St. Louis."

Weasel moved another piece. "Seems a shame."

Sallis said, "Yeah," clicking the Jolly Rancher against his teeth as he talked, "but what are you gonna do?"

"Just seems a senseless waste of human life."

"You whacked people before, Weasel." Holland moved his rook. "Why the tears now?"

"No tears," Weasel said. "I'm just saying it's a waste."

Holland took another piece. As the others put their money down, Holland looked up at Weasel. "It's the life we lead."

"*Sí.*" The Hispanic, Nardo Manzano, nodded curtly, placing money on the table. Holland regarded the man's broken face, battered from a hundred lost boxing matches.

Fix said, "Shame about Frankie, though."

Manzano spat. "Frankie got what he deserved." He glanced at the others, anger flashing in his eyes. "A son turning on his own father like that. It's, how you say, a *disgrace*."

Weasel moved another piece and changed the subject. "Hey, I don't know about you guys, but I think this new thing is great."

Sallis stopped clicking his Jolly Rancher. "What thing?"

"You know, working for the new blood, Fat Cat's sons."

Holland and Sallis exchanged a look. Sallis turned back to Weasel. "Yeah?"

"Sure," Weasel replied, risking a bishop out on the board. "I haven't been able to touch base with Gino yet, but I think working for him will be swell. He's gonna have himself some fresh ideas."

Holland and Sallis exchanged a second look. Sallis squinted at Weasel. "You realize you belong to Ritchie now?"

Weasel shot wild eyes. "What?" Sat up straight.

Sallis nodded. "Yeah, man, you're part of Ritchie's territory now."

Weasel slumped. Barely noticed Holland taking his bishop, the others around the table each laying another fifty bucks down. "Ritchie is crazy."

"I think Ritchie will do great." Fix stood and stretched his neck. "He may have a short temper, but that's the sort of fire this organization needs."

Holland took another of Weasel's pieces and more money hit the table. "Don't you mean *organizations*, plural?"

Fix jolted eyes back. "How you mean?"

"Well, when this was all Fat Cat's, we all worked for the same boss." Holland waited for Weasel to nervously move another piece, then took his queen. A hundred bucks a man hit the table. Holland sat back in the chair and glanced up at Fix again. "Once the dust settles, we'll all be working for different people. We're not the same club anymore."

Fix's eyes dropped. Holland could see that, clearly, this guy hadn't thought this new arrangement through. The weather was a tramp these days, and nobody knew which way the dirt would fly when the shovel came down.

– 40 –

Carla, with Carol and Ted, waiting. A pot of spaghetti cooling.

– 41 –

Across town, at the World Mission Church, Griggs checked his watch and cursed. Charlie turned to him, "What?" He had to shout over the growing rumble of the congregation.

"We were supposed to meet friends for dinner," Griggs winced. "I forgot to call Carla and tell her I couldn't make it."

Jordan held out her cell. "Here, call her now."

Griggs sighed loudly. "No, thanks." He grinned awkwardly. "That is a conversation I am not in the mood for."

Jurgens, his back to the wall, hands in pockets, leaned forward. "You know how it is, Tom," he said, smacking gum. "The longer you wait, the worse it gets."

"Thanks, Mike, but I'd just as soon wait."

The four were against the back wall of the church, a few minutes before service was about to begin. They had left some uniformed officers out front.

Griggs scanned the sanctuary. Amid the suits and dresses, he spotted Judge Reynolds scowling in one of the back pews on the right, sitting uncomfortably to himself, while those around him chattered it up.

Griggs tried to check as many faces as he could, trying to find anyone suspicious: the man close to the center aisle with the red bow tie, grinning; the woman in the third row with the outrageous flowered hat; the disheveled man by the side exit in a stained overcoat, ratty fedora pulled down to hide his eyes.

Taking in the décor, Griggs would have expected stained-glass windows, felt banners, harsh wooden pews, instead of bright red carpet and flags of the world. Padded pews, maybe fifty rows—a set on the left, a set on the right—tilted toward the stage at the front.

A big banner hanging behind the pulpit: "Jesus says GO, so what you waitin' for?" It seemed to be draped across some sort of Plexiglas water tank. Griggs didn't know what to make of that.

A group of men and women, six total, took the stage with microphones. Griggs saw a small band of musicians take their places stage right. A black man with dreadlocks pointed a finger toward the ceiling and shouted into his mike, "Are you ready to praise Him?" The churchgoers leaped to their feet and answered with a smattering of shouts and claps as the song kicked into gear.

A couple minutes into the song, Griggs noticed Charlie bobbing his head to the rhythm and mouthing the words. He leaned over, "You a fan of black gospel music?"

Charlie stopped bobbing with a puzzled look. "It's not black gospel, it's called praise and worship."

Griggs wasn't asking for a lecture. "Well," he faltered, "the church is black and the song was kinda grooving, so I assumed—"

"Actually, sir," Charlie cut in, nodding his head toward the people thumping and clapping and singing, "it's not an African-American church, either."

Griggs looked around. Sure, many of the faces were black, but there were also a lot of other kinds of faces—Asian, Hispanic, Greek, even white—it was the United Nations in here. For some reason, this church seemed to attract the immigrant community.

A couple more songs in, the crowd was still yelling and clapping. Griggs made a face and leaned over to Charlie again. "I don't get why they whoop and holler like that."

Jordan wrinkled her nose. "It's disgraceful."

Charlie was unfazed. "They clap because they love their Lord," he said. "Of course, in ancient times, clapping meant something entirely different."

Griggs cocked his head. "What are you talking about?"

"Well, today, 'clapping' signifies approval and appreciation," Charlie explained, slipping into the voice. "But when the Bible refers to clapping, it is an act of scorn or derision." He paused to allow Griggs and Jordan to keep up. "Back then, clapping was done by armies to discourage an enemy."

"I don't get it," Jordan said. "They were scorning God?"

"No," Charlie said patiently, "in the Bible, the reason clapping was an act of worship is because worship was a kind of warfare—a declaration that God is victorious over the forces of evil."

Jordan nodded. "Okay."

"Clapping is the sound of an army sensing the victory of its king."

Griggs nodded, turning back to the service. "I see."

He looked again at the faces in the congregation. Judge Reynolds was still scowling.

— 42 —

In a small room behind the sanctuary, Pastor Fresno Jones was getting ready, adjusting his robe, waiting for his cue. Most nights, about this time, he would be praying over the service and his message. Tonight, he was visited by Deacons Skillet Wilson and Carlos Rodriguez.

"You'll have to excuse me, gentlemen," he said, throwing the sash around his shoulders over the black robe, "but I got service. Besides, you two should be out front getting ready for the word." He could hear the stompin' and hollerin' through the walls of the study.

"I wanted to show you these." Skillet fanned a new set of prints on the pastor's desk. The crisp photos showed a variety of men entering and exiting Zoo Girls.

Pastor Jones frowned. "Now, Skillet," he said in his disappointed father voice, "you still taking those pictures? What I tell you?" He checked his robe and sash in the mirror. "I told you to wait until we can discuss this plan." He looked back at the pictures on the desk. "These aren't even license plates, these are people's faces. I don't know if that's legal."

Carlos leaned over the stack. "These are pretty sharp," he said. "This from a digital camera?"

"Yep," Skillet beamed, tugging at his lapels.

The pastor walked over and picked up the photos—a fat man, curly hair, T-shirt stretched uncomfortably over his beer belly; an older man, business suit, glancing around nervously; a fortyish man, tall, overcoat, in the process of wiping his hands with a moist towelette; a hippy, trying not to look sixty, jangle beads and everything. "Any these people threaten you when you took their picture?"

"Naw, Pastor, they don't even know," Skillet boasted. "I used a zoom."

Pastor heard the praise team wrapping up. "It's time to go," he said, putting the pictures back on the desk. He pushed both men toward the door. "We'll talk about this next church meeting." He slapped Skillet's shoulder. "I promise you—Lord willing—we'll bring it up next meeting."

He flipped out the light.

— 43 —

Ten P.M. After service. Preacher man had yakked forty minutes about this and that. Solo, wearing homeless guy's coat and hat—he'd used piano wire to kill the owner, so there was no telltale blood on the clothing—pulled the brim of the hat down a bit to shield his eyes from onlookers.

He had placed the cops in the back—including that chickie from the hardware store. He had also noted the boys in blue standing out in front of the church. Solo was reasonably sure the homeless ensemble he was wearing made him virtually invisible.

Normally, he would be too cautious to snuff a target with this many cops nearby, but a room this packed, a crowd this energized—this was gold. Besides, Solo wanted to get this name scratched off the list. Preacher man was triggering too many bad memories.

During the service—while preacher man hammered the pulpit with his fist and shouted about JEEZUS (he said it just like that, JEEZUS) being God in the flesh, came to Earth the first time to die for our sins, rose from the dead, ascended to heaven, and was coming back again in glory—Solo had been careful not to look directly toward the pulpit. If preacher man saw his face, this whole gig was over. A room full of cops might add a giddy thrill, but it also meant one wrong move was death.

Now, in the milling crowd following the service, Solo was hanging by the front fire exit. He watched the target talking with a man and woman, occasionally touching a shoulder, bowing his head and closing his eyes tightly, mumbling something at the floor.

Positioning himself by the side exit and having checked to make sure there was no fire alarm to trip, Solo had the door cracked open. Cool air rushing past him, he waited until he was sure preacher man had looked in his direction, then pushed through into the alley.

– 44 –

Pastor Fresno Jones loved these moments best. Following a message—when the power of the Lord had rained down, touched hearts, changed lives. These moments when people came forward to make a connection, to speak with the team of ministers, to pray with someone. This was where the action was.

He had just finished praying with a married couple. As they walked away, he looked over and saw his daughter, Amelia, waiting for him. He walked over, big proud father's grin, and hugged her. "And how's Amelia doing?"

Big grin, she hugged him back, squeezing hard, burying her face in his robe. He knew she loved the smell of the material. She said it made her feel safe. "I'm good, Daddy."

"No, you're wonderful. Where's your momma?"

"Can we go home, Daddy?"

"In a bit, darling. Where's your momma?"

"Back in the kitchen getting her Tupperware." Amelia pulled from the embrace and looked up with shining eyes. "Can we go home, Daddy? I got homework."

He grinned again. He loved his little girl. "When your momma's ready, we'll get out fast as we can."

He remembered seeing Homer go out the exit to the alley. "Actually, sweetie, I gotta go talk with somebody outside. I'll be right back."

"And then we can go?"

He touched her nose playfully. "Get your momma and I'll be right back."

He watched Amelia bolt for the kitchen, then headed for the side exit.

– 45 –

Jordan craned her neck. "Where is Reverend Jones?"

Griggs, eyes on Judge Reynolds (still scowling in his corner amid the hubbub), snapped eyes to the front. "Isn't he by the pulpit?"

"He and some of the other church leaders are ministering to the congregants," Charlie said casually, struggling not to slip into the voice. "You know, praying and stuff."

"I don't think so," Jordan said, alarmed. "I don't see him."

— 46 —

The alley ended in a brick wall, deep in darkness. The fire door opened, light and the gurgle of the crowd spilling out of the church as Pastor Fresno Jones stepped out. The door closed. In the moonlight, Pastor Jones glanced around the familiar alley—trash cans, puddles, rats—all which seemed so much friendlier by day. He looked toward the dumpster. His eyes adjusting, he saw Homer digging for treasure. "Hey there, champ," he said, walking toward his friend.

— 47 —

Pretending to dig through the dumpster, Solo heard a voice from behind, "Hey there, champ." Peeked at the silhouette behind him. Preacher man was alone.

"Homer, what you doing back—" Preacher man stopped when he saw Solo. Even in moonlight, he could see it was the wrong face under the hat. "Wait, I know you..."

"I got a message for you." The knife glinted. "From Fat Cat."

"You don't have to do this, son."

Solo grabbed the target's arm and pulled violently toward him with one hand, smoothly thrusting the knife forward into a yielding abdomen.

Preacher man grunted with surprise and pain, clutched Solo's arm as he fell. Solo, trying to pull his arm free, was surprised the man would be this strong.

Preacher man, gurgling blood, reached inside his coat—and pulled out the small Bible from before, from when they talked on the street.

He pressed it into Solo's hand and hoarsely whispered, "I...forgive you."

Died.

Solo let go of the man and stepped back. Dropped the knife, which clattered against brick.

What did that mean? Who did the guy think he was, forgiving him like that?

Solo was suddenly aware of blood on his hands and coat. For the first time he could remember, he panicked. Leaving the knife, shedding coat and hat, he grabbed tattered newspaper from the ground and began wiping his hands.

And ran.

~ Part Two ~

"...as if we were villains by necessity;
fools by heavenly compulsion."

—*KING LEAR* (Act 1, Scene 2)

~ ~ ~

It's getting harder to offer my hand / I pull them up gently, but
they fall down again / How much longer can I be there for
them? / 'Til my life is a wreckage, 'til I'm broken like them

—"BROKEN" © 2004 LIZZA CONNOR (ASCAP)

– 48 –

Scene of the crime. Going on one A.M. Uniformed and plain-clothes officers investigating the alley behind Mercy Street World Mission Church. As soon as Jordan—Detective Hall—had discovered the preacher's body in the alley, Griggs and team had quickly and discreetly blocked the area off and called in forensics specialists to comb the scene.

As the techs went about their work, the widow Jones and her daughter huddled to the side, blank faces. Griggs saw a couple of church members, older women in dresses, comforting them. The detectives had latched onto all the churchgoers they could, but most were long gone.

Griggs had called for help from specific officers, avoiding a general call to the station—hoping this particular scene would fall below the radar of the head of homicide, Detective Robert Utley. The people on the scene were good at their jobs, and Charlie was officially a homicide detective—on loan to Griggs for the joint operation. There was no danger of botching the investigation.

Everything was going smoothly until a rusted Ford Taurus screeched up and a familiar stubbled, bloated figure crawled out. "What's the story?"

Griggs rolled his eyes. "Utley, we're in the middle of something here." He wasn't in the mood for a turf dispute. Griggs and Utley had a history, and it was all bad.

"Looks like a homicide investigation," Utley replied, careful to spit his tobacco outside the perimeter. "Unless it turns out the reverend here was running an unlicensed bingo game for the mob, Griggs, I don't even know why you're here."

Before Griggs could stop him, Charlie grabbed Utley by the elbow, leading him aside. "Detective Utley, sir, we have reason to believe this man was killed by a member of organized crime."

"Look, Charlie, I only loaned you to Griggs because I think you're weird." He motioned toward the activity around them. "Just because you hear something on the police band—"

"Actually, we were already here," Charlie replied.

Utley raised eyebrows. "What do you mean by that?"

"Detectives Griggs, Jurgens, Hall, and I were here at the church earlier, watching the deceased. We believe that someone who was also here at the time may have perpetrated this killing, possibly as a contract hit."

Utley blinked. "Let me get this straight: When the man was allegedly *murdered*—you were all *here*?"

Griggs turned and walked away, fighting the urge to slam his head repeatedly against the brick wall.

Charlie was unfazed. "Yes, sir. We believe a significant part of this investigation—"

"Fine, Weird Charlie, stay." Utley sighed. "But stay out of the way of the real police work." Shaking his head, Utley waddled over to a uniformed officer. Someone continued snapping pictures from a variety of angles.

Charlie went to Griggs, who was pacing, hands on hips, staring at the alley's brick floor. Griggs glanced again where Mrs. Jones and her daughter stood. A uniformed officer was offering them coffee and blankets.

Jordan—where had she been?—came up to Griggs and Charlie, sniffling. "I let this happen," she whispered hoarsely. "First Tyler Smart, and now this."

"Jordan, you can't blame yourself." Charlie consoled her, awkward arm around her shoulder. "None of us expected it. Not like this."

Griggs, hearing her, blaming himself, turned and walked away. This was *exactly* what they expected. And they let it happen. They took their eyes off this sweet man who trusted them, and now he was dead.

Griggs turned toward the door back into the church, passing an assortment of cops meticulously doing their jobs. Doing fine without Detective Thomas A. Griggs.

Inside the church, a detective was taking statements from another church member, an older woman with a flowery hat. A couple more civilians waiting their turn.

In the pastor's study, Jurgens and another detective were talking with a grizzled old black man, white Brillo hair, the officer flipping through what looked like a stack of photos. The old man grinning, impatient to get them back. "And then I send a postcard and invite them to church."

The officer smirked. "They're gonna start coming to church, just like that?"

"As long as I help 'em see that God is watching, I done my part." The old man grinned. "If'n we get some converts out of the deal, all the better."

Griggs walked up, motioned to the pictures. "What's this?"

Jurgens gave a flash of alarm—he reclaimed his composure quickly, but it was there. "This is nothing, Tom," he said in a low, conspiratorial voice. "Just some tangent. You don't need to waste your time."

The other officer handed the pictures to Griggs. "Here, Detective Griggs, take a look." Griggs casually started flipping through. The officer pointed. "Guys coming and going outta some sorta girlie bar."

The old man was a little stressed, anxious. "Gonna check those license plates to get their address," he said. "Send 'em a copy of the picture with an invitation to church."

Griggs squinted. "Did you check whether this is legal?"

"God's laws are not the laws of man," the man beamed.

Griggs gave a puzzled smile. "Your reverend was killed earlier tonight," he said. "But you seem more concerned with whether or not we give you these pictures back, Mr....?"

The old man offered a wrinkled hand. "Deacon W.O. 'Skillet' Wilson. I know that Pastor Fresno is with Jesus. He don't need no savin'. These other men still in need of a rescue." He tried reaching for the pictures. "Now if you'll give me back—"

"Wait a sec." Griggs raised a hand. "I know this guy." Handed the photo to Jurgens, a snap of a heavyset man in a big fuzzy overcoat, a murderous gleam in his eye. "That's Dr. Bones," Griggs said incredulously, "Fat Cat's second-in-command."

"*Former* second," Jurgens corrected, fiddling with the button on his coat.

"Right," Griggs replied absently, already moving onto the next picture. "This looks like a couple of Russian mobsters, what's their names? Nickel and Dime."

The officer chuckled. "Nickel and Dime?"

"Yeah," Griggs replied, snapping his fingers. "C'mon, Jurgens, help me out."

"Oh, right," Jurgens nodded. "Nikolai and Dmitri something or other. *Tartikov* and *What's-his-name-sky.*"

A voice came from the doorway, "Nikolai Kozlov and Dmitri Sorokin." It was Charlie, in from the alley. The whiz kid continued, adjusting his glasses. "A couple of low-on-the-totem-pole ex-KGB, Red *Mafiya*–wannabes."

Griggs continued flipping through photos—twenty in all. "Gino Catalano and some'a his goons, Evil Duke Cumbee—at least a half-dozen mob guys." He looked up, tapping the pics against his other hand, thinking.

Jurgens frowned. "But Turk's club is a waste of time. We've been through this."

Griggs nodded. It was true, they had been through this. Their task force had limited resources—the irony of department politics is that with each success, the higher-ups considered the small group more obsolete. After all, they reasoned, each new arrest meant fewer bad guys left, right?

Between a department that kept cutting budgets and a judge that was slow to sign anything, Griggs and the others had to be economical with resources. And reports had shown that the high-class restaurant the Poignard and the low-class bar the Lonely Pony were the two must-watch locations. That's where the surveillance vans were parked.

On the other hand, Turk and the Zoo Girls club were close to the bottom of the list. Turk had long been considered a secondary player by the task force—they were convinced Fat Cat kept him around more for sentimental than for practical reasons.

But these pictures told a different story. Apparently, Turk was more plugged in than they had given him credit for.

"Somewhere along the way, Zoo Girls must've become mob central," Griggs said, handing the photos to Charlie. "Get somebody on these, see if any of these other guys are connected."

"It's not illegal to go into a club," Jurgens shrugged. "Tom, let's not waste our time here."

Griggs ignored him, tapping the stack now in Charlie's hands, the top photo a man in his forties, short-cropped black hair, overcoat, wiping hands with one of those antibacterial wipes.

Skillet, who had been quietly nodding, a step behind the conversation, now saw the pictures leaving his godly jurisdiction. "Wait! What are you doing?"

Griggs put a hand on the old man's shoulder, gave him a calm smile. "Sir, we need these for an ongoing investigation. The man who killed Reverend Jones may be in one of these pictures."

Skillet, seeing it was no longer up for debate, sulked. Shifting hurt eyes from Griggs to Charlie and back, he finally walked away, nodding and mumbling. Griggs didn't know whether it was a gripe or a prayer.

After the man had left, Jurgens leaned close to Griggs. "You really think the killer is in one of these pictures?"

"Nah," Griggs said, making a face. "But I do think these'll get us closer to Fat Cat." Feeling an important lead in hand, Griggs decided to drift back out to the alley. He found Utley and some others trading theories.

Suddenly, a voice came from the blackness, outside the circumference of the floodlights. "I think we have something." One of the forensics guys hobbled into the light on crutches. Short, neatly trimmed white hair crowning his otherwise bald head, wearing infrared goggles—Griggs thought the man's name might be Kralik. Crutches resting under armpits, rubber-gloved hands gripped tongs in one hand and plastic-bagged clothing in the other. The plastic bags seemed to contain a ratty olive green coat and a stained fedora. "The one item looks like it has blood. Hopefully, the lab boys can tell you whose."

Griggs crossed the alley in three strides. "Let me see those." He took the Baggies and held them closer to one of the floodlights, studying the color and texture of the items through shiny plastic. He noticed Charlie approach and nodded toward the evidence. "I saw this guy."

Utley popped up, attentive. "Yeah?"

"The guy who wore these—he was at the service."

"What, the gas station?"

"No, the church service. Looked like a homeless man."

"He didn't seem out of place to you?"

Griggs shook his head. "The reverend regularly helps at the homeless shelter."

Utley scribbled in his small notebook. "So now we're looking for one of the soup-kitchen regulars."

"No—a transient wouldn't drop a coat and hat. Somebody came dressed to kill."

Charlie's eyes lit up. "Our hitter."

Griggs nodded. "He was here. And I looked right through him." He heard a noise behind him and he turned to see Jordan, sniffling.

Utley grabbed at the plastic bags but Griggs held tight. "Thank you for an enlightening conversation, Organized Crime, but this is evidence in a homicide investigation."

Griggs, refusing to let go, stepped up to the other detective. He was a head taller than Utley if he concentrated. "We don't mind sharing information with your department, but I will not be frozen out. This is clearly part of our—"

Utley, face reddening: "I'll be danged if I allow a bunch of Elliot Ness wannabes who stood around and watched while this poor man—"

Kralik held up the tongs and yelled, "Children!" His voice echoed off brick, silencing Griggs and Utley, who both turned to the source. Kralik lowered the tongs, shoulders sagging. "I understand you boys feel the need to be testosteronic over this case, but if you're about done arm-wrestling"—he snatched back the bags—"the grown-ups need this evidence back at the lab." Adjusting his crutches under his arms. "The results will be available to both departments. Is that all right with the both of you?"

⁓ 49 ⁓

It was almost three o'clock when Griggs finally stumbled in the front door of his house. Dropping his keys on the end table by the door, he doffed his shoulder holster. He flipped through the stack of mail by the door, found another envelope from his dad. He tossed it into the box under the table, which was filling with unopened mail from his dad. Someday he would be in the mood, but not right now.

He heard the crackle of Carla's toes as she stepped into the living room. Light from the hall cut diagonally across the room. "Are you all right?" Her voice soft, weary, concerned.

"Yeah," he grumped, letting the door click shut behind him, fumbling for the lamp. "Got into a thing with homicide tonight." His head swirling, he was unsure how to articulate it all—Utley, Fat Cat, Dr. Bones, Gino, Ritchie, his unknown hit man. He burned with exhaustion, anger, humiliation, frustration—

"We missed you at dinner tonight."

"I'm not in the mood." He bulled his way toward the kitchen, Carla following.

"Not in the mood for what?"

"I had a pretty stressful night," he said, throwing open the fridge, poking through its contents. "I was at some idiot church service with people hopping and whooping and then a man I was watching was shivved tonight and then we were all out there in the alley and I had to see the faces of his widow and his daughter and know I let him die."

He grabbed a couple plastic bowls with meat and plunked them on the counter by the microwave. "So I'm rushing to find evidence when Utley shows up and pitches a fit because he wants jurisdiction over my crime scene."

Popped one of the bowls open, sniffed. Tossed it in the microwave and shut the door, punching up two minutes. As he listened to the hum and crackle, he looked back at Carla, who was leaning wearily against the counter. "So I'm out doing something important, dealing with real life issues," he was nodding savagely, "and I don't need someone ramming some made-up problems down my throat because I didn't go to the shrink and get on the couch and talk all about how I hate my father and how I don't communicate."

He focused on the microwave. "And if Ted and Carol are friends, they'll understand."

Carla sighed. "I know you do important work, dear." Speaking in low, controlled tones. "But you don't have to keep these hours all the time."

She nervously began pacing, fiddling with her hands. For the first time in weeks, she felt incomplete without a cigarette. "Tonight a man died. I get that. But just because you have an excuse *tonight* doesn't mean you have an excuse every time." She stopped and looked at him, her eyes boring into his. "I am important. I am your wife. We made a vow, remember? In front of a room full of witnesses? 'Til death do us part?"

"That can be arranged."

She shot an angry look. "What's that supposed to mean?"

"Nothing."

"No," she pushed, "you said it, it must mean something."

"It doesn't mean anything." The microwave started beeping and Tom impatiently hit the button before it finished. Grabbed the hot bowl and headed to the table, cursing the pain in his fingers, leaving the unheated bowl behind on the counter.

As he fled for the dining room, she stormed after. "You come back here, Thomas Griggs, don't you threaten me!"

"I was being dramatic." He plopped the bowl on the table, quickly turning back to the kitchen for a plate and silverware. Moving, always moving. "I was talking about taking my gun out to the pier and blowing my brains out." He stopped in the hall. "Isn't that what you want? Wouldn't that make your life easier? Then I wouldn't have to worry about any of this—Fat Cat, Dr. Bones, the contract killer, none of it." With thick sarcasm, "And then you could spend your three weeks in black as the dutiful widow and you're free to start fresh with the next man."

She slapped him, eyes ablaze. He clenched and unclenched his fist, imagining. Then walked away.

"Where are you going?" She followed, continuing to peck at him. "We are going to talk this through!"

"Carla, you don't want to be near me right now."

"This is always your problem." She bored in. "You only talk to me when you need something or you're yelling. You never talk to me like a person."

Tom plopped in the chair. Sulking. Wishing she would just go away.

"Okay," Carla said, voice quivering, "you missed dinner tonight. And you had a reason—I understand that." She bent on her knees by the chair, hands over his on his lap. "But you're late every night. And when you did have this emergency, you could have called. You could have saved me a lot of worry."

He didn't answer, glaring into the distance.

Carla was almost whispering now. "You're always so far away. Even when you're in the room with me, you're somewhere else. You're emotionally distant." She leaned forward. "Talk to me."

Breathing heavily through his nose, Griggs gripped the arms of the chair and launched himself to the center of the room. "You want me to talk? You want me to share?"

"You're yelling again."

He began pacing like a caged animal, throwing his hands in the air. "See? This is it. This is it right here—I'm trying to share, but I'm not doing it the way you want me to."

He stopped and gestured angrily. "You second-guess everything I do. I can't shop for groceries correctly, I can't do laundry correctly, I can't dress myself correctly, I can't do my job correctly—when will you get that it is entirely possible for people to do things in a different manner from you and the world won't stop spinning?"

He started pacing again, slower this time, methodical. Two fingers on his temple. "Every since Kayla Rae...ever since we lost..." His voice trailed off. He turned and saw Carla's eyes filled anew with dull, questioning pain. He knew his eyes carried that look, too.

They still blamed each other.

She whispered, "You always go too far." Bursting into tears, she rushed out of the room.

Boiling, he went to the front closet, found a box, and dumped its contents. Knitting supplies clattered to the floor. He stormed to the bedroom, ignored Carla crying into her wad of bathroom tissue, jerked open a dresser drawer, and started tossing items into the box.

She looked up and sniffled, fighting back tears. "What are you doing?"

"What I should have done in the first place." He wasn't sure what he meant by that, but he wasn't going to stop now. "I'm getting out of your way."

She stood from the bed, stunned. "What?"

He jerked open a couple other drawers. "You don't like the way I do things"—digging for shirts—"I'll just get out of your way and let you run things the way you see fit." Randomly grabbing socks and underwear and throwing them on top of the box. As the dresser bounced, items started to slide off the top. Tubes of lipstick, loose change, a small porcelain statue of Jesus. "Enjoy your new life."

Griggs stopped and looked at the growing pile of clutter on the floor. He bent and picked up the statue. Threw it across the room, porcelain shattering against the wall, fragments of Jesus on the carpet.

Griggs grabbed the box and headed out of the bedroom. "Wait," she pleaded, grabbing his arm. "I asked you to talk to me. How does this solve anything?"

He didn't have an answer. Fueled by stupid, nervous momentum, he grunted and shrugged her off. He left her stunned in the doorway, sobbing. Headed to the car, cold and sorry, unable to stop his forward motion.

Griggs threw the box in the passenger seat. Turned the key in the ignition, the car sputtering to life. The clock said it was 4:07.

Unsure where he was headed, he drove a while. Stewing. Knowing he was wrong, no idea how to go back.

The man does not forgive. The man does not blink. That would make him weak.

He eventually discovered himself pulling in at the police station. Carrying the box inside, he nodded to the graveyard-shift guys, who were still on for another hour. He headed for the men's room and stationed himself at the sink. Splashed water on his face.

Looking in the mirror, noticed stubble, realized he hadn't grabbed any toiletries at all. He mentally took inventory of what he needed: *razor, shaving cream, toothbrush, toothpaste, mouthwash, floss*—he sighed as the list continued—*dress socks, boxers, shirts, pants...*

He had a long way to go. Shouldn't have been so rash and stormed out, but if he backed down now, Carla would have the edge. He was not going to blink first.

— 50 —

Solo—slunk into the corner of his motel room. The blanket off the bed, wrapped tightly around him. How long since he'd been outside the room? Three days? Five?

Strewn throughout the room were empty bottles of whiskey and the remainder of his antibacterial wipes. He needed to go out at some point for supplies—whiskey, towelettes, jelly beans that weren't green—but couldn't bear the thought of venturing too far from the soap and water in the bathroom.

He ran his fingers through his hair. Greasy again already? When had he showered last? Once you started taking three or four showers a day, it made it difficult to keep track.

He licked his lips. The last of the whiskey had run out yesterday (the day before?). Empty bottles and beer cans punctuated the room.

From his hiding place, he looked over at the round table by the door. His list was on that table. Three names crossed off, three to go. Solo flinched. Is this what guilt felt like?

After he had offed the preacher man, he was so rattled he got himself a case of whiskey and a woman. Both were now long gone. How long had it been? Four days? A week?

This was crazy. He should not be rattled like this. Had to pull himself together. Get back to work.

Solo crawled across the room, stretched for the tabletop, and felt around for his crumpled list of names. He found the list, but his hand brushed against the pistol on the table. He needed to wash his hands.

As he lathered his hands in the sink, going through another two rounds of "Row, Row, Row Your Boat" in his head to make sure he washed long enough under running water, Solo looked up at the stubbled face in the mirror. How had his eyes gotten so red?

This was not how it was supposed to work. He was doing these people a *favor*. Shuffle off the mortal coil and all that.

Ignoring the silent figure in the corner of his eye, he leaned close to the mirror, rubbing stubble thoughtfully, mind drifting back. In thirty years of killing, it had never been like this.

He thought back to the guy who managed that golf course. New Mexico. Gus rarely gave Solo all the details of an assignment—it made the job less sticky—but somehow Solo had gotten the impression this guy was embezzling from the club. And since the wife owned the club, and since the money was funding the girlfriend's lavish lifestyle, it made sense the client would choose to avoid the slow wheels of justice and go for the shortcut provided by an independent contractor.

It had been best for everybody involved if it looked like an accident. Solo had arranged a scene where the cops were convinced the old man and the girlfriend, drunk and cavorting after hours on the course, had driven a golf cart right into the lake by the thirteenth hole. It had been a work of art.

Sure, it had turned out the man and the girl barely knew each other—it was actually the wife covering up her own indiscretions—but Solo had already moved on by the time it hit the papers.

Solo leaned into the mirror, pulling at his lower eyelid to check for redness.

He thought of the gig in Nevada, that accountant. That one he had no real details about, up to and including correct directions to the man's office. Solo couldn't remember why he was in such a hurry that time, not bothering to tail the target or anything, just trusting the client's directions, but it should have been simple. He was given a pass card to get in the parking garage after hours, take the elevators on the right to the third floor, second door on the left, the target would be working late. All Solo had to do was walk in, BAM, back down to the garage and away into the night.

As Solo left the corpse slumped over his desk bleeding, he noticed the nameplate didn't match the piece of paper in his hand. When Solo got back to the garage, he noticed the other set of elevator doors. *What the heck,* he decided, *I'm already here*—he took the second set of elevators and, sure enough, it took him into a completely different part of the building. He took care of the second guy easily enough.

As he had driven out of the garage that night, he had not been happy. He didn't like killing for free.

Now he came out of the bathroom, waving his hands dry; he didn't trust the towels to be clean anymore. He made the mistake of glancing back to the other corner, where his companion stood. Had been standing for several days now, silently. Was it a ghost? Hallucination? Vision? Pastor Fresno Jones, his lips moving soundlessly, praying or preaching or leaving a final message to his widow and daughter.

Solo looked away, heading back to his neutral corner.

He got back to the end table and stopped. Just stopped. There on the table lay the Gideons Bible *(hadn't he thrown that out?),* just sitting there, opened, as if someone had just come along and pulled the book out of the dumpster behind the motel and set it down there and plopped it open to some passage about judgment or wrath or something. When Solo glanced down, his eyes fell on a single sentence.

THOU SHALT NOT KILL.

～ 51 ～

At the Lonely Pony, the gunmen had set up the chessboard again. Weasel setting up the black pieces, Holland setting up the white, humming that tune again. The other guys around the table, money in hand, chose sides.

Holland's eyes on the board, his mind racing. Each new day brought more evidence of Fat Cat's legacy pulling apart at the seams. Holland needed to start working on his exit strategy.

He pushed out his pawn and nodded at Weasel. "Go." Weasel reached carefully, thoughtfully, moved a pawn.

Sallis, sucking on Jolly Ranchers, leaned in. "I thought of another one."

Holland moved another pawn. "Another what?"

"That sitcom *My Greek Wedding*."

Holland watched Weasel move another piece. Turned to Sallis. "Yeah?"

"Yeah, the movie had one ending, then the sitcom completely undid it. Stupid coda for a movie."

Holland turned back to the board, nodding. "Oh, right, right," reaching toward his knight. Put a finger on it, analyzed squares before moving. "*My Big Fat Greek Wedding* versus the short-lived sitcom *My Big Fat Greek Life*."

Sallis snapped his fingers. "That's the one."

Holland nodded, deciding instead to move another pawn. "I guess that would work."

Joe Fix popped more Sudafeds. "What are you nannies talking about?"

Sallis leaned toward him. "We was talking about spin-offs that contradict their source material."

"That's not a spin-off."

"Well, yeah—"

"If you're going to take it there, you might as well include *M.A.S.H.* and *The Odd Couple.*"

Holland watched Weasel move his knight out onto the board and said, "What you got against *The Odd Couple?*" Weasel looked up at him, made eye contact, smiled. Holland decided that if it came down to it, he would probably take him out with something close-range. A bullet to the forehead.

Fix waved his money to punctuate his argument. "They kept changing the back story. One day, it's like they first met each other in the army, then later it turns out they actually met on jury duty. The next time there's a story about how they met each other as children."

Holland slid another pawn out. "Actually, that's more a continuity problem." Leaning back, folding arms.

Sallis licked his thumb and counted money again. "Aw, I bet if you got the shows and watched them all together it would make sense."

"I don't know," Fix said. Holland decided if there were trouble with this one, he would probably try to kill the thick-necked man from the back; Fix's arms were too short to reach behind him.

Weasel moved another pawn, didn't even see the danger to his bishop. Holland took it with the next move and set the black plastic piece on the table next to him.

"What is that again, fifty?" Sallis counting out tens.

"*Sí.*" The Hispanic, Manzano, nodded, putting his money down on the table. The ex-boxer wasn't smart enough to betray anyone, just a child with big hammer fists. Problem was, if there were trouble, he would swing indiscriminately, taking down anyone within arm's reach. It was how Manzano had behaved in the ring, which more than one ref had found out the hard way—no reason to think he would be any wiser as a thug. Holland decided that if he needed to take care of this one, he would take Manzano out from across the room, preferably with a cannon. Just stay out of the man's reach.

Fix craned his neck around again. "Where are them burgers? I'm hypoglycemic."

Manzano looked at him. Spoke in his thick accent. "What is that?"

Fix stretched his arms, cracking his back. "It's like diabetes, only it's the other one. A blood-sugar thing." He pulled some more Sudafed pills out.

Holland glanced toward the bar, saw the bouncer—prettyboy, failed-linebacker type. Knife to the ribs would probably do it.

Weasel pushed another piece into play. Holland moved in his queen and said, "Checkmate." The room let out a round of groans and cheers; Holland looked up, surprised to see how full the room had become. The pile of money was pulled off the table, split among those who had sided with Holland.

Weasel vacated his chair and Fix took it, sitting opposite Holland. "I got yer number, man."

"I'm headed to the bar," Weasel said, locking eyes with Fix. "Win me some of my money back, man."

The game was over quickly—Fix took it in four moves. Weasel had only gotten back from the bar and here it was already over, Fix grinning up at him. "See, that's how it's done."

"What did you do?" Weasel, not happy.

"It's called a *blitzkrieg*," Fix bragged. "That's German for 'lightning war.'"

Weasel slammed his beer on the table. "You monk, your 'lightning war' only made me a hunnerd bucks."

"What?"

"You barely got any his pieces off the board," Weasel snapped. "Next time you play, take your time and get all the pieces you can."

"Look, I won," Fix whined. "Shut up and take your money and don't spend it all in one place."

"I don't got no choice but spend it in one place," Weasel growled, grabbing his money. "Next guy better win me a bigger scratch."

Fix craned his neck again for the bar, popping a Sudafed. "Where are those burgers? I got blood-sugar issues."

"You should put a lemon in your water," Manzano said. "It stabilizes your blood."

Right then, the girl showed up with their food. Holland grabbed his burger—Texas style, with an egg on it. He was in heaven, chomping and wiping yolk off his chin, when Sallis stood from his chair. "Hey, we gotta go."

Holland checked his watch and nodded. "Yeah." Clutching the burger in one hand, grabbing his jacket with the other, he followed Sallis out the back room into the bar.

As they headed for the door, he found himself still calculating his exit strategy. *How would I kill the bartender? The three guys at that booth? How would I get out the front door?*

As he planned it, move for move, Sallis interrupted his thoughts. "You seem awfully quiet." Sallis grinning.

Holland nodded, took another chomp of the brilliant burger and shrugged. As they hit the sidewalk, he decided he could take Sallis with an ice pick to the neck.

‒ 52 ‒

A week had passed before forensics allowed the Jones family to even think about a funeral for Pastor Fresno Jones. When Monday came, it was sunny as the throng turned out to the Mercy Street church.

Griggs was hanging toward the back of the sanctuary, standing in the same spot he'd occupied the last time he was here. His suit wrinkled like he'd slept in it.

While the celebration happened up front—*didn't these people know how to throw a funeral?*—his brain percolated with events of the past week. He had convinced himself that he was the victim, that Carla had thrown him out of his home, that it was Utley's fault the case wasn't going well, that he had every right to take the murder of the pastor personally.

Charlie had dragged Jordan toward the front as the congregation whooped and hollered through more of that music. Songs that Griggs couldn't begin to understand, about names and places of which he had not heard and in which he did not believe.

These people should be grieving, Griggs told himself. A good man was being laid to rest today while scum like Fat Cat was out free, living, eating, breathing—doing whatever he wanted.

The show had been followed by testimonials, which Griggs considered at least a bit more respectful. For an hour or so, congregants, civic leaders, and homeless people elbowed on equal terms as they shared their praise of the man in the open casket. Griggs saw Mrs. Jones and her daughter, sitting quietly in the front pew; they seemed more at peace than he expected.

As his eyes scanned the congregation, he saw other familiar faces. Judge Reynolds. Skillet, the old man who didn't want to give up his photographs. Even the chief of police.

One by one, a host of people spoke about Pastor Fresno Jones, about his great faith, about his commitment to excellence, about his service to the community and to the mission.

None of it, of course, would bring him back.

When the service finally broke up, Griggs counted at least a dozen more who were still in line hoping for the chance to speak their public goodbyes. The man had touched a lot of lives.

The pallbearers took the coffin down the aisle and out the door. Once it was loaded in the hearse, everyone headed for their vehicles, passing the flashes of cameras. Even the media had turned out.

In the car, as the parade of vehicles headed to the cemetery, Griggs asked Charlie about the group's behavior. Without blinking, the whiz kid replied, "They're celebrating because they know Pastor Jones is in a better place."

Griggs, unsure what he thought of that, was glad Jordan picked up the thread. "But if this minister is doing so much good work for the neighborhood," she asked, "why would God let him die like that?"

Charlie paused, choosing his words. "I'm not suggesting it all makes sense," he said, calmly, struggling not to slip into his lecture tone. "We're finite specks of created matter struggling to understand an infinite Creator. We can't wrap our minds around it." He looked at Jordan. "The things I don't understand, I leave to the Lord."

Griggs, driving, changed the subject. "Got any good leads?" He made eye contact in the rearview mirror with Jordan, who shook her head.

Charlie said, "We still have the other three members of that neighborhood watch under protective surveillance, but nobody has moved on them in more than a week."

Jordan folded her arms. "Maybe the killer is done."

Griggs shook his head, still following the parade of cars. "No, I don't think so."

Charlie shrugged. "Maybe we scared him off. We threw a pretty tight net around these people."

"We also threw a net around Pastor Jones," Jordan pouted. "And now we're driving to his grave."

The three were silent the rest of the way. Finally, Griggs turned the wheel and followed the line of cars into the cemetery.

As they walked in sunlight across grass, Griggs saw quite a number had come from the church. As the minister set up at the grave site, Griggs saw Earl "Dr. Bones" Havoc and some of his muscle, watching from behind the growing crowd, under a naked tree. Griggs looked at Charlie and motioned his head, and the two walked over.

As Griggs circled around, the mobsters made a show of not paying attention. He came up right behind the fat man in the coat and grumbled in his ear. "Come to make sure the job is finished?"

Dr. Bones turned and made a show of being baffled. "I'm sorry, to whom am I being addressed?"

One of the goons motioned. "This is Officer Griggs."

Griggs snorted. "*Detective* Griggs," he corrected.

Dr. Bones gestured with his hands, pulling off his hat and fiddling with it. "And why are you interfering with our grief on such a sad occasion, Officer Griggs?"

Griggs searched the man's eyes. Trying not to be distracted by the hat. He sucked in a quick breath, glanced back toward the grave site, then stepped up to Bones and locked eyes. "Maybe you and Fat Cat like to mix up the flowchart, try to make it hard to follow the chain of command, but we still got your number."

Close. Eye to eye. "You got the cops, you got the Feds and, for all I know, you got the Campfire Girls watching."

The men stared at each other for long, silent moments. Then Griggs stepped back. "Just waiting to bring you down."

Bones smiled. "I am sure you are mistaken, Officer Griggs." Paused, sizing him up. "We are, of course, willing to cooperate in any way. Good citizenship requires it. We're here to serve you."

Bones turned back toward the grave site, the goons following suit. "Now, if you will excuse us, officer, we are in mourning."

— 53 —

Solo had already used up all the motel stationery, was now ripping pages out of the phonebook, scribbling in the margins. There was no discernable rhythm or pattern, just a series of partially remembered names, misremembered towns, and acts of paid violence. Rocking himself neurotically, only occasionally glancing at the murmuring soul in the corner, Solo was struggling to make an exhaustive list of every murder he'd ever committed.

He had woken up with the memory of his first kill. Of having been locked in that basement for days, of hearing the doorbell, voices vibrating through the floorboards. As he heard the jiggle of the lock on the basement door, he hid in the darkest corner, away from the sliver of light coming through the narrow concrete window. They wouldn't take him without a fight.

Solo remembered that night—afterward, him covered with sweat and dirt, sitting in the backyard with the shovel, staring up at the crescent moon when his mother told him it was time to go. "Where are we going, Mother?"

Eyes glistening, she had smiled at him and patted him on the head. "The good Lord says to raise up a child in the way he should go, and someday he'll part from you. I think your time is come, Solomon." She had a strange look in her eyes, even considering the glint of the moon. Only later, after he'd made a few kills, did he understand what that look meant.

Sent out into the world, Solomon lied about his age and enjoyed a brief stint in the military, where he developed his talent. After he got out, he bummed around a while, killing freelance for sloppy money, until he hooked up with Gus and started getting jobs within organized crime.

But now—rocking, scribbling furiously on torn pages—he was trying to take account. He struggled with many of the details, going through several versions of some names and towns.

How many had there been? Hundred? Hundred fifty?

Barely remembered faces floated before his bloodshot eyes, accusers demanding blood, demanding vengeance. The mob prince from Phoenix who had turned to the Feds. The soccer mom in Memphis who had skipped town with her son after she'd lost custody. The fiancé in Rockford who wouldn't take a hint from his father-in-law-to-be and get lost.

So many forgotten faces, so many forgotten names, so many forgotten details. He was a professional. He had a job. It was never personal, it was just the job.

He didn't care about any of these people yesterday. Why did he care now?

Solo shut his eyes tightly, the images still clinging to his memory. He had to make it stop.

Clutching the papers close to his chest, his eyes took a vacant clarity. "Gus," he whispered at last. His mind reeling, he turned to the other side of the room, but preacher man was not there. "Gus," he mumbled to himself again, pushing himself off the floor and searching for his shoes.

– 54 –

Frank Catalano and Dr. Bones were in the back room of the Poignard having dinner with another of Pratt's guys, a man named Victor Leonard. Bones wasn't eating, Leonard had the chef's special, and Catalano was eating broiled chicken.

"I don't understand why we're having this conversation," Catalano said, wiping his mouth. "As I explained to your"—he made a disparaging glance at the muscle-headed goon standing, arms folded, behind Leonard—"*assistant,* I am no longer responsible for the quote–unquote day-to-day operation."

Bones watched as Catalano gnawed at a drumstick. Wiped his mouth on a cloth napkin. "You should be having this meeting with one of my sons." Smacking his fat lips. "The only reason I even deigned to attend this meeting is because of my great respect for your boss."

Bones bit his lip. This should be about him. About how, on the advice of Dr. Bones, Fat Cat had gotten the crazy idea to go into public office. How Bones should be in charge now.

Leonard sat back in the chair, confident. Bones considered having someone whap the smirk off his face. "Mr. Pratt prefers not to change horses, so to speak," Leonard said. "He still wishes to disentangle the misunderstanding since the previous changeover."

Catalano chewed. "When I took controlling interest of the business enterprise in question, I did not claim the baggage." Some wine to wash it down. "Whatever arrangements you had with the previous administration were quote–unquote null and void when the enterprise changed hands."

Catalano chuckled and took another bite. "Besides, I need the money," he said, chewing. "I got overhead."

Bones nodded toward Catalano. "Mr. Catalano here is planning to run for office."

Leonard smirked again. "What, you got your eye on the White House, Catalano?"

"In time." Eating, nodding to the man's dinner. "Try your Veal Galileo, Vic."

"It's Victor. And I can't help but feel like you're wasting my time, Mr. Catalano." Leonard pushed back in his chair. "I fly all the way out here from O'Hare as a representative of Mister Pratt's interests, and this is what I get. A lot of stalling, a lot of passing the buck, a lot of babble about a made man running for office like he got no skeletons."

Catalano pointed a stubby finger. "I don't appreciate your tone."

"When you replaced previous management, you did not gain ownership of this operation. You merely became custodian of the vineyard."

Leonard stood, pulled a cigarette out of his coat pocket. His goon approached dutifully, lighter raised. "Now, Mr. Pratt is not a greedy man. Most of the business can run however you— the custodian—see fit." He took a puff and blew. "But now you have elbowed your way in and wish to enjoy the fruits of Mr. Pratt's vineyard without paying the proper tithe."

Catalano violently pushed back from the table, face flushed. "Don't get brilliant with me." He stood and pointed. "When you step into my territory, your presence here is at my quote–unquote discretion."

While Leonard calmly savored his cigarette, Catalano stormed away from the table, clenching and unclenching his fists. Dr. Bones followed him over. "Boss, you can't let this weasel come in here and talk to you like this."

Catalano sighed, thinking. "This is exactly the sort of mess I had hoped to avoid. I'm making a different kind of life now."

Bones fiddled with his hat. "Step on this rat."

Catalano thought a second. Smiled. "Earl, what'd this guy call this place? You know, a garden or something."

"What? Oh—a vineyard. He likened your territory to a vineyard."

"Yeah. A vineyard." Catalano whirled around. "Vineyard, huh? You know what happens to grapes at a vineyard, right?"

Catalano snapped his fingers, didn't notice his men glance at Bones for approval before moving in on poor Victor Leonard.

– 55 –

Griggs had moved in with Jurgens. It didn't solve the problem of buying a whole new set of toiletries and grooming supplies—Jurgens had offered to lend what he had, but Griggs was squeamish about sharing—but at least the cramped apartment meant a roof over his head and cable TV. It was a far cry from the house Jurgens had had before his divorce, but it was livable.

Bonus, there was a Jimmy Stewart movie tonight. When the two had first started working together, one of the first things they had bonded over was a shared love of old Jimmy Stewart movies, especially the Westerns.

As Griggs sat on the couch, munching on Doritos, he heard a commotion by the kitchen window. Jurgens was spraying, spraying, spraying. Griggs asked between crunches, "What are you doing?"

Jurgens, eyes on the window, watching for something, "A fly got in here." Spray, spray, spray. "I hate that."

"Is that poison? You don't want that stuff in your lungs."

"Nah." Spray, spray, spray. "It's oven cleaner. If I can just hit the fly, this'll make its wings stick together." Spray. "When it drops I can catch it."

Griggs turned back toward the TV, grabbed the remote, started flipping. Behind him, the spraying continued. *Man,* Griggs thought, *the compulsions some people have.*

~ 56 ~

Solo wiped the receiver with his shirt best he could—it was all he had—and shoveled quarters into the pay phone. He nervously looked out the glass around the phone booth, but was certain all the suspicious looks were in his head. Maybe.

Through the earpiece, in some faraway place, the phone rang three times and the machine picked up. Solo hoped Gus was just screening his calls.

There was a beep. "Hey, Gus, this is Solo," he babbled. "Oh—sorry, I know you hate it when people leave names. But I got a probl—"

He was cut off by the sound of crashing and a voice jumping on. "Hold on, I'm here, I'm here!" A moment as Gus got himself situated.

Solo, feeling foolish, tried to play it casual. "Hey, Gus, what's tricks?"

"Fine, fine," Gus answered tentatively. "You don't sound so hot."

"No, I'm great, I'm dazzling." Awkward pause. "I need a favor."

"You know me, always ready to step in line with a favor. What's up?" Impatient. Was there a voice in the background?

Solo coughed. "Listen, Gus, I been trying to remember the jobs I done. Got fuzzy on some details, thought maybe you could go through your records and help me get some of the names right."

"I don't get it." Genuinely puzzled. "What you want?"

"You know, a list. All the people I killed."

"Are you crazy?"

"Why?"

"You're crazy now, aren't you?"

"Why?"

"You're the guy refuses to get a cell phone because you don't want a paper trail and you want to know if I keep *records?* Are you out of your *mind?* If somehow the Feds trail one of your jobs back to the home office in Lincoln, Nebraska, you think I want *paperwork?*"

Gus was pulled away from the phone by a female voice. Solo heard him say, muffled, "Not now, baby, I'm working through something here." Then Gus returned to the phone, agitated: "I know you're not this dumb, man. What's this about?"

"I need to go back." Through the glass, he could see a woman pushing a stroller in his direction.

"What, home?"

"No, back to each of the families."

"I hope I'm not tracking you here," Gus said, then asked, slowly, "You need to go back to *whose* families?"

"All the people I killed. I gotta make it right somehow." The woman and the stroller were closer now; their trajectory was clearly going to take them past the booth.

"Why would you do that? What is going on out there?"

"You wouldn't believe it if I told you."

Gus sighed. "I gotta tell ya—this is weird and dangerous. You need to pull yourself together, bro, finish your gig and get out of town. And forget this *list* crud. What if it falls in the wrong hands? You think about that?"

"No."

"What if the maid at the motel finds it? What if the list falls out of your pocket in a public place and someone finds it?"

"Look, I just—I'm working through something here," Solo strained, licking dry lips. "Besides, I don't know why you're making such a case. You gave me a list of the jobs I'm doing here in Kansas City."

"What, written down? I didn't know you had them written down!"

"I been talking about my list all along."

"I thought you were speaking figuratively," Gus said, "you know, like 'the check's in the mail' or 'a red light means stop.' Listen, what are you, at a pay phone?"

"Yeah."

"Do you have your list with you?"

"Back in the room."

"How about this other list?"

"They're both in the room."

"Okay, I'm going to say this slow enough you can hear me even through the pay phone there—you go back to your room, you take the first list, you take the second list, you take any list within arm's reach and you rip them into small pieces and then you burn the pieces and then you eat the ashes. *You got me?*"

Solo was silent a moment. Finally, "Whatever you say, Gus."

"You better believe whatever I say, because this is the stupidest thing I ever heard." Gus sighed, more patient now. "Maybe it was a mistake to send you on this whole project by yourself. I shoulda sent a team for the package deal like that."

"Naw, I'm fine," Solo lied. "I can do this." Stronger, if only in his own ears. "I can do this."

— 57 —

Ritchie woke with another hangover. Rubbing stubble on his cheeks, he tried to remember the events of the night before. How he had grown tired of cooling at Dr. Bones' house, gone stir crazy, in fact, so he and the boys had broken into the liquor cabinet. Drunk, they'd gotten it in their heads to go down to the Poignard, bust right in, make a show of strength. If it was the seat of Fat Cat's power, it would be the place to claim the throne, right?

Sure, at the time it had made a kind of sense, but in the light of day it just sounded stupid. Shuffling into the bathroom to throw up, Ritchie dimly remembered the clever finagling of Holland and Sallis that had deterred Ritchie and his boys—rerouted them, in fact, for the back room, where they would do the least damage.

Normally, Ritchie would consider such diplomacy a sign of weakness. But if he was going to run the show, he needed to start thinking of the high road. Stop making all his decisions with blood and fists, start thinking like the boss. Start thinking like the king.

Finished with this first bout of sickness—more would come—Ritchie needed to go back to Dr. Bones. Bones would point him in the right direction.

~ 58 ~

Griggs' office. Another meeting of the joint task force, cops and Feds comparing scant notes. Griggs paced. "I hate this."

O'Malley raised eyebrows. "Hate what?"

"This sitting around," Griggs said, stopping at the window. "Clucking like a lot of hens. Watching and listening like we can't do anything about it."

Jurgens pulled at the button on his jacket. "What else can we do?"

Griggs began pacing again, thinking. "We need more intel on these guys. All we have right now is enough to give 'em a few slaps on the wrist." He turned and looked deadly serious. "These are bad people. I want them off the streets for a long time."

"Well," O'Malley offered, "the new setup is just a pressure cooker waiting to explode."

"I have a question." Charlie half-raised a hand. "Why don't we have a bug in Turk's club?"

"It's Gino's club now," O'Malley answered, thumbing through a manila folder. "And we did have bugs there at one time—I don't know, maybe we still do. Never much use. We kept picking up background noise." He shrugged. "Music, boozies yakking, everything."

Griggs nodded. "Any chance we could try again?"

O'Malley pursed his lips, looked at the floor. "Best I remember, most of the problems were out on the floor. But the tech in the back office works great. It's a small, enclosed space, and the paneling is great for acoustics. When the door is closed, you barely hear the club."

"But you never got any good audio from the office?"

"Turk liked to be out where the action is." Checked the folder again. "By all reports, Gino likes it out in the club, too, where he can watch the place." He grinned. "The last good conversation we got from the bug in the office was an argument about the best flavor of Koogle peanut butter."

"You know, that wasn't actually a peanut butter," Charlie added in his lecture voice. "It was more of a paste."

Griggs cut him off. "At the risk of getting back on track, let's pretend we're here to fight crime, okay?" He sighed. "If we can't get audio because Gino does all his business out on the club floor, how do we get him to conduct his business somewhere else?"

Jurgens chuckled, "We could bulldoze the place."

Griggs smiled grimly. "Yeah, I'm sure Judge Reynolds would go for that."

Charlie's eyes lit up and he jumped out of his chair. "Wait a second, let's *control-alt-delete* here." Griggs made a face and Charlie explained, "I mean, let's rethink this." He paced, clenching and unclenching his hands, determining how to articulate his thoughts. "We convince him to move his operations to the back office."

Griggs shrugged. "What, we just go in there and ask?"

Charlie held his hands out dramatically. "These guys are always on the watch for surveillance, right? Under normal circumstances, we play like Cyrano and keep our distance so they won't spot any of our guys."

Griggs could not quite follow the literary reference, waved his hand, and said, "Go on."

"Suppose we press in—step up surveillance," Charlie said anxiously. "They'll be too nervous to keep meeting out in the open club area."

Griggs nodded. "I could see that working."

"Like herding cattle."

Jordan wrinkled her nose. "What do you know about herding cattle?"

Jurgens said, "Okay, let's say this thing works, we get them to move their business out of the front area. How do we make sure they go where we want? They could just pick up stakes and go anywhere."

O'Malley shrugged. "Anywhere they go has to be quieter than where they are now."

Charlie started pacing again, snapping his fingers. "Okay, okay, we can do this," he said, thinking aloud. "We need a pretend surveillance team to spook them—but a *second* team hanging back in the bushes." He stopped pacing and snapped his fingers one last time for punctuation. "*Surveilling.*"

Griggs made a thoughtful face. "And the second team watches so that, wherever Gino moves his business, we can follow." He laughed. "Good, Charlie. I like it a lot."

Charlie grinned like a ten-year-old.

~ 59 ~

I can do this, Solo told himself as he unrolled the blanket he had retrieved from the trunk of his car and his arsenal bounced on the unmade bed. A quick inventory of the ammo netted a hundred bullets for the .38, about fifty shells for the .410 revolver. He had a couple clips for the .32.

His hands shook as he took some of the guns apart and cleaned them. Should have been an easy thing, like butter, but in his current state of mind all bets were off. He decided to clean the automatics, too, mostly to kill time. He loaded the weapons, clumsily dropping bullets and clips on stained carpet.

He stopped several times to wash his hands, each time careful to lather and then rinse for the correct length of time. It wasn't something you had to sing out loud, necessarily, but you had to go through it in your head. Twice.

When he looked up at the mirror, he caught another ghostly glimpse of good ol' Pastor Fresno Jones watching from the corner. Still moving his lips, making no sound at all. But when Solo whirled around he was alone.

Across the room on the end table, the Gideons Bible appeared to be turned to a different place now. Where had that come from? Hadn't he ripped it up, burned it, thrown it out? The past few days were hazy, but Solo was sure he remembered the thin pages tearing easily, the tough binding less so. He was too far away to see where the pages were turned now, and he wasn't going to look.

As he sat on the bed with his gun blanket and weapons, he thought about the next name on the crumpled list. Thought about looking in the man's eyes, offering to set him free from this mortal coil, the target slumped to the ground with empty eyes, bleeding into the earth from whence he came. It was the way of the world.

Solo had done this so many times, had long ago gone numb with practice and experience. But right now he just felt nauseated. He tried to imagine the mark's eyes, but they kept morphing into the eyes of Pastor Fresno Jones.

Solo's hands began shaking again and he felt the siren call of the corner of the room, a good corner for shivering, and suddenly longed for the safety of his quiet time with the stale pies in the basement of his childhood home and it was then that he knew he couldn't do this. Not like this.

Rattled as he was, Solo needed a couple more kills under his belt before he would be free to get on with his life. Then he would close his eyes and good ol' Pastor Fresno Jones would fade into the gray and become another half-remembered detail for his scribbled memoirs.

No, he needed to make this kill—but doing it in close quarters was no good. Knives, no good. Handguns, no good.

I need a rifle, he told himself. I'll get a rifle and I'll go old-school sniper on this guy. Just like in the army. He might not have been the best marksman in the army, but Solo had certainly proven to be the coldest.

He could do this next job. Track the prey, get the lay of the land, find the best vantage point, make the shot, BAM.

Scratch another name off the list.

Solo went to the pay phone and made another call to Gus. This time he was able to say everything was cool; Solo just needed a rifle and ammo without going through the usual legal channels. Gus, relieved, set up a drop.

Solo smoked to look casual, like he was loitering, until a kid in a greasy T-shirt, strawberry fields on his arms, came and handed over a gym bag. Solo didn't know what arrangement Gus had made with the kid, but he didn't ask for anything and Solo wasn't in the mood to offer.

Solo stamped out the cigarette on concrete with his heel and he was in business. He could do this. Time to take care of Judge Hapsburg Reynolds.

— 60 —

A call from a pay phone. A diner two blocks from the police station. A man shoveling in quarters and punching up numbers.

A gruff voice answering, "What have you got?" Earl "Dr. Bones" Havoc.

The man at the pay phone says, "I know how you can set up Gino."

– 61 –

In the car, Solo punching buttons on the radio until he could find something good. He stopped when he heard the familiar melody and bang of KISS, something from *Destroyer*. Solo cranked up the big rock crunch loud, savagely nodding to the music as he pumped himself up for the gig.

Got to the courthouse about noon, parked in a pay lot down the street. Solo walked up the sidewalk, eyeing buildings along the way, looking for rooftops, vantage points.

He analyzed the steps leading toward the entrance but didn't figure the target would come and go by the front door. That would be too open, too vulnerable, too accessible to drunks and fools with a grudge. Anyone could just march right up and make trouble.

Solo lit another cigarette—look at me, I'm casual, everybody just keep casual—and decided there must be a parking garage in back. He wondered whether blueprints might be available online; it looked pretty easy on TV. Solo didn't have Internet access, nor the patience or wherewithal to find a city clerk and beat the info out of him.

He took a walk, nonchalant, just a tourist taking a smoke and a walk, careful not to bump into any uniforms. The front would be guarded. There would be metal detectors inside. As long as the target was on the job, the man was sitting in a fortress.

Solo, checking his watch, decided the target wouldn't get off work for a few hours. So he strolled to the nearby drugstore.

They didn't sell comic books and they were out of the antibacterial wipes, so he grabbed a newspaper, a Mountain Dew, and a pack of Dentyne.

Returning to his spot across the street from the courthouse, he picked a bench and sat in the sun, twisting the cap off the green plastic bottle and wiping the mouth of the bottle with his shirt. He wasn't sure whether he was adding or subtracting germs with that move, but at least his germs were better than somebody else's. He took a swig, enjoying the fizz and citrusy goodness.

He unwrapped a piece of the Dentyne and popped it in his mouth. The sharp cinnamon burned his tongue, mixing badly with the Dew, but something about the act of chewing made you seem more casual.

Solo killed the afternoon flipping through the paper, paying careful attention to the funnies and the sports. The weather was cool and sunny—not bad if you were wearing a coat.

Checking his watch again, Solo decided maybe he should consider finding the target's residence. Sure, if he just waited a few more hours, he might be able to just follow the man home. But Solo was feeling jittery, needed to keep moving.

Since the assignment had been to kill the targets on the job, the information provided by the client did not include the judge's home address. But given his current state of mind, Solo was ready to expand his options.

He walked a few blocks, began looking for a phone booth. Ripped a page out of the phone book, showing three addresses attached to the same name. It was possible that Judge Reynolds was unlisted, that all three were false leads, but it was all Solo had for now. Coordinating the listed addresses with his maps of Kansas City and nearby communities, Solo spent the afternoon scratching possibilities off the list.

First residence, about forty minutes west, a battered trailer with a plastic sunflower spinning in what could be loosely referred to as the yard.

Second address led to a house that was at least a step up, a crummy tan-brick one-story box with unmowed lawn. In fact, the lawn mower sat in a dozen pieces in the carport, soaking in a pool of oil and abandonment.

Solo began to feel he was wasting his time, but the third address seemed viable. Gated community. Nice houses. Lovely trees.

Solo parked across the street and hoped this was the place. Smiled as he analyzed the row of trees behind the property. If the target's house was one of those along the back row, all the better.

He drove the twenty-five minutes back to the courthouse. Only way to determine for sure whether candidate Number Three was the right house was to follow the target after work. But making the trip ahead of time gave Solo an edge—if the scenery began to look familiar, he could relax and hang back.

Stationed back at his bench, across the street and up the hill, Solo flipped to the next page of his paper, glancing quickly at the fortress again. Realized he was nervously snapping his gum. Forced himself to relax.

I can do this. I can do this.

– 62 –

Dr. Bones, with his thugs in a car heading to Zoo Girls. Asking why Solo hadn't finished his job yet. "Don't know, sir," the driver, a beefy Hungarian named Lugo, answered dutifully, eyes in rearview mirror. "Haven't seen him around in more'n a week now."

Dr. Bones cursed. "Where is that dirtbag keeping himself?"

Both thugs in front shrugged, Lugo and the thick-necked Joe Fix. Bones sighed. "Okay, we need to get Gino to talk to us in the back room."

Fix, in the passenger seat, turned toward Bones. "Where do you mean?"

"The place where we're driving right now, you nimrod," Bones shot back. "Back room of the Zoo Girls."

"Why, Dr. Bones?"

" 'Cause I say so," Bones replied. "Our friend inside of law enforcement says the Feds have a listening device in there." He smiled. "Everything we say in that room goes on tape."

Lugo asked, "What if Gino don't wanna leave his table? Can't we just record him there?"

"The microphone don't work there."

"Why not?"

Bones smacked Lugo in the back of the head. "What am I, Regis Philbin? I'm telling you boys, no matter what, we push Gino to the back room of the club. I got things to tell him."

They continued in silence, Dr. Bones gazing out the window, alone with his thoughts. Then Fix, popping Sudafeds, turned again, "Won't that mean we're on tape, too, Boss?"

"No, because you idiots don't say nothing, understand?" Then, more pleasantly, "It's all worked out. This is all about getting that crudball Gino outta the way."

Lugo nodded, made a turn. "Whatever you say, Boss."

Dr. Bones poked Lugo on the shoulder. "Pull in here."

As the car pulled into a parking space, Lugo asked, "You wearin' a wire, Dr. Bones?"

"What do you mean, am I wearing a wire? What am I, a pansy? You think I'm a pansy?"

Lugo looked down at the steering wheel, sheepish. "No, Boss." Fix occupied himself with looking at the fire hydrant outside his window.

Bones sat back. "I ain't no pansy."

- 63 -

Inside Zoo Girls. AC/DC blasting out the speakers, "Big Gun," girls writhing as Dr. Bones and his soldiers met Gino at his usual table, the corner booth. "Dr. Bones," Gino greeted, breaking into a smile, no doubt considering the return of Bones to be an endorsement, "what brings you here to my humble abode?"

Bones motioned toward the office in the back. "We should really move off the floor here." Yelling above the music. "It's not safe to talk out here."

"Nah, man, this is great," Gino yelled, leaning back, stretching his arms across the booth. "These are all my peeps," he said, nodding toward the losers on the main floor. "None of them would give us trouble."

Even if not for the plan, the noise would have been enough to drive Bones to get things moving. Without explaining himself, he began checking under the table and then along the wall behind Gino, everyone watching with puzzled interest.

Bones found what he was looking for in the light fixture over the table. For the sake of drama he yanked at the lamp, grunting until he ripped it out of the wall. Chunks of plaster flying, chips landing in the drinks.

He held the lamp in one hand, the small attachment in the other. "As long as we stay out here, you're in trouble." He nodded toward the back again. "Let's go back to your office." Gave that snake smile. "Trust me."

Gino's group quickly gathered their belongings, ashen-faced. At first, they wanted to leave the building, run outside, and find a new hangout, but Bones smoothly herded them to the back, where he assured them they would be safe from prying ears.

The office was a mess, the desk a pile of folders and papers. Bones positioned Gino close to where he knew another listening device was located. Closing the door, Bones pulled off his fedora and held it in his hand. "Back here we can talk."

Gino paced. "Who gets off invading my space out there?"

Bones grabbed Gino by the shoulders, eye to eye. "That bug was for Turk. But Turk was a nobody, so they stopped paying attention." Almost the truth.

Bones let go of Gino and walked a few paces, then turned and pointed. "I got a hot tip for you, Gino."

The younger man relaxed. Sat in the desk chair, locking fingers behind his head to prove how relaxed he was. "What?"

Bones glowed. "A major shipment of heroin."

Gino made a face. "Heroin?"

"Worked out a deal with the Chinese." Bones stopped in front of the desk. "For a percentage, we take the product off their hands and make a fortune on the streets."

"I don't know." Gino cocked his head like a spaniel. "Pa didn't like to get into drugs."

"What do you think I am, dumb or something?" Controlled menace in his voice. Gino stiffened. "Now, you listen to me," Bones said, leaning in, pointing two fingers on his right hand. "This is what I got for you. Now forgive me, but your father never worked the junk because he never had the guts."

Then Bones softened, breaking into a smile. "But you're better than that. You are the king now. Reach out and grab it."

Gino stood and moved closer to Bones. Sighed. "Okay, Bones. If this is what you think."

"It's what I think."

— 64 —

Ten minutes after six, Judge Hapsburg Reynolds drove his Ford Explorer out of the parking garage. Solo, in his nondescript Dodge, was positioned to follow. As they wound their way through traffic, Solo trailed him, hanging back three cars, four cars at a time, switching lanes at random intervals. As they hit rush-hour traffic, there were some touch-and-go moments, but Solo hung with the target.

They left the city limits, headed in a direction Solo had not been. If the good judge was headed home, that meant Solo had spent the afternoon visiting the houses of strangers.

The drive went on another forty-five minutes to an hour. They reached a remote area, climbing steadily through hills, all the while Solo drifting further and further back, hoping not to give away his presence.

They passed the occasional cabin or trailer home. Solo glanced down at the fuel gauge, wishing he'd filled up before they took off.

The climb was steep and dark, Solo's old Dodge wheezing to keep up with the Explorer. As the snow began to fall, the only light now came from the moon and the Explorer's headlights ahead. And they were getting farther and farther away.

With each turn in the road, Solo worried he would lose the judge or, worse, get lost altogether. He was relieved when Judge Reynolds finally pulled into a private road—what looked to be a gravel driveway.

Solo drove another quarter mile or so, parked off the country road. He doubled back on foot, lugging the gym bag, the metal parts inside banging intermittently against his leg. He embraced the pain. It helped him focus, helped him ignore the gnawing at his soul.

As he trudged up the hill in the dark, Solo buttoned his coat, pulling up the collar to fight the bitter wind. The crunch of gravel forced him to head for the grass, where he found the crunch of his shoes on dead leaves and branches nearly as bad. Solo cursed and slowed his pace to keep the noise down.

Light pooled at the top of the hill, a nicer house than you'd expect this far from civilization. The Explorer and a PT Cruiser parked out front. Solo doubted this was the target's residence, but didn't know whether this was a visit or overnight stay. Long weekend? Tryst?

If Solo had his act together, he would have just stormed into the place, no fear, just kick the door in, grab the judge by the arm, drag him outside kicking and screaming, press the .32 in the man's face, give the customary "You're welcome" speech, and head off to the nearest tavern for onion rings and a beer.

Under normal circumstances, the thought would thrill him. Right now, the idea made Solo vomit in the grass. He hit his knees, retching, the pressure behind his eyes making him feel his head might explode.

Afterward, he wiped his hands on leaves off the ground, wishing the antibacterial wipes had been in stock at the drugstore. He didn't have anything to rinse the taste out of his mouth; he spent the next several minutes spitting, trying to salivate the wicked taste out.

Eyes adjusting to darkness, he could finally make out shapes in the moonlight. He saw a narrow entry through a thick patch of naked trees, leading to higher ground.

Following the path, he ended up at a vantage point that made him feel pretty good: far enough from the house so no one could see him setting up, but where the scope gave him a great view of the front door.

From here, he saw the house—saw the lake off to the side, shimmering in moonlight—saw the cleared space for the backyard. As long as the judge didn't have some underground-tunnel exit, everything would be fine. Dandy.

Sparkling.

— 65 —

Holland and Sallis were stationed again near the entrance of the Poignard. They occasionally acted as greeters, nodding and smiling politely at guests, holding the door.

It was cold tonight, Sallis was rubbing his hands and watching his breath. He turned to Holland, who was humming that tune again. "You gonna make music all night?"

"Sorry," Holland replied, brushing blond hair out of his eyes, "I can't get it out of my head."

"What is that again?"

"It's from *Singin' in the Rain*."

"I thought 'Singin' in the Rain' went different than that."

"I didn't say it was 'Singin' in the Rain,' I said it was something from *Singin' in the Rain*. It's a musical. It's got lots of songs."

"Oh." Sallis, still rubbing hands, blew on them. Didn't help. "So, which song?"

"I don't remember."

The two were silent again, watching the street out front, watching cars and pedestrians pass by. Sallis, clicking a Jolly

Rancher in his teeth, turned back to Holland, trying to think of something to talk about, anything to keep his mind off the cold. "Read anything good lately?"

Holland nodded. "Some Japanese guy, I forget the name. But he's good." He smiled at an attractive brunette and her older companion, held the door for them. Once they crossed the threshold, he let go of the handle. "I like that he doesn't explain everything."

"What do you mean?"

"You know, a lot of novels you read and put them down and you're just done. Ready to go on with your life." He rubbed his nose with the back of his hand. "But this guy, he puts in a lot of texture, stuff you can't stop thinking about, even after you put the book down. Like a loose tooth you can't stop thumping with your tongue, you know?"

"Yeah, I guess," Sallis said, still rubbing hands. Thinking about a hot sandwich. "You ever read that book, *The Da Vinci Code*?"

"It was okay."

"There was some big controversy, I guess."

"Yeah."

"What was that about?"

"It was about people being stupid. Just because a character in a book says somethin' don't make it so. Today's readers ain't sophisticated enough to distinguish between the voice of the author and the voice of the character."

"People are stupid."

"They're the worst."

Then they saw a familiar figure shambling up the sidewalk toward them, Turk, mumbling to himself. Sallis intercepted him before he made it to the door. "Whoa there, old-timer," Sallis said, baring teeth in an awkward grin. "Where're you going?"

"Got me business with Frank." A husk of his former self.

Sallis and Holland exchanged looks of pity. Sallis said, "I don't think that's a good idea."

"No, you don't understand, me and Frank got business." Turk's eyes darted back and forth, trying to make contact with either of the men. "Business."

Holland pushed Sallis and Turk aside to allow some patrons to pass into the restaurant. He nodded a greeting before turning cold eyes back to Turk. "You gotta go, man."

"But me and Frank, we go way back," Turk pleaded. "We got blood that goes back to the beginning."

Holland shoved Turk away from the door, directing him down the sidewalk from whence he came. "Now, you know the drill—the boss don't want to see you no more." Holland leaned in close and whispered in Turk's ear. "Now, we're supposed to pop you we even see you around here. But we'll stretch our necks here this once."

Holland whirled Turk around to look him square in the eye. "Next time, you won't be so lucky." Pause, searching to see if he'd made contact. Put a hand inside his coat, hand on his heater. "Don't make me pull this gun. You know what Chekhov says, right?"

– 66 –

Next morning. Solo at his perch on the hill, staring through the scope at the cabin. Judge Reynolds had been there all night with a young blonde Solo could not imagine was the man's wife.

Solo rubbed tired eyes. He had assembled the rifle in the dark, had watched through the scope off and on, even after the lights had gone out at three A.M.

He had again briefly toyed with the direct approach, just kick in the door and finish the job, but dropped the idea before it made him vomit again. Solo felt stupid and broken, needed to make this kill, needed to prove he wasn't washed out.

Around six A.M., give or take, Solo watched through the scope as Judge Reynolds and his woman, both in robes, frolicked around the breakfast table. They must have had a great view of a lake through the dining-room window.

The judge came out front seven-thirty A.M. in his suit, headed for the office. He and the woman, sharp blue dress, out in the driveway, talking, chatting, planning, hugging. Solo could not have had a better shot.

Solo watched, counted for no particular reason, felt the rifle in gloved hands, felt the pressure of the trigger. The crosshairs zeroed on the target's head. He adjusted, compensating for wind and gravity.

I can do this. I can do this.

Solo rubbed his tired eyes again, then carefully re-aimed for the target. Clean. Easy. No problem. No problem.

Solo jolted as he saw the third person. Standing near the others, to the side, not interacting in any way, staring right toward him.

Pastor Fresno Jones. Staring.

~ 67 ~

"Now why would Bones say that?" O'Malley was meeting with Griggs and Charlie, sharing the transcript of Bones' pitch to Gino. Including details of the job.

It was the weirdest thing. Here the task force had been in a bunch, trying to figure out how to maneuver Gino into his back office so they could get him on tape. And for some reason, Bones had done the job for them: had herded Gino back to the office, had positioned Gino so close to the mike that this new transcript had every word. You can't buy luck like that.

He went on. "I can't believe Gino would be dumb enough to get into drugs at this point. Fat Cat has always stayed out of narcotics."

O'Malley touched a hand to his chin, thinking. "The junk trade is not worth the trouble, no matter how much it brings in."

Griggs wrinkled his brow. "But organized crime was built on drug trafficking." He turned to Charlie, the whiz kid. "Help me out here, Aaron Sorkin."

"Actually," the kid lectured, "organized crime was built on liquor trafficking during Prohibition. Before the 1920s, the Mob was just a nickel-and-dime operation."

The kid continued, picking up steam, "Thanks to a handful of picketers who convinced Congress it was possible to legislate morality, Prohibition led to a business model that catapulted the Mafia into an empire."

"Exactly," Griggs said, feeling vindicated. "If it worked with alcohol, it should also work with narcotics."

O'Malley shook his head. "It's a different world out there, Griggs." He stood, walked to the window, squinting into sunlight. "While many of their criminal enterprises can be kept quiet, the drug trade attracts the most unstable people."

Charlie nodded. "It also puts you out in the open. Selling drugs means you have to be on the street, sooner or later." Muttering to himself he added, "Not to mention the neighborhood-watch angle."

Griggs turned to him. "What was that?"

"When it's about gambling or prostitution," Charlie said, "the neighborhood moms and grandmas shrug and think it's a shame, but at least it's just the bad people doing bad things."

"And?" Griggs felt like the dumbest person in the room. Didn't like it. It reminded him of marriage counseling.

"But one key component of the drug trade is that they come after your children," Charlie said, "drafting them as employees or hooking them as clients. When it strikes that close to home, parents find the courage to step up and get involved."

"Yeah," Griggs said thoughtfully, looking down at the transcript again. Pause. "Which brings us full circle."

O'Malley turned to him, piqued. "Yeah?"

"Why would Dr. Bones tell Gino to get into the junk business?"

— 68 —

Frankie Catalano had found Turk crashing at his sister's house out in the suburbs. She didn't want to be involved with Turk's profession, with his lifestyle, but when Turk suddenly found himself on the outs with the organized-crime community, she couldn't very well turn her own brother out in the cold.

Frankie had found Turk sitting in the living room by the fire, an afghan pulled tight around him. "This is gonna sound crazy," he began.

Turk regarded the young Catalano. Frankie was like a nephew to him—Turk had watched him grow up, had posted his first bail. He said, "After these past couple weeks, what's one more crazy thing?"

"You know how sometimes you gotta do something bad to fight an even bigger bad thing?" Frankie, sitting on the couch, was aware that Turk's sister was hovering nearby, out of vision but never out of earshot. When she had found him at the door she had been rude, convinced Frankie was here to drag Turk back into the old life. "It's like that thing they say, you have to start a fire to fight a fire?"

Turk, looking in the fireplace, snorted. "What do you mean, start a fire?"

"Seriously, it's a thing they do. When there's this big fire, one way to fight it is start another fire. I don't remember the explanation, I'm not a scientist, but it's a thing they do. Or like when they fight a disease by putting another disease in your body."

"Sure." Turk nodded uncertainly. "But what's that got to do with us? You joining the fire department or something?"

Frankie shook his head. Took in a breath, sucking in his cheeks, then blew back out dramatically, watching his breath interact with the fire. He stood and walked toward the hearth, moving closer to the heat. The crackle of burning wood was soothing. "We gotta go to the cops."

Turk didn't answer. Frankie wondered if the older man hadn't heard what he said. But when he looked over, Turk was gripping the afghan with white knuckles. Finally, the old man rasped, "Are you crazy?"

Frankie shook his head, held his hands close to the fire. The room was warm but he was chilled to the bone. "It's like I said, you gotta do a bad thing to make a worse thing go away."

"I should just pop you right here. Dump your body in the sewer out back."

Frankie heard the gasp of the woman eavesdropping in the next room, ignored it. "Nah, man, we go to the cops and we, what do you call it, we stipulate."

"Stipulate?"

"We make it clear we aren't turning against Papa," Frankie said, the words coming out all in a rush. "We tell 'em we want immunity for Papa, this is all about Gino and Ritchie and Dr. Bones."

Turk looked at the fire again.

Frankie continued. "Between us, we got the evidence, we got the knowledge. We got the edge. If the cops want to play with us, they gotta play by our rules."

Turk tilted his head slowly to the left and to the right, trying to orient himself in this new world...this new world where he would even consider going to the cops. Frankie could see the wheels turning, could see the tide shifting, could see the wind blowing in a new direction. "C'mon, Turk, these guys are no good. They have turned Papa's head in some strange place. How else you explain he turns you and me out in the street like this?"

Turk nodding. "That's right."

"There's no reason Papa would have turned like that, unless those guys confused him with a lot of sweet words. As long as they're in there and we're out here, Papa is in trouble."

"Yeah," Turk still nodding, talking to himself now. "We'd be helping Frank."

We can start a fire, he thought, looking back at the hearth. The only trick was not to get burned in the process.

~ 69 ~

Solo had napped in the woods before heading back to his car, driving back down the hill. He stopped at a tavern a couple miles from the judge's country home, a shack called The Swig. Parking in the gravel and heading inside, it took a second for his eyes to adjust to the indoor light. He took a stool by the counter.

Took an inventory of his wallet. His cash reserves were running low. He needed to hang onto a ten for more towelettes and another ten for a box of Icy Hot patches—staying on that hill overnight had done a number on his back.

He was down to less than a hundred bucks. Back when he expected to finish the gig, expenses were no big deal. Now, Solo had some hard drinking and hard thinking to do. And less than a hundred bucks.

"Whatcha need, sailor?" The woman behind the bar looked like she had seen prettier days. Maybe it was the early hour, maybe it was Solo's burning eyes. He was exhausted.

He tried winking and it came off as a twitch. "Jack Daniels," he answered in a cracked voice. When the drink came, Solo didn't even make eye contact. "Can I get some eggs?"

"Sure, you want the special?" He looked up with questioning eyes. She added, "Eggs, toast, bacon, American fries."

Solo looked down again, realized his back was to the front door. Stupid. "Sure," he said, rising, grabbing his glass, "the eggs runny and the bacon crunchy." He glanced around, pointed to the back booth. "I'll be back there."

"Sure thing, hon."

Back in the booth, he took a sip and grit his teeth as he thought about his predicament. There would be repercussions. A man does not retire from this line of work. If Fat Cat or his soldiers should decide he was weak, they might assume Solo could also turn state's evidence. He would never do that, but they'd never allow the risk.

As a freelancer, Solo hadn't just worked with one family, he'd worked with all of them. Now they'd all think he was a risk. Coast to coast.

The tavern door opened, light flooding in. A shadow entered, went for the bar, started chatting it up with the lady. She called him "sailor," too.

Solo returned to his drink and his worry. Maybe he could explain himself. Explain this setback, this psychological glitch where he was worthless for anything he had ever been good at. Maybe they would take it in stride, be patient. After all, he had done them a lot of good in the past. *Sure, Solo, no problem. You just need a vacation.*

He took another sip, grimaced. Anything he told those people at this point would mean a one-way visit to one of their construction projects.

He pulled out the newspaper clipping again. He never did find out how the trial turned out. Whether this woman was convicted or went to prison. Whether she was still alive. Whether she could be who he thought she might be.

The waitress came back to the table, a greasy plate in one hand and silverware in the other. When she set the plate down, she dropped the silverware on the bare tabletop. "Anything else I can get you?"

He grabbed her arm. "I can't use this silverware. It's touched the table."

"I wiped the table down this morning."

"Just bring me some napkins and another set of silverware." He looked up with pitiful eyes. "Please."

She sighed. Chomping on gum. "All right, hon." She walked away.

Solo found himself thinking about the clipping again. What if he did make a break for Priest Pointe, Kansas? He was this close already, just a couple hours away. He didn't have enough gas to get there, so he'd have to steal a car. But he had to focus. F-O-C-U-S. Had to rein in his scattered thoughts.

He needed to talk to Gus. It would be a risk—in this line of work, every friend is another potential knife for your back—but Solo was too rattled not to trust Gus this one time.

He needed quarters. He also made a mental note to get phone cards, the kind that reroute your long-distance calls and gave a false reading to caller ID.

The woman returned with some napkins, laid one down, and carefully and conspicuously placed his fork and his knife and his spoon on top. She stood back and grinned. "You gonna be okay now?"

He looked at the plate and up again. "You got Heinz 57?"

— 70 —

That night. Griggs looked through Nighthawk tactical night-vision binoculars toward the rail yard outside the city. The bad guys were still waiting for Gino and his men to show up.

"Hey," Charlie said, "let me see."

Hoping it wouldn't lead to another round of "Charlie Knows More Than You Do," Griggs handed the field glasses over. Surrounding them were all manner of armed agents in black clothes and black masks and goggles. O'Malley had set up the small army, courtesy of the FBI and the DEA. Griggs wasn't quite sure who they answered to—and once the operation was over, he didn't know who would get the collar, either. He tried to convince himself the question mark didn't bother him.

Hunched in the darkness, he turned to Jordan again, trying not to sniff her hair. "She never listens, is the thing."

She frowned at him. "What?" Sotto voce, nervous they might break their cover.

"My wife. She never listens, she never understands."

"Griggs, I don't know whether I should—"

"I do all this work, I work hard to keep the streets safe." He gestured around at the other agents. "We all do." He saw Charlie trying not to listen, trying to keep watch through the glasses. "She has her own selfish needs, she blames me unfairly for the loss of our daughter, she drags me to counseling, she even drags me out with her friends, the better to gang up on me."

He didn't notice how uncomfortable Jordan was feeling. Didn't notice the growing number of agents focusing less on their surveillance and more on his chatter. "She expects me to be home all the time, I tell you that?"

"Actually, I think—"

"Here we are, middle of the night, freezing in a train yard because we have to save the city from gangsters, she's wasting her time teaching and knitting." He spat on the ground. "Not that she ever finished anything."

Jordan leaned in, spoke in a soft voice. "Have you considered your wife's side at all?" She looked to see whether she was disturbing the others. "She just wants more chances to talk." She looked around again to make sure the bad guys hadn't arrived yet. She turned back. "It doesn't do any good to talk to me about this. You need to be talking to your wife. Talking *with* your wife. Not at her."

Griggs felt his blood in his cheeks. This wasn't the sympathy he was expecting. "I didn't ask for a lecture."

Charlie dropped the field glasses and scooted closer. "You know, I have a theory," he said, handing the glasses back to Griggs, who turned away from Jordan and looked over the yard as the kid continued. "I think the reason God made Adam head of the household over Eve is because he wanted to punish them both by putting the dumber of the two in charge."

Jordan wrinkled her brow. "What do you mean?"

Griggs could see the Chinese gang clearly, could see the two leaders, Alan Chin and John Lee. To be honest, he couldn't tell them apart. The one with the shaved head was smoking, leaning against the black car, while the one with the goatee paced. A variety of others were clustered nearby, hanging out by a series of boxcars off the main track.

"In the Garden of Eden," Charlie continued, "everything was perfect. The only real command for Adam and Eve was to not eat the fruit from the tree of the knowledge of good and evil."

"Oh, the apple, right?"

Charlie chuckled at Jordan. Griggs was growing to hate that chuckle. "Actually, we don't know anything about what it looked or even tasted like."

Jordan nodded. "Okay."

"So the serpent came along and convinced Eve to eat the forbidden fruit. Now, notice this: The serpent had to *convince* her, go through a whole conversation, a series of back-and-forths, syllogisms, to convince Eve to do the wrong thing."

Griggs turned from his glasses. "Doesn't sound so smart to me."

Charlie pointed an "Ah" finger upward. "But with Adam, it didn't require all this intellectual trouble. All they said to Adam was, 'Here.'"

"And?"

"So I'm saying that Eve had to be outsmarted, but the man was too lazy—or too dumb—to require the trouble. So when God threw them out of the Garden of Eden, I believe God deliberately put the dumber of the two in charge as punishment." He grinned at Jordan. "In fact, most times, men would get into a lot less trouble if they would just listen to the women."

Griggs saw lights and a cloud of loose snow on the road in the distance. Gino was coming. He turned from the glasses to glare at Charlie. "You're not married, right?"

Charlie dropped the stupid grin. "No."

"When you've been married a few years, get back to me." Griggs picked up the walkie-talkie and spoke into it. "They're coming." Alerting cops and federal agents in black wearables and masks. "Let's roll."

— 71 —

Five minutes after the scheduled time, Gino and his men got out of his limo and a second car, strode across the platform toward the Chinese gang. Gino assumed the men approaching were the two that Dr. Bones had told him about, John Lee and Alan Chin.

"Hey, fellas. What's the haps?"

The one with a goatee said, "You're late."

Gino smiled, wondering briefly about their chain of command. Decided he didn't care. "Just wanted to make sure we weren't followed." He laughed, trying to put the Chinese at ease. Something about them made him nervous. Was Bones sure about this? Maybe he should have come along.

In the harsh floodlights the Chinese had set up, a forklift brought a pallet of unlabeled silver cans. Could be drugs, could be green beans. Gino motioned with his head and one of his men grabbed a can off the pallet, shoved a big hunting knife through the lid. The man pulled the knife out and smelled the powder, tasted it, smiled as powder drifted in the wind.

Gino smiled. This could work. This might just be his—

Helicopters swooped in, billowing snow and flooding light. Men in masks surrounded them, rifles poised, barking orders. The Chinese dropped weapons and raised their hands, Gino thinking they'd set him up.

He was clustered with his own men, cowards with hands over their heads. As a small group of plainclothes detectives strolled toward him, Gino tightened his grip on the weapon behind his back. Hoping the cops couldn't see.

One of the plainclothes stepped to the lead, flashed a badge, made eye contact. "Gino Catalano, I'm Detective Tom Griggs and you are under arrest."

Gino, breathing heavily, adjusted his grip on the gun, hand shaking, thoughts of his father and Bones and humiliation coursing through his veins. The cop with the big mouth continued in a dull, sing-songy tone, "We have you surrounded. You aren't going anywhere. You have the right to remain silent—"

Gino, hyperventilating, pulled his gun and fired twice, missing bigmouth but hitting one of the plainclothes agents to his side, the cop grunting and flopping back.

He fled. Bursting through the cluster of mobsters, he jumped into the darkness at the edge of the floodlights. There was a hail of gunfire, bullets whizzed past, he felt a KER-CHUNK pop his left calf. And he fled.

Behind him, bigmouth said, "Everybody back, I'm on him!"

He was crunching across gravel, stumbled across railroad ties in the moonlight. Could hear yelling and barking behind him, heard the hum of copters circling somewhere in the distance. If they spotlighted him, he was done.

Gino tried to control his wheezing, was conscious of the gravel as he ran. Wishing the snow softened more of the sound. He saw blood on the ground. His own. Not just from the leg.

Leg throbbing, he stumbled across tracks. It occurred to him to just follow the tracks out of here, it would keep him from getting lost out in the woods. He was limping when the tracks began to shake.

Gino could see light pooling around him. Flashlights? Choppers, circling overhead? Felt a whoosh, heard a wail, noticed something bearing down on him. He jumped and rolled, the train whizzing past, clatter, clatter, clatter.

In agony, he pushed himself off the ground. Woozier by the minute, he staggered toward a string of boxcars, attempted to crawl into the nearest freight car. It was closed, he couldn't figure out the door in the dark, he crawled under.

Pulling himself up on the other side of the car, he was lost. Wondering if he was trapped. He turned and saw a ladder on the side of the car, started heaving himself up. He heard steps in gravel approaching quickly, fired a few shots blindly under the car. Heard people diving for gravel.

Climbed the ladder, wasn't sure where he planned to go, knew if he could just get on top, he could get his bearings. Struggled to climb, strength failing him, imagined he could feel the blood oozing out of him, wondered if this light-headed feeling was how it worked, almost lost the grip on his gun.

Reaching the top of the boxcar, Gino searched for an opening, thought maybe he could hide. If he could just sit a second—just sit and stop bleeding. He found a hatch, grabbed the handle, it wouldn't give. Setting down his pistol, he grasped the hatch handle with both hands and tugged hard. No good.

He heard the black-and-whites rushing in, sirens blaring, lights flashing. Heard helicopters buzzing around, searching with floodlights. Heard footsteps again, running on gravel and snow.

Gino started crawling across the top of the car, wished the train would just go and take him somewhere, anywhere, but the cops and Feds probably had all the engineers locked tight, out of the way.

He heard someone climbing up the ladder from where he'd come, had his gun ready. Nervous, hands shaking, leg throbbing, he fired prematurely, warning the guy on the ladder.

Voice came from the edge, "Police! Freeze! You're under arrest, Gino Catalano! You have the right to remain silent!" Somebody too young to be out on a night like this. "Anything you say can and will be used against you in a court of law. You have the right to an attorney—"

Gino pushed himself up, limping across the top of the car, following the voice. *I'll kill you, cop.*

Suddenly, a voice behind. "Put the gun down, Gino." He turned and saw the main cop from before, bigmouth. "Nobody's gonna hurt you. Put the gun down."

Gino could hear his own wheezing, could feel his pulse in his ears.

The cop, gun trained on him, spoke again, "Drop it. Now."

Gino screamed and brought up his own gun. Before he could get off a shot, Griggs shot him three times square in the chest. The impact threw Gino over the side of the car and he landed splat in the gravel and snow.

Griggs went to the edge of the car, saw Jordan checking the fallen body of Gino Catalano, now surrounded by a growing crowd of cops and agents. Panting, he holstered his gun and wondered whether Charlie was alive.

– 72 –

Solo called to give Gus an update.

"I can't do the contract." Simple, to the point.

Gus took the news badly. He was a businessman, and this was bad for business.

After an earful, Solo didn't feel like going back to the motel, didn't know where to go. He was a stranger in town, didn't want to run into any of Fat Cat's people, didn't want to run into cops or Feds or gangsters or anyone else. He walked and drove the streets of Kansas City all night. All over.

Finally found himself in front of some church, Fisherman Methodist. How did he get here? He found an empty bottle in the gutter out front, it was green, he couldn't read the tattered label, swung his arm back and planned to heave it at the brick building.

Then he stopped. Thought. Considered. Decided.

He was going to have it out with this God once and for all.

Glancing around to make sure no one was watching, he stealthed across the lawn and headed to the front double doors. Locked, locked.

Apparently, God was closed for the night. Typical. Solo turned his collar up and stalked back into the bitter wind.

– 73 –

Detective Jordan Hall rode in the ambulance with Detective Charlie Pasch. The paramedics had done everything they could. As one of them monitored his blood pressure, Charlie drifted in and out of consciousness. It was a wonder he wasn't dead.

Hall wasn't feeling so good herself. She had never seen so much blood.

Charlie stirred again. When he saw her, his eyes lit up. A bit. "Jordan...Hall..." His eyes flitted, his brain processing something. "Hey...Hal...Jordan..." His eyes closed. "Never noticed that about your name before," he whispered before he was out again.

It was now in the hands of the hospital and God.

— 74 —

The sky was dark for Gino Catalano's funeral on Friday. Everyone was there.

Afterward, as Dr. Bones followed Frank Catalano to the car, he felt like he was on a tightrope now, playing all sides. It was a lot of work pushing a man off the ledge, especially if you intended to convince him it was his own idea.

They got into the limo. As soon as the door shut, Bones said, "You need to respond to Gino's death or lose the respect of the men."

"What are you saying?" Fat Cat had never looked so weary.

"If you don't respond in kind, the whole system will disintegrate."

"I don't know."

Bones exploded, pushing before the old man had a chance to recover from his grief—he needed the old man to get worked up, to lash out without thinking. "You wanna be mayor? You wanna be governor? You wanna be man-about-town?" Bones raised his voice with each possibility. "Prove you can be a father and take care of this."

"Why can't you take care of this?"

"Because it needs to be you, Frank—everyone needs to know that you are not a man to be trifled with. They need to know that nobody messes with Fat Cat." Bones dared to speak the name to his face. Knew it would get the man's blood moving again.

As the car followed the procession, Bones pushed again: "If you don't take care of this, Ritchie will think you don't care. He might reason, why should I care for my father if he don't care for his son?" Bones licked his lips. He hadn't expected the death of Gino to come so easily, but maybe this grand opportunity would put his own plans back on track. He had spent all this time angling for the batter's box, to mix a metaphor, all this time convincing Fat Cat he should hand off the power and run for office, become legit—

He thought back to a conversation with his own soldiers. One asked why he didn't just kill Fat Cat and step up. But, as Bones explained, this is a new age: The old ways don't work like they did. If they simply whacked the boss, who knew what would happen? No, this was supposed to be smooth. Who knew the idiot would leave it to his no-good sons?

Ever since Fat Cat had tossed his power to the wind, grabbing back the reins had been like trying to wrangle smoke.

"I try to be a reasonable man," Catalano was saying now, looking out the window at passing cars as Bones brought his focus back. "I try to form a legitimate life strategy, I pass off the enterprise to my family—and this cop kills my oldest son dead." He looked at Bones with sad eyes. "My Gino, dead. A father ain't supposed to outlive his son."

Bones leaned forward, feeling a crackle of excitement. "So what do we do?"

Fat Cat leaned forward, fire in his eyes. "You listen to me, Earl—you get that contractor on the phone and you tell him that if this cop is going to take away my family, then we are going to take away his family."

Bones pulled out his cell. Had Gus on the line in less than thirty seconds. "Tell your boy that Fat Cat has another job for him."

- 75 -

Solo had spent the evening cradling the gun, considering. His life was over. Couldn't imagine where to go from here, how to get there. Wondered if the gun could resolve him faster.

But after a couple hours of inactive cuddling under the watchful eye of silent-lip-moving Pastor Fresno Jones, Solo realized he still couldn't shoot anyone in this state of mind, not even himself.

The TV on in the background, some old black-and-white monster movie, he wondered if he might fare better with a razor. One good slit, pool of blood, and then he would be swallowed in sweet blackness. He hoped.

Hoped.

Had to be better than the hell he would go through if the families found him.

Crawled to the bathroom, dug through the toiletries, found a dull disposable razor. Sat back against the wall, breathing deep, breathing hard, trying to focus his thoughts, trying to figure out how to extricate the blade from the plastic housing.

He couldn't let them find him. Couldn't let the mob guys find him.

Eventually, he sighed, dug for the rusting can of shaving cream. If he couldn't end a life, maybe he could find a new one. He reached up for the sink and pulled himself up, looked at bloodshot eyes in the mirror. Filled the sink with hot water, steaming up the mirror.

He took a handful of shaving cream, ran it through his hair.

− 76 −

"Unbelievable." Bones pacing the floor at his garage, processing the news from Gus.

The Hungarian, Lugo, cocked his head. "What?"

"Our crudball hitman has taken himself some AWOL." Bones could feel his blood rising. "Just jumped out of the stream, just like that."

He stopped, held his hands out. "A professional." Shook his head. "A professional is supposed to do the job." Started pacing again. "This ain't professional."

Fix felt his pockets to find some more Sudafed pills. "So, let's get someone else."

"I don't got time for this. I'm trying to work angles here, I got angles to work, and now this guy I'm counting on steps out of the game and expects me to pick up the slack." Bones shook his head again, in his own world. "This ain't professional."

Lugo said, "Well, he got most of them, right? Put the fear of God in those do-gooders?"

"He had three of the original contract left, but that's not even the problem. I've finally got Fat Cat pushed to the ledge, but I can't make him jump unless we can add these two more to the list."

"Two more?"

"Yeah, the cop in the hospital and the wife of the cop who shot Gino dead."

"Why we gotta mess with the guy in the hospital?" Lugo didn't sound sympathetic, more like it was an imposition.

"It seems like a nice favor in Gino's memory. It's like we're helping him finish off his final act on this earth."

"Sure thing, boss," Lugo said. "Why don't we just do it? Me 'n' Fix, we go over, WHAP, done for, you know?"

Bones still pacing, still cloaked in his own thoughts. "Catalano," he spat. "Still can't believe he gave it all to his two no-good sons."

"At least it was only two of them," Fix offered, encouraging. "Frankie is out of the picture."

"No," Bones grumped, "as long as Frankie is alive, Frankie is part of the picture. If he ain't *with* me, he's *against* me. And last I heard, he ain't with me. Got it?"

Both men nodded, Fix said, "Sure, boss."

Bones spat. "And now this hit man leaves us high and dry."

Lugo raised an eyebrow. "You want us to take care of him?"

Still pacing. "We can't let this stand," Bones said to the men. "Make an example of this guy—and finish his original job. Get some more out-of-town talent if you have to."

"Let's make sure we got it straight," Fix said, counting on his fingers. "We whack the three guys left on the original list, we whack the cop in the hospital, we whack the wife of the cop who shot Gino dead, and we whack the original contractor who should have done it all for us in the first place."

"Yeah, yeah," Bones replied, feeling better. He snapped his fingers and pointed. "But don't turn your back on this thing," he said. "We need to be more personally involved. That was our mistake, we brought in this guy and then we trusted him and turned our backs and this is what happened. So if we bring in outsiders, it's purely to keep ourselves arm's length from this stuff." He put on his hat and adjusted it. "But no further than arm's length, got it?"

- 77 -

Shaving his head had been a lot more trouble than Solo had expected. After some time with the razor, he finally limped to the motel office and demanded an electric shaver. He labored all through the night, infused with nervous, sleepless energy.

He collapsed around nine A.M. the next morning, slept a few hours before he woke again. When he rubbed his head, the rough patches of hair confused him at first, until he remembered and shuffled to the bathroom mirror to check his work. Trying to finish the job, he still had trouble getting the hang of translating the mirror image into real action, crooking his neck and twisting his arms in weird contortions to reach.

Finally, he lathered up his head again, used the disposable razor to polish it off. Eventually satisfied the job was passable, he felt a jolt of remembered urgency. He needed to get out of town. Fast. He lurched for the bed, started grabbing things.

When he reached the nightstand, he was confronted with the Gideons Bible again, sitting open. Solo glanced around the room, but his phantom stranger hadn't put in any guest appearances for a while. With shaky confidence, he grabbed the Bible, threw it again in the trash. If he was leaving town, it couldn't possibly bother him anymore.

His bag haphazardly stuffed, Solo sat on the edge of the unmade bed to plan. Maybe he should get out of the country. He wondered whether it was a problem that he didn't have a passport. Didn't have a credit card, didn't have any unnecessary forms of ID. Solo had been a cipher all these years, wandering beneath the radar. Normally, the situation gave him peace of mind. Now it just limited his options.

He grabbed the maps off the bed. From what he heard, there was no problem crossing into Canada or Mexico without a passport; the only problem was in coming back. But, unless all of organized crime was scheduled to fall in a hole tomorrow, coming back wouldn't be an issue.

He didn't know what he'd do for money once he got out—wash dishes, shovel rock, train elephants. He only had the one marketable skill, but you couldn't really advertise "professional killer" in the classified section of the *Thrifty Nickel*.

He flipped a coin. Heads, Canada. Tails, Mexico. The coin landed tails. But he didn't want to learn a new language or drive through Texas, so he started checking the Missouri map for northbound routes.

As he traced out a route with his finger, he noticed the other folded map, a dog-eared corner sticking out of his coat pocket. He pulled it out and gingerly opened it—a ragged map of Kansas, disintegrating from the many times it had been opened and refolded. A red ink circle scribbled just millimeters to the right of where Priest Pointe should be listed.

Solo closed his eyes, thought of that trip he had promised himself so many times. When he'd gotten the call to come to Kansas City, he had toyed with taking some time after the killing was over to cross the border into Kansas and find Priest Pointe, to try and find this woman and see whether they were related. See whether she was his mother.

But the job had not ended well and now there was no time for family reunions. You can't get a job training elephants in Canada if you're dead.

He needed to figure out his best shot to the border, the smartest way to get there without leaving a trail. If even one guy could figure it out, it would bring the mob hammer down before he could see it coming. The mob didn't forget. It was what gave contract killers like Solo job security.

– 78 –

Back when Charlie had first handed over the stack of photos, he had wondered why it was taking the lab techs so long. "Why don't we just scan all these in and let the computer ID them?"

"This ain't *CSI: Kansas City*, Mr. Spock," had been the reply. "We still do things the old-fashioned way."

So much had happened since then. Had happened to Charlie.

Now, finally, Special Agent O'Malley and a detective, big grin on his face, came back to Griggs and Jurgens with the stack of photos, now with some of the dots connected.

"Nickel and Dime," O'Malley said, pointing at the first one. "A couple down-on-their-luck ex-KGB, ex-Russian Mafia."

Griggs nodded. Charlie had pronounced it *Mafiya*. "Tell me something I don't know."

"Okay." O'Malley leaned in, murmured in a conspiratorial tone. "They were looking to start a protection racket in town."

"They went to Turk for some pointers?"

"Not exactly," O'Malley snickered. "They went to shake him down."

"I bet that went well."

The detective spoke up, "This could explain why one of their associates—another Russki—turned up dead."

Griggs turned to him, wished he remembered the man's name. "I don't suppose he turned up conveniently dead right there at Turk's club?"

"Nah, he was out at a dump site a few miles away."

Griggs pointed to the next photo, a tall man in a suit. His hair styled like he was a used-car salesman. "Who's the guy?"

"Local preacher, Daniel Amos Webster. Had no idea he had a camera on him or he woulda gone to another strip joint."

Jurgens shook his head. "You'd think a reverend of all people would know someone is always watching."

Griggs nodded, flipped through more photos—Dr. Bones, Evil Duke Cumbee, a couple more mob guys. Pointed to the next photo. "And this guy?"

"Local used-car salesman, works down at Uncle Fred's Used Cars."

"Hey, Tom," Jurgens said, chomping gum, "ain't that where your old man used to work? Before he took all that money and ran off with the saleslady?"

Griggs ignored the question. Pointed to another photo, a man with close-cropped hair, wiping his hands on a towelette. "This guy?"

O'Malley shook his head. "Don't know yet. Can't find any records locally. Still waiting for info from out of state."

Griggs looked at the face, thinking. Wait a second. Why hadn't he noticed it before? "I've seen this guy somewhere." Lightbulb. "At the service the night Jones was killed. But he wasn't dressed like this, he was"—thinking...wait for it—"dressed like a bum."

The detective without the name crooked his neck to look at the photo in Griggs' hand. "What is he dropping there?"

Griggs squinted. "I think it's one of those wet naps, like you get at the chicken place."

Jurgens chuckled. "Coming out of a club like Zoo Girls, I'd wash my hands, too."

O'Malley snapped his fingers. "Antibacterial wipes. Like my wife always has for the kids." He tapped the photo. "If this guy is the hired killer we been having trouble with, maybe he left behind some of these in the evidence pile."

Griggs doubted. Shrugged. "Can't hurt to check."

— 79 —

The bus station, heading out of Kansas City, Missouri. Destination, anonymity. Earlier, before choosing this method of escape, Solo had briefly entertained a complicated zigzag strategy, stealing cars every couple hours, taking off in a different direction each time, circling, doubling back. But he didn't need to take off his shoes and socks to realize the math was too complicated. It would just take too long.

Finally, he had decided the smartest way to leave town would be rather ordinary. Get a bus ticket. The ideal thing, if he'd had enough cash, would have been to get several bus tickets, all headed in different directions. But money and time were tight. Sure, he had money stacked up in his accounts— what was left after the bookies got their share—but there was no way he had the nerve to try and access any of it now. Who knew who was watching the banks, maybe they had some kind of tap on his account. All he had available in the world was on his person.

He'd been at the depot all afternoon, debating with himself, checking the signs to see how far north the money in his pocket would take him, checking his maps to make sure he got a bus heading in the right general direction.

He watched the buses come and go, weighing the risk of being trapped if somebody tracked him down. The bus could quickly become a moving coffin if he was inside and some of Fat Cat's boys pulled alongside with automatic weapons.

Another bus came in and he watched the passengers disembark, one by one. Old man and old woman. Couple of teenage girls. Fat guy in a brown shirt.

Solo jolted as he saw the next two passengers, a tall guy dressed like a Mennonite and a younger guy in his twenties, styled blond hair like some guy from the movies. He didn't remember their names, but he'd seen them around.

Professional killers.

Solo looked around the depot, considering his options. He had already ditched his car, and the afternoon crowd was too thin to just blend in and walk away.

Solo ducked into the men's room, a long row of sinks, urinals, and stalls. He paused before one of the urinals, a trough with water glugging down the rear porcelain. Solo turned toward the stalls, stooping to see which were empty.

Proceeding along the row of doors, Solo selected the stall at the end, furthest from the entrance. Before he pushed his way into the stall, he heard two men enter. Glancing at the big mirror over the row of sinks, he saw the killers, chatting, the blond one lighting up a cigarette. Solo wasn't sure whether they were after him specifically, but their sudden presence in Kansas City could not be coincidence. And if they were his replacements, better to be safe than dead.

Blood and fear rising in him, Solo took action before he had a chance to stop himself. He strode toward them purposefully, game face, and without a word, grabbed the blond by the hair on the back of his head and slammed his face into the mirror, glass and blood splattering in the sink. The kid slumped.

The other man whirled and barely had time to register Solo's face before the two were in a savage, wordless struggle in the close confines of the lavatory. The man reached for a gun inside his coat, but Solo was ready for it, a head butt followed by a hard kick in the knee, reaching to keep the man's hand from getting inside his coat. Solo shouldered the man, a pistol clattering to the tile floor.

The struggling men bounced off the door of a stall, then Solo succeeded in grabbing the man's scarf and pulling it taut. The Mennonite was probably more accustomed to using the scarf on others, had never considered the odds of it being used against him.

The man struggled, clawing at the scarf around his neck, face reddening, Solo pulling harder and harder. Then he saw a flash from the motel Bible, THOU SHALT NOT KILL, and he saw Pastor Fresno standing in the corner of the men's room, watching.

Solo grunted and let go. The man fell to his knees, panting, pulling at the scarf, rubbing his neck, cursing in spits and gasps. Solo knew the enraged bear was not going to kiss and make up, kicked the man in the ribs, and then pulled his own .38 and pointed the barrel at the man on the floor.

THOU SHALT NOT KILL.

THOU SHALT NOT KILL.

Mind whirling, Solo had just enough presence of mind to pocket the gun, kick the man again to give himself a head start, and walk briskly to the lobby again. As he walked away, trying to look calm, look normal, *nothing to see here, folks, just another tourist like you,* he heard a commotion behind him pooling around the entrance of the men's room.

Solo finally sneaked a peek, saw a couple of uniformed cops running into the bathroom, where some innocent passerby must have stumbled across the two contract killers. Solo was lucky he had stepped out just in time. If he had stayed long enough to make the kill, he would have been just as caught.

Given that both men were loaded for business, the cops would see the need to pick them up, would assume the two were fighting each other, would never guess the need to find their attacker.

Solo knew he was free for now. But for how long?

He made it to the parking lot before he had to vomit.

— 80 —

Solo pulled out the phone card from the drugstore, squinted at fine print, started punching in numbers. Eventually, he got to the part where he was actually making a long-distance call. The phone rang three times before Gus picked up.

"What?" Busy, caught in the middle of something.

"Hey, Gus, guess who?"

"What, you finally crawled out from under the bed?"

"I just had a meeting with some of my co-workers. I figured they worked for you."

"What, are you at the airport?"

"Bus station."

"Oh, okay."

"They here to finish my job? Maybe finish me?"

There was a hesitation on the line. Then Gus sighed. "I won't lie to you, Rain Man, you're on the dinner menu along with the rest of the original cast."

"I'm out, Gus. The family don't need to worry about me."

"You know how it goes, Solo. These people don't like loose ends. That's what kept you in caviar and comic books all this time. Well, now you've jumped columns and instead of being the guy who ties the loose ends, you're the guy they think needs tied off. To coin a phrase."

"Fine. No hard feelings. I'm a big boy."

Gus sighed again and whistled through his teeth. It made a noise into the receiver. "Given our long and lucrative friendship, I'll give you this. For old time's sake."

"What's that?"

"You have a clean opening to get out of Dodge if you leave right now. And I mean *right now.*"

"Why's that?"

"Right now, all the shooters are headed to off some cop's wife."

～ 81 ～

Holland turned the wheel of his maroon Chevy Lumina, heading in the general direction of John Calvin McCoy Elementary School. He flipped on the radio, a familiar guitar riff echoing through the speakers.

Sallis lit up. "I love this song. Zeppelin, right?"

Holland chuckled. "Nope." Female vocals kicked in, singing a completely different melody. A male voice started to rap over that. "It's some rapper, Terror Glass-P."

Sallis, game, tried nodding along, just couldn't get into it. "I hate it when they do that."

"What?"

"You know, take one song and write another song around it."

"It's the way of art," Holland said, eyes on the road. "Everything comes from somewhere."

"I don't know."

"The trick is whether they can actually say something new. They don't always do." Holland looked down at the gas gauge. "Aw, crud, remind me to stop at the gas station."

Sallis, clicking a Jolly Rancher in his teeth, leaned over to see the needle. It looked full from his angle. "What, you need a candy bar or something?"

"Low on gas," Holland replied, squinting at sunlight through the windshield. "I think."

"What does the needle say?"

"The gauge doesn't work right. It only goes from full to about half-empty, then starts climbing the other way again. 'Full' could just as easily mean the tank is empty." He stopped for a traffic light. Turned to his partner. "I can't remember the last time I got gas, so that probably means I'm empty."

Sallis nodded, looked out the window. Then furrowed his brow and looked back at Holland. "You are going to stop for gas on the way, then, right?"

Holland nodded his head. "Sure, sure."

"Because it would be pretty bad if we ran out of gas afterward, know what I mean?"

"Sure."

"Because someone is bound to find the body, it being the middle of the day like this."

"Sure."

"And if we're sitting in a car that's out of gas just a couple of blocks—"

"I said *sure*."

The conversation stopped as Holland drove on. Sallis watched the trees going by, piles of dirty snow melting along the curb. They were in a suburb, he didn't know the name. He turned back to Holland. "So why are we doing this?"

"Bones got his reasons."

"But do you know the reasons? I mean, this doesn't strike me as the wisest course of—"

"They had a couple of out-of-towners lined up for the hit, but something happened at the bus station and the cops picked them up. So we have to step once more into the breach." Holland pulled the turn signal, waited for traffic, made a turn.

"Bus station? Why would a couple of professional killers be coming in on the bus?"

"I just report the facts, I don't explain them." Holland gave Sallis a silly grin as he pulled up in front of a school and announced, "We're here."

The two men started checking their weapons. Sallis said, "What's her name again?"

Holland pulled a folded piece of paper out of his shirt pocket. "Griggs. Carla." He held the paper up and smiled. "We even have her room number."

– 82 –

Griggs was at his desk, poring over files, re-looking at photos. Trying to wrap his head around this new deal of Fat Cat.

The Kansas City PD and the Feds together over the past few years had successfully put away significant organized crime figures, an equal-opportunity assortment of ethnics and immigrants and homegrown bosses and lieutenants and soldiers. Frank Catalano had been the grand opportunist who filled the vacuum, amassing power, growing in influence among the various crime factions with interests in KC.

He already had so much in his grip. Then murmurings among intelligence, shared information from colleagues in the FBI and DEA, that Fat Cat had bigger aspirations. A matter of weeks ago, he'd thrown the reins aside, splitting what he allegedly considered the day-to-day between two of his three sons.

Why? Griggs felt like all the pieces were there on the desk, but didn't know how the jumble fit together.

What are you planning, Fat Cat? What bigger picture do you have in mind? Why hand off the territory to two of your sons? Why Gino and Ritchie, but not Frankie? Where are you getting your inside information? Judge Reynolds? The Feds? The cops?

Griggs looked at the face of Earl "Dr. Bones" Havoc. How was he taking all this? The man could not be happy about being passed over. He had to be planning trouble. Whatever else happened, Griggs knew to keep his eyes on Dr. Bones.

And now that Gino was gone, what next? There would likely be repercussions. But what? And where?

And even as Fat Cat had handed off the reins, he seemed to have some bigger plan in mind. But what?

Griggs sat back in the chair and stewed. He had not been to see Charlie yet, wondered how the kid was doing. Griggs had avoided visiting the hospital, had felt weird, felt responsible for the kid getting shot.

Jordan—Detective Hall—was really shaken up by what had happened at the rail yard that night. But the events had also galvanized her somehow. Griggs saw in her a strength he had not seen before.

Griggs was pulled out of his thoughts when the phone rang. He picked up, barked, "Griggs."

There had been an incident at John Calvin McCoy Elementary School.

– 83 –

Solo in a stolen car, fresh from the bus-station parking lot, foot on the gas, turning toward John Calvin McCoy Elementary School. Information in hand from a reluctant Gus. Sirens, flashing lights as he slowed, drove by. The yard full of people, cops, teachers, custodians. A pair of EMTs carrying a body on a stretcher, the face covered.

Too late.

~ 84 ~

The Griggs home. Carla had called in sick for the third day in a row, had begged off with a headache and gotten Mrs. Gill to cover for her again like she had all week.

She had run down to the store for grapefruit and toilet paper, had plastic bags hanging from her wrists as she fished for keys in her purse. A credit card fell out and hit concrete. Trying not to lose her balance, she went to one knee, picked it up with two fingers, and slipped it into her pocket for now. Unlocked the front door. Maybe grapefruit would help her feel better. She would not be able to skip out many days like this before the administrator would step in and say something.

Since Tom had left, she had initially felt a sense of relief—as if she could finally cut her losses and get on with her life. But there was a sense of stress percolating in the back of her head. Building, causing her to feel tense all the time.

If Tom wanted to be an idiot, it was a free country. He was free to be an idiot.

But instead of closure or release or any of the other kinds of relief she expected, she just felt a strained emptiness. Hollow.

She hadn't expected that. She was supposed to be strong. She had married relatively late in life, her mid-thirties (which, granted, was not as late as it once was). Unlike some of her friends who had gone to college seeking their "Mrs. degree," she had a life. She was a person, didn't need a man to make her complete.

As she peeled the grapefruit over the kitchen sink, she failed to look out the window and see the first car, the brown sedan. Three men in trench coats were getting out. She sucked on the citrus, worrying over how many times she could pull a sudden exit at school before the administrator's patience was used up. She needed to get her head straight. If Tom wanted to ruin his own life, fine, that was his problem, but she couldn't let him ruin hers, too.

Vaguely aware of footsteps out front, she threw a couple of unfinished knitting projects off the chair and plopped down, kicking her feet up on the ottoman. As she sucked on the grapefruit pieces, she began to relax. Grapefruit juice was trickling down her chin when she heard a terse knocking at the door.

Catching the stray juice in her hand, she mumbled through a full mouth, "Just a second." Maybe it was somebody from the school, checking up on her. Dropping the grapefruit on a plate on the end table, she wiped her hands with a wet paper towel as she went to the door, mentally rehearsing a properly sick tone of voice. Since people always assume you're less sick than you really are, you have to overcompensate to get the appropriate level of pity.

As she unlocked the door, she began, "I appreciate your—" and stopped cold when she saw the strange man at the door, saw the man's face, chiseled lines competing with pockmarks, balanced somehow by cold, gray eyes, a broken nose, and a clean-shaven head. A shotgun at his side. In an emotionless, husky voice he said, "We don't have much time."

Everything began moving in slow motion for Carla—him reaching, clutching her arm in an iron grip. She pulling back, kicking at the rug by the door for traction, reflexively looking for a blunt object within reach.

The gate at the end of the sidewalk creaked, and Carla and the stranger both turned to see two men step into the yard, trench-coated thugs striding toward them with purpose. The man gripping Carla's arm pushed her back and she was tumbling to the hardwood floor, knocking over the end table. There was cannon fire and the picture window exploded, glass flying through the living room. She covered her face with her arms as the man kicked the door shut, twisting the deadbolt and drawing the chain.

Carla on the floor, arm across her face, looked up in shock at the man standing over her. He reached out and said in an unhurried voice, "The door won't keep them out." She grabbed his hand and he pulled her up.

She ran for the dining room, the man following, pumping the shotgun. Behind them, more explosions, the splintering of what had been the front door.

Through the dining room, through the kitchen, headed for the back door. Behind her, more explosions, the end of her fine china.

Reaching the back door, Carla was reaching for the knob when a dark face appeared in the window. She shrieked, fell, tripping on one of her half-finished knittings. The dark man elbowed the pane, glass shattering, and he reached through the jagged hole and inside, twisting the knob.

As the door opened, the stranger who was saving her burst into the room, held up his shotgun at the newcomer. Hesitated. What was he waiting for? The newcomer brought up a pistol and the shaven-headed stranger dodged bullets, diving behind the recliner.

As the newcomer started to turn toward Carla, she grabbed the knitting needle off the floor and jabbed him in the leg. He howled and stumbled back, dropping the gun.

The stranger saw his opening and jumped from behind the recliner, leaping at the newcomer and slamming the shotgun into his head, knocking him down. He slammed the shotgun down on the man's head again.

Regaining control, he grabbed Carla by the hand, dragged her up and out the door. They ran across the backyard, past the neighbor's clothesline, then circled toward the front. A heavyset man was leaning against a maroon Lumina, lighting a cigarette. The stranger fired his shotgun in the air. The heavy man bolted, diving behind bushes.

The stranger yelled for Carla to get in the Lumina. She opened the passenger door and jumped in, slammed the door and ducked, preparing for the worst. She heard gunshots around her, peeked out the window. Saw the other killers coming out the front door, firing in her direction. She noticed the neighbor, old Mrs. Simpson, peering from behind her curtain. *God, please don't let these men see her watching.*

The stranger appeared at the driver's side, cranked the ignition, and put the car in reverse. He deliberately slammed the vehicle into the other car parked out front, aware of the other killers coming across the yard. They started firing at them, the back window shattering as the stranger stopped the car, put it in drive, stepped on the gas.

As they peeled out, a passing car got in their way, swerved into the bushes and ran aground. One of the shooters stepped over, pulled the dazed man out of his car and shot him in the head. As he was getting behind the wheel of the car, Carla shivered and turned away, sobbing as her rescuer continued driving.

Then she noticed all the blood.

~ **Part Three** ~

"It is the folly of the world, constantly,
which confounds its wisdom."

—OLIVER WENDELL HOLMES

~ ~ ~

"Who'd have thought a person had
to worry about character?"

—OLIVER WENDELL WEEKS
(Ed McBain, from *The Frumious Bandersnatch*)

- 85 -

It had been sunny and warm. In fact, it was hot as an oven here in the basement, sun leaking through the narrow concrete windows.

How many days had he been down here? It was easy to lose track, alone in the dark with the smell of rotting fruit pies.

He was napping when he heard the doorbell, then voices vibrating through the floorboards. Solomon held his breath, listening. Shoes clattered across kitchen tile, headed for the basement door.

This was it, he feared, *she's sending me away.* His dear mother, tired of suffering disappointment, had finally sent for people from the state or the church to take him away.

He had already grown big enough that she could no longer physically force him into the basement for his quiet time. But he was still cowed by the sheer force of her presence and, frankly, wanted to keep the peace. He had already lost one parent.

But she was still disappointed, making a point to remind him of that often.

He heard vague words through the floorboards, couldn't make out the direction of the conversation. But there was no mistaking the vibrations of footsteps leading toward the locked basement door.

When he heard the rattle of the knob, Solomon hid in the darkest corner. They wouldn't take him without a fight.

The door opened and light burst from the kitchen down the stairs. "Go on down to the sitting room," he heard his mother say to the visitors. "I'll bring some tea down shortly."

"Yes, ma'am." A man. Uncertainty in his voice.

An unsteady foot creaked on the top stair, soon joined by three more feet creaking down the wooden slope. Two people.

"When you get to the bottom," he heard his mother encourage them, "flip the switch at the end of the stairs."

Solomon, hiding, wondered why she would say that. She had not yet changed the bulb from that time he had killed the cat.

As soon as the two strangers were several steps from the top, Solomon's mother slammed the door, locking them in the darkness, with only the dim light from the crack under the door and tiny basement windows.

The man shouted while the other, a woman, shrieked and clomped clumsily back upstairs, pounding on the door. "What are you doing?"

"You both need some quiet time with Jesus," Solomon's mother cackled through the solid wood. "Now, I'm gonna go watch my stories, and when I come back we can discuss what you cultists have learned."

Solomon heard their whispers, their strategies, their panic in the dark. Could smell perfume and fear. He knew what he should do. What would make his mother proud.

When his mother came back later—had it been an hour? a day?—she confronted Solomon about what he had done. "I am very disappointed, young man."

She helped him bury the bodies in the basement, again stealing over in the middle of the night to get dirt from next door, from old Mrs. Wilson's rose garden—where his father had been laid to rest all those years ago. Old Mrs. Wilson always bragged on her rose garden, never realized why her roses did so well.

That night, covered with sweat and dirt, Solomon had sat in the backyard with the shovel, staring at the crescent moon while his mother told him it was time to go.

She had a look in her eyes.

– 86 –

Carla checked her watch. She was driving, scared, didn't know where she was going. She nervously checked the rearview mirror, didn't know what she was looking for. Tom had never trained her in the art of losing someone if they should choose to follow you. Trailing, tailing, whatever they called it.

All the times Tom brought his work home, he never once brought home anything useful. Never brought her survival skills, how to know if someone is following you, what to do if a man is shooting up your house. What to do if your passenger is quietly bleeding to death while you're driving down the highway.

Carla and the bleeding man had already been on the road, what, two hours? They were heading west. According to the map she had pulled from the bleeding man's coat—saw it sticking out of his pocket—somewhere along here should be Priest Pointe. He had phased in and out of consciousness, had refused to be taken to a hospital, had mumbled his need to go to Priest Pointe. It had seemed as good an idea as any.

There were lingering doubts. Who was this man? Why had he been to her house? What if he were working with the shooters? But there remained her blinding fear—and the simple fact that when everyone else was shooting up her house, this man had come and taken her out of harm's way. He was bleeding to death because he had rescued her. In her frazzled state of mind, it was all she could cling to.

In the back of her mind, as she checked the rearview mirror for the forty-seventh time, she knew her reasoning was shaky. But someone had tried to kill her, for Pete's sake, had burst into her home and shot up her china, the china passed down from her grandmother. She had a good excuse to be rattled.

Back when they had peeled out in front of her house, all those men shooting—*peeled out, does anyone use that term anymore?*—the strange man had kept enough presence of mind to drive them out of the neighborhood, but not even as far as the interstate, before he got too woozy to keep going. He had pulled over, she had jumped out and run around to the driver's side, pushing him to the passenger side as best she could.

Her first thoughts had been to find help—police, firemen, ambulances, anything. But the men with the guns had piled into the beat-up car, others had run for another car, presumably parked behind her house. Had given chase. Gripping the steering wheel with white knuckles, she had ducked this way and that, in and out of traffic, her eyes burning with fear and adrenaline, until she thought she'd lost one or both of the cars. But she wasn't sure. She kept glancing at the rearview mirror and seeing phantoms. Every time she thought of pulling over, of turning off the highway, she would look again, certain she saw one of the cars.

She wanted to dig for her cell phone, but her purse was back at the house. When people are shooting up your grandmother's china, it's surprising the things you leave behind.

She looked again at the bleeding man in the passenger seat. He clearly had needed medical attention, but who knew whether the bad men had still been right behind them even then.

Or were behind them even now.

So she drove. Too afraid to stop, too afraid to turn around, too afraid to think. Flee. It was all she could do.

It was dark now, moon glinting off patches of unmelted snow lighting her way. Occasional headlights coming up behind and passing. The lanes going the other way were separated from her by a large strip of land with trees and rocks and such.

Throughout the trip, she regularly flipped the knob on the car radio, had trouble keeping a station for any length of time. Right now, she had country music on the radio, which made her think of quiet nights listening to old records with her grandparents.

Carla glanced over at the man in the passenger seat, wondered if he was alive. She thought about praying as she squinted at the green signs marking the highway, marking the exits. But she hadn't been on a first-name basis with God since she was a little girl. So she put her faith in the laws of physics and in the green signs marking the highway. She wouldn't feel safe until she reached the spot marked on his map. Maybe it was his home base.

Nosiree, this was not the time to put faith in some never–never land. She had men with real guns after her. She wasn't going to trust anything she couldn't see for herself.

She glanced down at the gas gauge. They were fine. Almost a full tank of gas.

– 87 –

Griggs checked his watch. He sat on the arm of his TV chair, surrounded by detectives and Feds running around dusting, scraping, gathering evidence.

He knew the statistics: If you hoped to find a missing person, find your leads within the first thirty-six hours. After that, the best clues evaporated. It was almost eight P.M., about four hours since someone had broken into his home and stolen his wife. About three hours since he had stormed into Fat Cat's office and had to be dragged out by officers, Catalano shouting threats of a lawsuit.

At first, Griggs had tried to fight the Feds on taking over the case, but O'Malley had pulled him aside. "This is in Carla's best interest, Tom," he had said. "These people do this all the time. They can look at the evidence objectively."

Jurgens had thrown a fit. "Cops should do this. This was a personal attack against a cop, against his home. If we let outsiders do this thing, how is it gonna make us look?"

But in the end, Griggs sided with O'Malley. Something about it felt right. Jurgens had stormed off, who knows where.

All Griggs knew is he wanted his wife back.

At the crime scene—his home—they'd dug bullets out of the wall, laid fragments of china and tchotchkes out on the carpet in a pattern, dusted for prints, scraped blood off the wall by the back door, searched the house for bodies and clues. Someone had found the broken statue of Jesus in the trash and added it to the pile of evidence. Griggs didn't correct them.

Now, the Feds and detectives were canvassing the area, searching for clues outside, questioning neighbors. On the dining-room table were burgers and donuts.

O'Malley entered the living room and found Griggs, nodded a greeting. "How you holding up?"

Griggs felt weary. "Been better." He looked up hopefully. "Got anything?"

"We're still running the numbers, but we have some leads. That time of day, most of your neighbors were out, but we were able to get some preliminary IDs. There were five to seven people out here, some of whom were probably Fat Cat's boys. There was some sort of dispute, gunfire, and something of a demolition derby outside."

"Demolition?" Griggs furrowed his brow. "What?"

"There were two people fleeing the scene—got in a car and used it to bash one of the other cars before they peeled out."

"Two people?"

"Yes, it looks like Carla was taken. Or escaped." O'Malley pursed his lips. "With somebody else."

Griggs stood, stretched his legs. Walked through the damaged house. "So they didn't just come to *take* Carla." He motioned toward the burst wall, the splintered front door. "This wasn't for show. They were trying to hit somebody."

He whirled and looked dead at O'Malley. "They were trying to hit Carla."

"I think so." O'Malley pointed along the wall. "There is a pattern through the house, from the front porch all through to the back door in the kitchen. A moving target." O'Malley winced, realizing how cold it sounded, but Griggs closed his eyes and nodded, and O'Malley went on. "Carla obviously kept moving. And she and whomever else got out the back door, overpowering somebody there to get out—"

"Why do you say that?"

"The pattern of violence indicates it was somebody entering from the outside who was attacked, beaten hard enough that they were in no condition to simply run outside and jump in a car. No, whoever left that blood on that wall had to be carried off."

Another agent, suit and tie, entered and added, "Or stored in the shed."

Griggs and O'Malley looked over. Griggs said, "I don't own a shed."

The agent thumbed over his shoulder. "Your neighbors do, about three doors down. We found a body, pretty battered. If it doesn't turn out to be kitchen-wall guy, then this would be the coincidence to end all coincidences." The agent grinned. "My guess is whoever was here tried to take him away rather than leave him as evidence, but he became too much of a burden."

"Hiding evidence," Griggs said, nodding. "Because if they just shot him here, it would be a big calling card who was here."

"Right," O'Malley agreed. "I thought the mob was smarter than this. I mean, I know they have a long history of whacking and extorting and all sorts of bad things, but usually they try to be more discreet about it. These past few days have been some of the sloppiest I have seen."

Griggs started pacing, thinking. Getting his mind back on Fat Cat got him off worrying about Carla. Worrying where she was, worrying what they might be doing to her, worrying whether she was sorry he'd left. "For one, Fat Cat isn't running a traditional Mafia organization," Griggs said, gesturing. "But even less so the past couple weeks."

He stopped and held out his arms. "Think about it. He gets some grand scheme in his head, whatever it is, and hands off the reins to his sons."

"But not all his sons, only two of them," O'Malley said. "Whatever that's about."

"Right," Griggs nodded, "whatever that's about." Pacing again, O'Malley and the other agent watching. "So you suddenly have this splintering, and nobody knows quite for sure who they're working for anymore."

"Okay."

"But by all accounts, Fat Cat still seems to be handing out orders. As if he thinks he's still in charge."

O'Malley nodded. "Sure."

"And you have Bones, a guy who was a shoo-in to be in charge, you know he's not taking this sitting down."

"Okay."

"So you have multiple streams of information running through the system," Griggs said, picking up steam. "The guys lower down on the totem pole, all they know is what they're told. They don't know what's coming from who, they don't know what to believe. But afraid to question, because they know the next guy is just looking for an excuse to step on them and move up."

O'Malley nodded again. "Say someone passes along a ridiculous order where you're shooting up a cop's house in the middle of the day—"

Griggs snapped his fingers. "Even if they think it's stupid, they're not going to be the ones to say."

O'Malley smiled. "They're not going to be the ones to say."

The agent watching them struggled to follow the train of logic. Finally coughed politely and asked, "But where does that leave Mrs. Griggs?"

— 88 —

Detective Jordan Hall checked her watch as she strode down the hospital corridor amid competing odors of disinfectant and new carpet. Visiting hours were almost over. As she passed the row of doors for private rooms, bits of audio drifted out, old television reruns and cable game shows and prime time news programs.

Reaching the private room of Detective Charlie Pasch, she entered and announced, "Back for one last visit, Charlie-Boy."

She stopped. He was not alone. There was a woman, graying hair, likely late fifties, and another woman who was perhaps thirty, when the light hit her right. All eyes turned toward Jordan as she grasped at words. "I-I'm sorry, I didn't—"

Charlie sat up in bed, coughed. "Detective Hall!" The bandages on his head still an eyesore. At least the swelling in his face had gone down. "This is my mom and my sister."

The elder of the two women said, "Good to meet you," then gave Charlie a smile. "Well, it's getting late. We'll leave you to your friend." She went to kiss Charlie on the cheek and whispered loudly, "Is that *her?*"

Charlie's face grew red. "Thanks for coming, Ma," he coughed, voice still weak. "I'll see you later. Thanks, Deana."

Heading for the door, the two women waved at Charlie. As they passed Jordan, the mom gave a knowing smile, but the sister sort of sized her up. It made Jordan uncomfortable.

When they were alone, she asked Charlie, "How you feeling, Champ?"

"They say I can go home pretty soon. Apparently the worst is past."

Jordan nodded, glancing around at the flowers and balloons. Since none of the boys at the station had sent so much as a card—*men*—these must have come from family. She took a whiff of a floral arrangement. Daisies? Nice scent, whatever it was.

Jordan realized she was still nodding. Then she said, "Oh!" remembering the brown bag folded under her arm. "Brought you something to read."

She deposited the package on the table by the bed. He reached eagerly; his coordination was still slow. He slid out a stack of reading materials: *Starlog, Shonen Jump,* a variety of comic books.

"I didn't know what you had," she explained, "so I got what looked interesting." She reached for a copy of *Betty and Veronica.* "And, of course, what looked interesting to me."

Charlie smiled, leaned back, eyes flickering. "Thanks." He *must* be exhausted, if he was too tired to flip through comics.

"This was really cool." He paused, searching for words. "Coming to visit, too."

She smiled, walked to the window, looked outside. "Any of the boys been to see you?"

"Nah." He fumbled with the plastic cup by the pitcher. She came to the rescue as he continued. "Been busy, I guess."

She poured water into the cup, making a mental note to check for a vending machine on the way out. She handed the cup to Charlie, nervous he might drop it. "Not even Griggs or Jurgens?"

Charlie sipped the water desperately, then set the cup on the table and leaned back again. "No big." Smiled gently. "I'm sure they're thinking about me."

Jordan went to the window again, looked down at the street, three stories below. In the night, headlights flickered to and fro.

"Hey, um, Detective Hall?" He paused, started again. "Jordan?"

"Hmm?" She turned from the window.

"I know things are kind of crazy right now."

"Sure," she said. "Mainly, still trying to figure out what Fat Cat's doing. It's like he's gone crazy and all his guys are scrambling to make sense of it all. Everyone jumping around stupidly because everything is off balance for them."

Charlie tried to chuckle. *"Striving to better, oft we mar what's well."*

"What's that?"

"Shakespeare."

They talked a while longer, about country music and football and even, God bless him, Jonny Quest. Anything to keep their minds off the shooting in the streets.

When Jordan checked her watch again, visiting hours had been over for some time. "Listen, I'm supposed to go. Anything I can bring you tomorrow?"

He fumbled for words. At last, "Can't think of anything."

"Any music or anything?"

"My mom is already bringing over some of my CDs. Evie Tornquist, Al Green, P.O.D."

"Okay, I have no idea what you just said, so I guess she'll have to take care of all that." She smiled. "You look good."

"Thank you for lying." His eyes flickered again. He was having trouble keeping them open.

She made an awkward gesture for the door. "So I'll let you sleep and catch you later."

"Hey, um, Jordan."

She stopped. *Oh, no.* "Yes?"

"When I get out of here, do you think we could, I don't know, get dinner or do something?"

She sighed and offered a weak smile. She wrinkled her nose and said, "You've been through a lot, Charlie. Maybe now is not the best time."

He put on a brave face and it broke her heart. She turned again for the door. "I'll visit you again tomorrow."

At the end of the hall, she pressed for the elevator. As she rode the elevator down, she was full of mixed feelings. The little twerp who read comic books and quoted Shakespeare as easily as *Star Trek* was starting to grow on her, but the family thing kind of freaked her. When that thing had happened with his mom and sister, Jordan was struck with painful memories of every visit home for Christmas. The hollow feeling in her stomach reminded her why she never got involved. With anyone.

As she exited the elevator and crossed the lobby, she glanced back and saw another set of elevator doors closing. It was only a glimpse, but she saw the pair of stone faces headed upstairs.

⎯ 89 ⎯

Carla pulled in at the motel around nine P.M. As soon as she had dragged him into the room, she had gone right into the work of nursing the wounds of her unconscious protector. She had only a vague idea how to care for him without taking him to the emergency room or even a doctor, but she drew on bits of memory from overheard conversations, when Tom and his cop friends were hanging around on beer-and-barbeque football weekends. Challenges about who had seen the grossest wounds, the most unfortunate circumstances following a wound, all sorts of knowledge she never thought she would put to use.

But here she was—a greasy motel next to a truck stop, Kansas, middle of the night trying to save the life of a total stranger who had dragged her out of the house while gunmen destroyed her grandmother's china.

She had expected more trouble at the desk, but her practiced lie went unused. The small man behind the counter merely looked at her through dull glasses, nodded, handed her a key.

The real trouble was dragging the man into the room. During the trip, she had stopped a few minutes to pack the wound under his trench coat with cloth she had bought at the gas station. She'd worried about using the credit card, but had to take the risk.

Now, in the motel room, looking at the man lying on the bed, she ripped up a bedsheet to clean and wrap the wound, wondered again who he was. Had Tom sent him? Was he a detective? A government agent?

After fiddling with the music button on the digital clock, she bathed his wound with warm water from a bowl, Joe Christmas playin' on the radio. Every time she heard a strange noise outside their door, she glanced over at the man's unholstered pistol, which sat atop his rumpled clothes on a chair near the bed.

Running fingers lightly over the vicinity of his wound, she felt burning. She moistened her fingertips with saliva, continued the examination. The bullet had entered in front, had come out in back. There was the danger of infection, and her stranger had lost a great deal of blood.

She left him long enough to walk to the truck stop, thrilled to find milk and linseed oil to make a poultice to fight the infection. She also bought tea, but when she got back to the room she realized there was no way to prepare it.

She patted beads of sweat off the man's brow before applying the poultice. He jerked and grabbed her wrist before she knew he was awake. There was a frightening moment as their eyes locked before he seemed to regain his wits, panting for dear life.

"We're safe." She realized she was panting too. "I don't know what I would have done if you'd died."

He tried to rise, fell back. She adjusted the sheets around him. He coughed, "W-where are we?"

"There were men shooting and—"

"I know that."

"So you drove off—"

"I know that, too. Where?"

"Somewhere in Kansas. A truck stop."

His eyes drifted closed, then jolted open. "Kansas? Why are we—?"

Something about his tone of voice frightened her. "You told me to come here," she said, fumbling around the bed to find the map tucked in his coat. "I assumed this was where you wanted to go."

He continued his labored breathing, staring occasionally at the ceiling. He grunted.

She dropped her head. "I mean, I was scared, and I didn't know how fast or how far to drive before they caught us, I didn't even know who they were—"

"Where. In. Kansas."

Blink. "You said Priest Pointe." She tried to keep her voice calm. "You said."

He didn't answer. He had drifted away again.

She wondered how safe they were. Whether bad men were going to burst through the door any moment.

She went to the phone by the bed, stretched the cord across the room. She called the police station in Missouri, hoping to reach Tom, tell him she was alive and in Kansas, but he wasn't in. She didn't want to leave the message with just anyone. Didn't want to leave any voice mail for someone to intercept. The woman on the other end of the phone waiting for her next request, Carla said, "How about Detective Jurgens—is he there?"

Pause. "Yes, ma'am. I'll transfer you." Carla sighed with relief.

Hearing the familiar voice on the phone, she gladly gave him their location. He told her to stay put, he would take care of everything.

Having done all she could, she crawled into the empty bed and pulled the covers tight. Once the lights were out, however, she knew this arrangement could never work. She crawled back out of the bed, dragged the thick blanket across the room, positioned the chair to face the door. Made sure the gun on the table was within arm's reach. Practiced grabbing it, pointing it toward the door.

Her last thought as she drifted to sleep in the chair was a quote from an old movie: "He who travels fastest, travels alone."

～ 90 ～

Jordan had her gun in hand as she raced up the hospital stairwell, two and three steps at a time, counting doors at each flight. When she reached Charlie's floor, she peeked into the hall, making sure the coast was clear, nervously flexing her grip on the pistol.

She didn't see anybody in the hall, didn't hear anything, stepped gingerly onto tile. She was in a different part of the hall than before, had to map out her location in her head.

Down the corridor, the elevator door was closed. Maybe they didn't know yet where they were going. Maybe they weren't coming for Charlie. Maybe she was mistaken and they were just regular joes, come to meet one of their stone-faced friends. *Sorry, detective, we just broke curfew because we were out late feeding orphans and walking old ladies across the street.*

Jordan stepped down the hall, walking lightly, holding her breath, listening. Arm bent, gun in the air. Other hand out for balance, ready to pounce, jump, whatever it took.

She thought about Charlie, helpless in bed, too weak to read his comic books. If these were mob guys, come to whack Charlie out of some misplaced knee-jerk reaction because of what happened to Gino, he wouldn't stand a chance.

Maybe it was a mistake.

She watched room numbers as she sneaked down the hall. Charlie's door was around the next corner. She peeked around, coast was still clear. Wished someone had thought to put a guard on Charlie's door, but who would have expected this?

Hopefully it was a mistake.

She came past the nurses' station, badge handy. First nurse or doctor she saw, she would instruct them to call Security.

Jordan couldn't bear the thought of anything happening to Charlie. What would his mom think of her now?

God, please let it be a mistake.

– 91 –

Terry the Weasel waited in the empty hospital room as another nurse passed. He would have thought a hospital wouldn't be so populated after hours like this. He and one of the new guys, Zimmy, were slinking across the second floor before heading up to the cop's room on the third floor. The plan was to circle and double back; it had just seemed like the right thing to do at the time.

But if every time they turned a corner there was going to be another orderly, another nurse—*don't these people ever go home?* "I don't know about this," Weasel grumbled.

"What?" Zimmy, with his dopey grin.

"Nothin'."

"No, man, tell me. I want to know it all."

"This isn't how we used to do things," Weasel sighed. "Public place like this, all these witnesses."

"Don't worry about it," Zimmy shook his head, gave his dopey grin again. "Everyone is asleep. Don't you know? Hospitals always keep the patients too doped up to cause trouble."

Weasel grimaced. The kid was wrong, but he was wrong about a lot of things. This wasn't the place to get into an argument with him. Not to mention, he was an oak tree who walked like a man.

They reached the stairwell without incident and headed up to the next floor.

~ 92 ~

Jordan shook Charlie. "Charlie-Boy, wake up!" A nurse was running for Security, who in turn would call the cops.

Jordan's job, right here, right now, was to simply keep Charlie alive. She didn't know for sure he was the target of a hit, it didn't make sense, but the second she saw those faces, something had kicked in. She didn't want to call it intuition—if only because the boys at the station would never let her live it down (never mind how often they played their own hunches).

But the second she'd seen those faces, she'd had a bad, bad feeling.

She shook Charlie again, harder, and he stirred. But she could tell he was in no condition to run. He was groggy when she was visiting, even worse now that he had been asleep.

This probably was not good for someone recovering from a head injury.

Jordan heard noises in the hall, rushed to the door to check. Peeking into the hall, gun held firmly, she saw the stairwell door at the end of the hall. She saw the door open. She saw the stone men step out, guns in their belts.

Jordan jumped back into Charlie's room, eyes flickering, darting through her options. Whatever she was going to do, she had to do it quickly.

A standoff in the hallway would be bad. Two of them, one of her, a narrow corridor that would only help their aim.

No, she had to take them by surprise.

She didn't dare peek out again. But she noticed the window across the hall—if she focused, she could see reflections in it. Could see small figures stealthing up the hall toward her.

Coming to see Charlie. She knew it.

She looked around the room. There wasn't much in the way of hiding places. She closed the door to a crack, then ducked in the bathroom, leaving its door also open a crack. If God or the fates were with her, they would go straight for the man in the bed. Would never expect someone hiding in the bathroom after visiting hours.

In the dark bathroom she crouched, ready to spring on iron-coil legs at whatever came her way. Gun firmly in hand. She couldn't see it in the dark, but the feel of the grip in her hand gave her courage.

She heard a murmuring. It sounded like Charlie stirring. Was he saying her name? Was he asking for her?

Then she heard a competing set of voices, men who thought they were whispering, too dumb to realize how much sound carries when halls echo like these.

"There used to be a certain way of doing things," one of them was saying. "A sense of decorum."

"We're gangsters," the other one replied. "How can—" He stopped speaking. They were in front of Charlie's room.

One of them entered. She heard breathing, sounded like it must be a huge man, she wondered how she would be able to fight a man like that. For the first time, her courage faltered. She gripped the gun tighter.

She was about to push out into the room when she heard him stepping the other way, back to the hall. Outside, she heard him say to the other, "I think this is the one."

Now both men entered. They were headed for Charlie when one, the smaller one, said, "Hey, check the bathroom."

"What? But I don't gotta—"

"Listen to me, check the bathroom."

The larger man, an ox, sighed an ox sigh and clomped toward her. She was in battle stance, facing the door.

This is it. This is it.

At the last second, she changed tactics and put her back to the front corner, inside the door as it pushed open. Waited for him to step in, flip on the light. This way, instead of stopping him dead in his tracks she could—

As he stepped forward, weight on his front foot, she grabbed his wrist and yanked as hard as she could. Using his own weight against him. The ox stumbled and banged against the toilet.

Not giving him a chance to get his bearings, she kicked the gun out of his hand, elbowed him in the back, flipped around and kicked him in the face.

He slammed against the wall and slid down, dazed.

It had taken about three seconds, but enough time and enough ruckus to draw the attention of the other killer. She whirled around, gun trained on the door. Dropped to one knee, putting her beneath his firing line.

Then a man in the doorway, gun in each hand, must have thought he was John Woo, he blinked and fired wildly and she fired once, twice. He crumpled to the ground.

She suddenly felt hands at her neck, big hands, she tried reaching around with her gun, firing behind her, couldn't make the shot.

The ox man started shaking her, enraged, and she dropped her gun. He reached for it and she kicked it away, out the door.

Jordan tried to stand, tried to lift him, but his weight was on her. It was one thing to try judo when the opponent is in motion, but when he's dead weight, there's not much you can do. At least, not that she had learned.

She tried an elbow to his ribs and must have hit a sore spot because he bellowed and let go. She was crawling for the door, skittering before he could grab her ankle, was pushing out of the bathroom when she heard cannon in front of her, behind her the dull thud of a body dropping.

She looked up. Charlie, groggy, leaning against the door frame, barely standing. He had one of the guns in his hand, she didn't recognize it.

She stood, gasping for breath, looked back and saw the ox man crumpled in the corner, unfired gun in hand. Open eyes of a dead man.

She went over and hugged Charlie. "Thanks."

He let out a breath, blinked heavily. About to collapse. Smiled a charming smile. "*Now* will you go out with me?"

– 93 –

Next morning. Frankie had put out the first feeler, had been careful about making that first call. After all, so many were on Papa's list of "friends," he didn't want to be sloppy, just walk in the front door of the police station and announce his and Turk's plan. No, he had to, what do you call it, "strategize," had to be smart.

That's when he decided to go right to the heart of the enemy, go right to the men who were dedicated to bringing Papa down—surely, they would see the value in a truce. After all, this deal would get them not one, but three guys right up at the top of the chain. Surely, they would see the value in that.

Frankie hid behind his menu. The diner was greasy but it was about the only place he could think of where he wouldn't run into the wrong guys. Sure, there were members of the family everywhere, but the ones he had to worry about would never be caught dead in a place like this. He had shooed away the waitress twice already, then ordered eggs and sausage and got a refill on his coffee.

He checked his watch, peeked over the menu toward the front door. Frankie had stayed away from the Feds, didn't want to get in with the government—a local cop would have a much easier time bending the rules if it meant cutting a deal. He would run the offer past the cop, then report back to Turk in a couple of hours.

Turk had been worried they would get shoved off into a witness-relocation deal, but Frankie was sure they could make another, what was it, "stipulation," that he and Turk would get to stay in Kansas City. Once his Papa saw this was him being rescued, all would be jake.

Frankie peeked at the door again, saw a man in a suit jacket glance around the joint. Frankie waved him over to his corner booth. When he had put in a call with the cops, he had asked for the man in charge of the organized crime division. The head guy was out, but they had sent him the next best thing.

The man approached the table, tugging at the button on his suit jacket. "Frankie Catalano? I'm Detective Michael Jurgens." The detective looked around the diner and motioned toward the door with a nod. "It's kinda crowded in here. Maybe we should go outside."

– 94 –

Solo was dazed when he first woke up, thought at first he was still in that rat motel outside Kansas City. It took him a few moments to orient himself, fragments of memory coming back to him, of the rescue at the cop's home, of the strange drive through the country, of a midnight surgery. Of the woman who had kept watch at the door.

He didn't know where the woman was.

He looked in the bathroom mirror, saw a face pale and drawn. He examined the wound, a hole drilled through his left side. The wound bled as he wrapped a towel tightly about him. He washed his hands thoroughly, then meticulously wiped blood off the sink with tissues. Flushed them down the toilet.

He looked at his hands again—thought of all the germs, the blood, the tissues, the handle on the back of the toilet—and washed his hands again. Looked at the bar of soap, wondered where it had been, grunted and grabbed an unopened bar and ripped it out of the package, washed his hands again.

There was a noise from the door. Solo jumped out of the bathroom, immediately tried to take an inventory of his weapons. He had no idea where they were. He saw his overcoat draped over the chair by the door, hoped it still held some of his toys. He limped toward the coat, but the room started spinning and he stumbled and fell.

The door opened, bursting light accompanied by a cold blast of air. It was the woman. "You shouldn't be up," she griped, setting something on the table by the door and stepping quickly over to Solo, helping him stand and limp over to the bed.

"You need to rest," she said. "I have coffee and breakfast."

"I can't."

"It's all right." The woman patted him on the chest like a nurse. "You've got to lie still."

As Solo lapsed back into sleep, Carla still had her hand on his chest. She wondered about this man on the bed, noticing bruises, scars, knuckles grazed.

Carla went to the table and pulled out a fried-egg sandwich, unwrapping it. She stared at the man from across the room as she ate, sitting in her post again by the door. She felt in her coat pocket for the gun she had taken with her. She'd spent the whole visit to the truck stop charged with a giddy thrill of having a gun in her pocket. Was it illegal? Could anyone tell she was *packing*? She felt a wicked sense of empowerment.

The man on the bed, eyes still closed, stirred and said, "Can I have something to drink?"

"Do you want coffee or some water?"

He was silent a moment. What was working in that mind of his? "What do you mean, water? Is it bottled?"

She felt in the bag and pulled out a plastic bottle. "Yes." She took him the bottle, helped him sit up.

He gulped desperately from the bottle. Belched. Fell back to the bed and drifted away again. Carla watched him a few moments, and then returned to her post by the door.

– 95 –

Seeking refuge, I stealth down the hall, sneaking past the familiar drunk sleeping on the floor, snuggled next to the saxophone case. I can't see his face, but I recognize the rose petals strewn about.

Pushing through the door, I scan the restroom, watching for thugs and germs. A dwarf with a shaved head and multiple piercings sits on a chair in the corner, using a device on his naked arm. Smoke seems to rise from his work.

A second man enters, this one older, losing his hair, bent-rimmed glasses, going straight for the sink. I think it's an actor from a movie I can't place. He ignores the bald man in the corner, looks right up at my reflection in the mirror and smiles. "There are so many unnecessary germs," he says. "There is no excuse for uncleanliness in any area of life."

I smile, continue polishing my gun. "I know what you mean." I holster my weapon. "I don't wash my hands without washing my hands afterward."

The man smiles, tapping one finger to his forehead. "Clean hands are the cornerstones of a polite society." Returns his attention to the sink. "The prince of darkness is a gentleman."

What? I pull my weapon from its holster. "What?" Glancing in the mirror, adjusting my hat. "What did you say?"

The man is still lathering his hands. "King Lear." Still lathering. "Act three, scene four." Lathering. "Or, if you prefer, The Goblins, by Sir John Suckling."

I relax, lowering my six-gun. "You can't be too careful," I say. "When you're on the road, these mall restrooms are not clean."

I look over at the other man, the one in the corner, notice multiple piercings around my head and across my naked chest. Smell flesh burning.

"There was this guy in Toledo," I chuckle, turning back to the man at the sink, "public restroom, men's room at the airport, I tell ya, airport restrooms are the worst, and I was the next guy in line for the stall. When he came out and I saw what he did, I could have strangled him right then and there."

"What happened?"

"I strangled him right then and there."

I move to the next sink, start pumping the soap dispenser, aware of all the germs from all the previous men's room occupants pumping on that soap dispenser before they had washed the germs off their hands. It is a conundrum I cannot deal with.

The man at the sink is still lathering his hands. "Maybe you should stop complaining." The tap water circles the sink, gurgling down the drain. "Maybe you should invent something."

That young priest from the confessional, Father Mac, he offers me some candlesticks, brass or gold or whatever they are made from, but I shoot him dead. Or knife him or club him or something.

I look at my cupped hands, blood dripping from the dispenser. "Like what?"

"Oh, I don't know, something that teaches urinators a lesson. Men too stupid to lift a lid. Men who don't have the coordination or the brains God gave a diseased monkey. Men who should be taken out to the dumpster and beaten to death, literally to death, a rock taken to their empty heads and smashed against their skulls again and again and again—"

"What would I invent?" I glance around nervously, see the men from the bus stop, each grinning as they pass, headed for the empty stalls behind me. One has shards of glass sticking out of his face, doesn't seem pained.

"What would you invent?"

My hands are under the rinsing water, healing water, cleansing water, but the water runs red, swirls like the Red Sea unparted, swirling, red, swirling. "What would I invent?" I glance in the mirror and see faces, the room suddenly full of men and women, strangers I have killed. I try to remember names. I look down in the sink, the red water swirling, red, swirling.

"What would you invent?"

I pump the dispenser again, more red foam covering my hands, gurgling, foaming, gurgling. I hear screams from behind me and see the thugs running out the door, soaked, and I know suddenly, know completely, that my invention has worked. They will never leave the lid down again, will always remember what it is like.

The older man next to me has left the sink, is pumping the paper-towel dispenser with his elbow, always with his elbow, don't want to get germs from the handle on your clean hands, water dripping down his wrist as I pump the towel dispenser with my elbow, always with my elbow, and the man is gone as I am toweling my hands and headed for the door.

Noticing the door has a handle inside, you have to pull on the handle to get out, I calculate how many unwashed hands have grabbed that handle, how many stupid, stupid men had left the germ room without washing their hands, turn back and elbow some more towels out of the dispenser, grip the handle with the towel insulating me from the germs.

I look back at the dwarf tattooing himself in the corner, the smell of burnt flesh sickening me. My eyes flicker and our eyes meet before I look down at the tattoo.

THOU SHALT NOT KILL

I am opening the door, find myself face-to-face with the preacher man, what was his name? Behind him are every man, woman, and child I have ever killed, some I don't even remember.

I slam the door shut, still inside the germ room, my back to the door, breathing heavily, looking back at tattoo dwarf and read

YOU CAN'T WASH YOUR HANDS

— 96 —

"I gotta wash my hands." Jurgens, leaning in the chair, sat upright and stood, heading for the door.

"Little early, don't you think?" Griggs and Jurgens were alone in the office, had been shooting the breeze because Griggs was too nervous, too distracted not to. "Pizza will be here soon."

"Fine, I'm getting a smoke, too." He stopped at the door, putting a hand on the jamb, and looked back. "Hey, if the delivery guy gets here," he said, nodding toward the jacket draped over his chair, "grab the money out of my pocket."

"What, the great Detective Michael Jurgens is *paying?*" Griggs grinned the first time since Carla had been stolen. "What's the occasion?"

Jurgens dropped his smile, a sadness in his eyes. "I just thought I would." Ducked into the hall.

Griggs sat back in the chair behind his desk, swiveled to look out the window. It was a dirty winter day. But somehow it seemed colder inside. Jurgens had been a great comfort, staying close to Griggs' side this whole time. A great friend.

The phone rang. Special Agent Martin O'Malley, FBI. Griggs felt his stomach rumble, wondered when the pizza would arrive. He had been running on fumes and caffeine for what seemed like days now; anything in his stomach would help at this point. "O'Malley, what you got?"

The Fed had regret in his voice. "I wish it was more. But we do have some more info on the guy in the photo. We think we have a positive ID from one of your neighbors."

Griggs leaned elbows on the desk, phone in one hand, covering his tired eyes with the other. "So they saw Fat Cat's guys out at the house? I thought we already assumed that."

"No, no, no, man—we have a positive ID of the guy you saw at the church that night."

Griggs, eyes popped wide, sat straight up. "Say again?"

"The guy with the hand wipes, we have what we think is a positive ID from one of your neighbors. They say he was bald, but something about his posture—"

"So this guy was one of the shooters?" Griggs' mouth was desert-dry. His stomach rumbled again. "One of the guys who shot up the house?"

O'Malley paused. "We think he was the one with Carla who drove away."

Griggs sagged. *What?* "So what are you telling me?"

"We haven't connected all the dots yet, Griggs, but we have reason to believe that your contract killer is the same man who grabbed your wife."

There were voices in the hall, someone getting directions, then a kid popped in the room, carrying a big square thermal bag. Griggs held one finger up for the kid to wait a minute while he continued on the phone. "Are you saying he kidnapped Carla? But why? Is Fat Cat hoping to hold her for ransom?"

"We don't know at this point, Tom," O'Malley apologized. "There doesn't seem to be any indication she was actually kidnapped. All the forensic evidence, all the testimony, seems to point to a group of shooters tearing through your house."

The kid with the pizza was fidgeting, made Griggs nervous. But Jurgens should be back in a second. O'Malley continued, "For whatever reason, a man was seen rescuing your wife from said shooters. And if this ID is correct, the man who saved your wife was your contract killer." Pause. "*Is* your contract killer."

Griggs blinked heavily, violently, trying to process this information. This didn't make any sense. This didn't make any sense. This didn't make any sense. "But the shooting at the school has to be related." He found a pencil, checked to see if it was sharpened, started doodling on a pad as he pieced all these things together in his mind.

O'Malley, still on the line, said, "At this point, the investigative team believes it was a case of mistaken identity at the school—"

"I gathered that."

The pizza kid was antsy, driving Griggs nuts. Nodding to the kid, he placed the receiver between his chin and shoulder. Rolled his chair toward Jurgens' jacket, watching to make sure the cord didn't drag the phone off the desk.

The voice on the phone said, "But, Tom, look at this fact: If the intent of the whole group was to simply kidnap your wife, they would have kidnapped the wrong person, not murdered her. There were two factions out there, two sets of gunmen working at cross-purposes."

"Working for Fat Cat," Griggs grumbled, "getting back at me for—"

"We still don't know for certain who was involved," O'Malley continued. "Could be *La Compañia,* could be Greek or Russian."

Griggs stretched for the jacket, grabbed it off the chair, and pulled it close. Started feeling in the pockets for money. O'Malley continued, "All we have pieced together is that somebody—who, at this moment, could possibly be your contract killer—intercepted Carla and got her out of harm's way. Barely."

Griggs pulled out a wallet, flipped it open for the money. A wad of cash and paper fell to the floor. He said to the phone, "Hold on a second." He set the receiver on the desk, bent down, and grabbed the money. Gave the kid what he needed, the kid gave him the pizza and the change.

Griggs picked up the receiver again and said, "I'm back." He started flipping through the bills, arranging them to place back in his partner's wallet. Some ones, fives, a couple of tens, a yellow note with scribbling on it, a message.

O'Malley, still on the line, said, "We're working several leads to figure out where they might have headed afterward, where they might be hiding out."

It said CARLA.

"Tom?"

"Hold on a second," Griggs said to the phone, reading the secret message. It said PRIEST POINTE, KS, and a motel address and even a phone number.

Griggs was startled by a voice behind him. Jurgens had returned. "So, what's the damage?"

Jurgens.

Griggs dropped the phone and swiveled, jumped from the chair. He roared, grabbed Jurgens by the shirt, pinned him to the wall, elbow to the Adam's apple, his partner barely able to croak. Through gritted teeth, he said, "We trusted you! *I* trusted you!"

Griggs pulled away. Exhausted, spent, needing to focus what strength he had left on rescue. Let revenge come later. The bad guys surely had a head start; Griggs didn't know how much time he had.

Jurgens, massaging his throat, croaked, "Tom, you gotta understand—"

Griggs clenched his fist and swung, smacking Jurgens dead across the face. He fell hard, banging his head on the wall of the empty room.

Griggs didn't have time to check on him, grabbed the phone, "O'Malley, I know where Carla is. I don't know how much time we have."

O'Malley, left on the line all this time, was flabbergasted. "What? But how?"

Griggs looked down at Jurgens, still lying out cold. He spit on the man's tie and said, "Jurgens told me."

~ 97 ~

Solo woke from the dream with a jolt, wondering where his scribbled pages had gone. In all the excitement, in all the confusion, he had dropped his project. But after that dream, he knew it was time to get back on track. That dream...all those faces in the hallway. The priest with the candlesticks, the image of his father sleeping or dead in the hall. So many details...they must mean something...something deeper...

Then he remembered where he was, where they were, that it was "they," him and the woman he had rescued in a fit of insanity. Had rescued from the mob.

He noticed movement out of the corner of his eye and sat up in bed suddenly.

"You're awake," she said. "How do you feel?"

He shook his head, tried to shake the cobwebs. "How long have I been asleep?"

She checked the digital clock on the table. "Several hours. Almost a day."

He looked and saw his big .38 revolver lying atop his folded clothes. The woman had been looking at it, fascinated, picking it up, setting it back down, picking it back up, admiring the craftsmanship, the weight, the power. She asked without looking away from the gun, "Who are you?"

Solo's voice cracked. "You know what you're doing?"

She shook her head, tentatively, and Solo held out his hand. Mutely, the woman handed Solo the pistol from arm's length. Giving her another look, Solo snapped open the cylinder and shook out the heavy, copper-jacketed rounds into his palm. She asked again, "Who are you?"

Ignoring the question again, he snapped the cylinder closed again, then nodded to the woman. "Come here."

She edged closer.

He asked, "You ever handle a pistol like this?"

"No."

Solo noticed the smell of her hair. "What's your name?"

"I thought you knew."

"If I knew, I wouldn't have asked."

"Carla."

"Carla?"

"Carla Griggs."

"Okay, Carla, the first thing—"

"What's your name?"

"What?"

"You saved my life, you dragged me out of a house while they were shooting up my china, I don't even know your name."

Their eyes locked for a long, uncertain moment, then he grumbled, "They call me Solo."

"Solo?"

"Are you going to let me teach you this or not?"

She nodded. Solo offered an awkward smile as he focused on the pistol, demonstrating as he cocked and uncocked the gun. He wordlessly handed it over to Carla, butt first. "That's something."

"What?" She tried to imitate Solo's expertise, his ability to smoothly do the action one-handed, but she was clumsy about it. Relieved she hadn't been called upon to shoot someone while he was recuperating.

"Armed men in your house, shooting to make you dead, and the thing you focus on is the plates."

She finally managed to get the thing cocked, using both hands. Solo reached to guide the muzzle away so it wasn't pointed at him. She felt stupid, embarrassed, moved to the edge of the bed to practice privately.

He watched from behind, still under the blankets, gazed at the contour of her back. Said at last, "I need to stretch my legs. I guess those are my clothes over there?"

She nodded toward the pile on the chair. "Your clothes were stained with blood. I soaked them." She turned her attention back to the pistol in her hands. "They should be dry enough."

— 98 —

Jurgens was still dazed as Griggs dragged him off the floor, out of the office, and down the hall. Clutching him tightly by the arm, pushing, shoving him hard against the desk of another detective. "Read Jurgens his rights."

The other detective had been in the middle of a sandwich at her desk. Puzzled, she looked up at Jurgens, saw his eyes clouded, saw the blood trickling down his chin. "What's going on?"

"We'll start with a charge of conspiracy to commit murder," Griggs growled, marching away, leaving Jurgens behind. "We'll work on the complete arrest report when I get back."

The other detective stood and took Jurgens by the arm. Called after Griggs. "Griggs, where you going?"

"I'll file a report when I get back!"

And was out the door.

～ 99 ～

A car full of gun monkeys, headed down the highway, following directions from their cop informant. Lugo behind the wheel, Fix on the passenger side, still popping Sudafeds like candy. In the back: Ritchie Catalano; Nardo Manzano, the Hispanic ex-boxer with the battered face; a guy named Phil Duncan, a real Chuck Connors type, a patch hiding one eye.

They drove a while in silence, the car smelling like stale beer and popcorn. Finally, Fix announced, "I don't know how they were supposed to know the old bat at the school was the wrong lady."

"That's a *muy* big mistake," Nardo said. "They should have known she was too old to be the right one."

"Sure," Fix said, "but the past few days everything's been a blur, right? We got hired help coming and going, refusing to do their contracts, other guys coming in and getting busted before they even get out of the bus station—"

"Yeah," Lugo broke in, "why were they at the bus station? Don't hit men get paid better than that?"

"I don't know why the bus station," Fix continued, "I'm just saying, we're all running around scattered, we don't know which way is which, it makes perfect sense to me that when you suddenly have to switch who's up to bat, he's gonna swing at the wrong pitch. So to speak."

Lugo checked the mirror again. "Maybe." Glanced at Ritchie, saw him fuming in the backseat. What was on his mind?

Lugo almost wished that tip hadn't got to Bones, telling him where he could find the cop's wife and the contract man who had run out. If that call hadn't come through, they'd be back in the cage playing chess and guzzling beer, not out here across the state line in Kansas, digging deeper holes for themselves.

— 100 —

Solo woke up again. Scanning the room, he saw that the woman was gone. He dragged himself out of the motel bed, shuffled naked across dingy carpet, headed for the mirror to check his wound. He posed, modeled, positioned his fingers to mock a gun, challenged his reflection—"How do you like me now?"

Looking in the mirror, the hole in his side looked better than it felt. He felt weak, too weak to be up and around. But who knew how far behind the killers were?

He knew what he needed: He needed to get out, outside, needed to stretch his legs, needed to breathe what passed for fresh air around here. That's what the doctor ordered.

Shuffling across the room to the chair by the door, he found his clothes, gingerly put on his shirt, grunted as he pulled on pants. He picked his socks off the floor, sniffed carefully, wished the woman had rinsed them, too. He turned them inside out and sat on the bed so he could put them on.

How long would it take the killers to find him and the woman? How long would it take the bad guys to track them down?

Solo had left a contract unfinished. Worse yet, he had interfered with the operation. He shook his head, cursed at the empty room. Must have been out of his mind to interfere, to run in there and grab someone marked for death.

Yes, there would be people coming. Bones had to make an example of them.

Besides, the mob had a long memory. Solo couldn't count the number of times he was assigned to finish off thought-to-be-forgotten business. Someone had squealed, someone had miffed a gig, someone had left someone else holding the bag. Someone thought they'd gotten out free and clear, were relaxing somewhere, sure that nobody cared about little ol' them.

Sure, the client might not assign the contract right away, might bide their time, wait until the investigation was over, wait until Lady Justice had turned her blindfolded gaze the other way, wait until things cooled off.

But they never forgot.

Solo remembered at least one time, something like ten years had passed. The pigeon surely felt a sense of relief, had by then decided the storm would never come.

But the storm always comes. If you build on the rock, you might come out okay. But these people never build on rock.

And the storm always comes.

Solo was shaken out of his thoughts when he heard a rattle at the room's door. He flinched, once again realized he had no idea where his guns were, made a decision right then and there that he would from this point on always have something useful within arm's reach. For all the good it would do him.

The door opened, light and cold air violating the warmth of the room. Fortunately, it was the woman again. She smiled uncertainly. "Feeling better?"

Solo sat on the corner of the bed, returned to putting on his smelly socks. "Guess so," he grunted. "Where you been?"

"Just out walking in a big circle."

"Big circle?"

She nodded. "There's not much within walking distance." She motioned toward the curtained window, as if he had X-ray vision and could just look through the wall and see where she was pointing. "The truck stop, the little store, big square block of concrete."

"Concrete?" Left shoe. "What do you mean?"

"You know, the truck stop," she said. "It's a big parking lot. Big square of concrete, asphalt, whatever it is. Surrounded by a lot of tall grass."

Right shoe. "What about the highway?"

She shook her head. "There's just a road." Shrugged. "Doesn't look like it heads much of anywhere."

"I thought you said we were at Priest Pointe." He thought of the map, wondered where it was tucked now.

"That's the exit we took," she said. "But then you get down here and the town apparently is a few more miles down the road. It's one of those lonely roads that leads to nowhere."

"I don't think I know what you mean." Shoes on now, he was working up the energy to stand up.

"Then look for yourself."

"That's the plan." Hands on knees, he felt a lifetime of bruises and scars rush at him all at once. He'd been shot before, this should be no big deal.

Of course, he'd never been in a corner like this before. Before that preacher man had done his number on Solo, he could have his back to the wall and would have no problem shooting, knifing, or clubbing his way out with an iron pipe and be on his way, careful when you step on the carcass, sir. He could instantly size up any opponent and calculate what would maim, disable, or kill the quickest so he could move onto the next thing.

He wobbled toward the door, the woman stepping in to help. He waved her off. He had to do this on his own. Had to focus. Had to be strong.

Because the storm always comes.

― 101 ―

Griggs was in the car, driving, driving, driving. Focused on his rage, his mission, his journey. Didn't have the presence of mind to check on details, to call for helicopters, to fill out the arrest report on Jurgens. Somewhere in the back of Griggs' mind, he knew O'Malley would handle it.

Griggs would focus on his rage.

He had crossed into Kansas forty minutes ago, had already tried to call the hotel number on the sheet of paper. Nobody had picked up. He tried Carla's cell phone again. No luck. He again tried the number on the slip of paper. Seventeen rings. Nothing. You would think there would be an answering service of some sort, even if meant the gal working the front desk.

Griggs had a map and a vague idea where he was going. The signs along the highway didn't say anything about Priest Pointe yet, but if he read his map right, he was still headed in the right direction.

Still clutching the cell, he punched up some more numbers, got an operator. "This is Detective Thomas Griggs of the Kansas City, Missouri, Police Department," he said, trying to sound as official as possible, not like a man on a blood mission. "I need to get in touch with law enforcement for Priest Pointe, Kansas."

There was a pause, and she put him through to the sheriff's office in that town. The phone rang several times there as well. There didn't seem to be a machine or answering service there, either, so Griggs slammed the phone shut and threw it on the passenger seat.

His rage continued to boil in his blood, thoughts of Carla, helpless, terrorized, thoughts of Charlie in that hospital, damaged, knocking on heaven's door. Then he thought of Jurgens, weasel, liar, traitor. Griggs mentally cataloged all the good times, trips to the batting cage and cookouts, the times he and Carla had had him over to dinner at the house, how Jurgens had stood with them when he and Carla got married. How Jurgens had leaned on Griggs during his divorce.

And he had betrayed them. Jurgens had betrayed his friends, his co-workers, his fellow detectives, the Feds, his country. Had given comfort and information to the enemy. Had helped the enemy slip ahead, slip through the net, time and again. Jurgens was responsible for that poor kid Charlie dying in the hospital. Jurgens was responsible for his poor wife, Carla, responsible for whatever she was being dragged through right this moment.

His cell rang and he picked up. O'Malley. "Where are you, Tom?"

"Somewhere in Kansas."

"The state?"

"I crossed the state line a coupla minutes ago." A coherent thought bobbed to the surface. "I put Jurgens into custody and took off for a town called Priest Pointe."

"Custody? What do you mean?"

"Detective Jurgens." Griggs bit off each syllable. "I arrested him."

"I don't understand," O'Malley said, puzzled. "Didn't he give you that lead for Carla?"

"No," Griggs sighed, too impatient to admit his blame for the miscommunication right now, "the person he gave the lead to was Dr. Bones."

"Got it." There was a noise on the line as O'Malley barked orders to someone else. Then he returned. "Listen, Tom, we have federal agents en route now," O'Malley said, in a calming voice, clearly trying to talk a man off the ledge. "They are going to secure the area for us."

"Make sure they stay out of my way."

"Tom, don't make this—"

"They have a head start, O'Malley," Griggs cut in. "I don't even know when Jurgens passed this info to Bones." Griggs' voice dropped low. "I don't know how much time we have."

"All the more reason to step back and let the Feds take care of this."

"How can you say that?"

"This is not new information, Tom," O'Malley said. He paused. "You get in the middle of this, Carla is as good as dead."

Griggs ignored him, felt his heart pounding in his chest, felt his breath exploding in hot bursts. "Fat Cat wants to start a war? I'll give him a war."

"Detective Griggs, this is not the time to get all Van Helsing on their—"

"I'm losing you." Griggs slammed the phone shut and threw it on the floor.

– 102 –

Holland and Sallis in a diner, waiting for someone to come take their order. Holland now humming something else, looking forward to another brilliant Texas Burger. In the rush before, he hadn't really gotten to enjoy the last one, had had a hankering for another ever since.

Sallis pulled a half-dissolved red Jolly Rancher out of his mouth and set it on his napkin. "Hey, what's that thing you say about the guns?"

"What do you mean?"

"That thing about Chekhov. Is that a *Star Trek* thing?"

"No," Holland smiling, looking up from his menu. "Chekhov is a Russian playwright from like the 1800s." Eyes back down. "He said if you have a gun in the first act of the play, you better use it by the end."

"Oh."

The waitress came, took their order, went away again. The two men were silent a while, then Sallis asked, "Hey, what's with that guy knocking on *The Odd Couple*, huh?"

"Yeah."

"You know what I liked on that show? That one where he said, 'I have some green juice and some brown juice,' and the other guy said, 'What's the difference?' and the first guy said, 'About two weeks.'"

"Uh-huh." Holland was glancing around the diner. You can never be too vigilant.

"Funny." Sallis chuckled.

"Yeah, they did that joke on *Punky Brewster*, too."

"What do you mean?"

"Like word-for-word, they repeated that joke on *Punky Brewster*," Holland said, looking over at Sallis across the table. "I immediately recognized it from *The Odd Couple*."

"Huh."

"Like I said, it's all been done before."

— 103 —

Solo and the woman had taken the car another twenty miles or so deeper into the territory, away from the main highway, away from civilization.

Solo's mind drifted to another time, another small town, a little spitball called Shirley, Missouri, the town even the locals nicknamed "Surely, Misery." On the run from Russian mobsters—a story in itself—he had ended up in the small town, had stumbled across an old mark who had faked his death and got away. The thought of the whole escapade gave him shivers.

He looked over at the woman driving. The first time his eyes were clear, she had finally grilled him hard for information. He was slow on answers, but managed to grunt out enough satisfactory information to convince her they should both lie low and keep their mouths shut. He didn't think she would call the cops.

When he started to get his strength back, he had made a pass. She cut him off cold. Then he caught a glimpse of preacher man out of the corner of his eye, decided not to press the matter. Also decided he was too baffled with his new life trajectory to know what to do with her.

"You can't come this far and not find out for sure," she had said. She had also turned up the heat, hot air blasting out the vents. She told him if he was going to have his window down in the middle of winter, she needed to keep warm somehow.

"Sometimes a person is better off not knowing," he had answered, ignoring the sight of his breath. He was trying to watch for landmarks, didn't want to lose track of himself—that could get a man killed—but out this way a landmark was a water pump or broken-down farmhouse or a few cows. The air was cold but it invigorated him. He rested his eyes.

— — —

Carla had driven past a few more water pumps, a few more broken-down farmhouses, a few more cows, when the man rasped, dry throat, "Are you watching the mirror? Making sure nobody is following?"

"Out here?" She didn't know why, but she kept to herself the fact that she had called her husband, had talked with his good friend Jurgens. That even now, the cavalry should be on the way. Maybe this guy would be happy, but there was something about him that troubled her. Still, she felt too connected, and too vulnerable in this strange place, to leave his side right now. Whatever danger he posed, she was safer with him than out with those men who had shot up her house.

But she trusted her husband and the police back in Missouri far more than she trusted this complete stranger. "Why would anyone think we took this exit? Wouldn't they expect us to head to another big city? Try and get lost in a crowd?"

The man rested his head on the car seat, window down. "Can never tell," he said at last. "Although they probably think we're headed for Mexico." More cows passed on the right. "Or Canada."

"Isn't that a little cliché?"

"What?"

"Skipping the country? Besides, if we were skipping the country, why wouldn't we go to Italy or France, maybe—"

"I was headed for Canada," he cut in. "That's where I was headed when I got sidetracked." He let the implication hang in the air.

She didn't know how to answer that. She watched the road, tightly gripping the wheel. The weather seemed clear today, but she didn't want to risk hitting a patch of black ice on this lonely road. If they ran off the road, who knew where they would find help out here?

Eventually, they came upon a cluster of muddy white buildings. Looked like a small town as they drove in, reminded her of something out of *Andy Griffith* or *The Waltons*.

Carla pulled in front of the wooden sidewalk that connected a series of storefronts. She turned off the ignition and pulled the keys. "I guess this is it."

Solo didn't answer, just squinted at sunlight out the passenger window, elbow hanging out, right hand gripping the top of the passenger door.

Carla looked around for gas but didn't see a station. Fortunately, they still had almost a full tank. Wow, this car had some good mileage.

Solo opened his door and stuck his foot out, testing his leg against the gravel. He was still sore from inactivity, but the walk should do him good. He felt his pockets for cigarettes, found none, ambled toward what looked like a drugstore or gift shop or something.

As he opened the door, there was the little rink-tink-tink of a bell. *Another angel got his wings,* Solo thought grimly, looking around for someone. He finally heard a noise to the side, saw a burly man with white hair huffing as he carried a crate from the back. Dropped it *thump* on the counter, pulled a handkerchief out of his pocket, and dabbed his brow.

The old man was noting something on a pad of paper when Solo walked up and faked a grin. The man seemed to believe it, broke into a grin of his own. "Hey, there," the man said. "Can I help you folks?" His eyes darted friendly back and forth between Solo and Carla, who had walked up close behind him.

Solo didn't correct the man's impression. "We're looking for a woman." He reached for his newspaper clipping.

− 104 −

Special Agents Gregory and Wheeler drove their black car in the general direction of Priest Pointe. It was a small enough town that they had trouble locating it on the map. But now they were relatively sure where they were going.

— 105 —

"I don't see her out here."

Carla watched Solo crane his neck, taking in the small cemetery, surrounded by a council of dead trees. He could probably see all the headstones from his vantage point. But he had read all of them, she had watched while he had walked from grave to grave, reading off the names.

The man back at the store didn't know what had happened to the woman in the newspaper story. When reminded of the name of the day-care center, the one mentioned in the article, he had scratched his head, remembered it was located in this church here in the middle of a big plot of land. Seemed to recall that the place had been closed down by the state. He gave them directions and here they were, had found a cemetery out back.

Solo pulled the clipping from his pocket to check the name in the story again. Compared it with the names on the gravestones.

"Maybe she isn't here," Carla said.

"I said that."

"No, I mean, maybe she isn't dead," Carla added, inflating her words with a hopeful tone. She put up a hand to shield her eyes from the sun. "Some people live, you know."

"Not in my line of work."

He didn't elaborate, and she wasn't sure she wanted him to. This mysterious stranger who had saved her. Her own husband had left her, left her to the fates, to the killers, like he had left their daughter that fateful day. Her own husband had left his wife to die and this man had come out of nowhere and saved her. Rescued her.

Was he FBI? CIA? Some glamorous black-ops group like you see in the movies but the government denies exists?

She wondered why he hadn't made a pass at her. He started that one time, but she'd rebuffed him and he didn't seem to want to try again. Was she unattractive?

And why did his eyes keep darting around a room like he was looking for somebody? It was like he expected somebody to walk out of a wall or something.

But Tom was still her husband. She had left a message for him, he should be here anytime.

As the stranger made a second pass among the gravestones, double-checking names, she turned and looked at the landscape. They were in a sort of valley, the cemetery at the bottom, a little white church sitting at the top of the hill. There wasn't another house or building in sight for maybe miles. As the snow had thawed, the road leading in had become muddy, horribly muddy.

She looked back at Solo, as he called himself, saw he was growing distraught. As if he were at wits' end, having been under the strong impression that finding this person's gravestone would make it all work. She caught his eye and said, "Maybe we can find somebody up the hill," nodding toward the church.

He didn't say anything, but the look on his face indicated the notion did not thrill him. He sighed and, eyes darting around again for whatever phantom, trudged up the hill.

She followed, feet slipping and sliding in mud. There should be a walkway; maybe they were approaching from the wrong direction. As she looked around again, she wasn't sure where else they could have approached.

Reaching the top of the hill, she could see the church was dark. Solo tugged fruitlessly on the locked front doors. Nobody home.

He seemed unsurprised, went around the corner, maybe looking for an open door.

She heard the crashing of glass, heard a *whump* of something hitting hardwood inside. Through the narrow window along the door she saw a shadow, coming closer. Then a click at the door handle and the left door swung open. Solo stood, ungrinning, holding the door wordlessly until she entered.

— 106 —

Lugo went into the store while the other killers stood around the car outside, taking a smoke. Lugo didn't like them smoking in the car. As he was fond of saying, he didn't mind guns, but cigarettes could kill ya.

Back when they'd reached the motel right off the exit, they had stopped, found nothing. The kid behind the counter had been no help. They drove down the long road toward this town, had stopped at every building that seemed to have people. This little patch of civilization, a series of storefronts, was their third stop out on this road.

When Lugo came out, Duncan let out a sigh and dropped his cigarette to the ground. As he ground it out with his boot heel, the others followed suit.

Lugo was grinning. "The old dude saw a man and a woman. Gave them directions to some church."

Fix chortled. "What, Solo found religion?"

Ritchie spat. "Before sundown, Solo's gonna be seein' God face-to-face." He stepped for the car door and opened it. "He might as well call ahead."

— 107 —

Carla had gone back to the car, wanted to drive back to the motel, see if Tom had called. Without her cell, her only hope of hearing from the outside world was if Tom called.

Behind the wheel of the car, she turned the key. The engine turned over, but the car wouldn't start.

— 108 —

"Have a drink. It's my only quote–unquote weakness." Frank Catalano motioned toward the wine glass in front of Colin Pratt, the son of the out-of-town boss. Catalano, Bones, and Pratt were having dinner in the back dining room of the Poignard. Catalano had been surprised at the sudden appearance of yet a third representative from Chicago, flying in to "clean up this misunderstanding" once and for all.

No misunderstanding, Catalano told Bones before the meeting, except the boys in Chicago seemed to take an awfully quote–unquote high view of themselves.

The younger Pratt sipped from the glass, nodded in appreciation. "You know why I'm here."

Catalano jabbed a fork into his salad, shaking his head vigorously. "I can't imagine," he said, "but we are pleased to welcome an esteemed representative from our friends in Chicago."

Pratt set the glass down, folded his hands. Grim. "We sent two others," he said. "You done wrong by them both."

"I surely do not know what you mean," Catalano said, stone-faced, jabbing again at his salad. "If your boys ran into some unfortunate weather in our fair city, I cannot be held responsible. Quote. Unquote."

Pratt, also stone-faced—two could play this game—sipped again from his wine. Ignored the thugs in each corner of the room. Kept mental tabs of his own man, who he'd left standing by the door to the hall leading to the bar.

He set the glass down. "I will not be tangled up in your web of deceit," he said, checking his temper. "I am here on business for my father. The terms are more than reasonable for all parties involved."

Pratt thought back to Fat Cat's predecessor, Gregor Chak, thought back to the business arrangement between Chak and his father. The two organizations had made a mint on a toll-call scam, ripping off users of psychic lines and dating services to the tune of a hundred and twenty-five million.

"It's a lucrative business," Pratt said in a flat voice. "But you threaten to bring the whole operation down. This opportunity is bigger than any one city. It only works if we pull together."

Catalano ripped a piece of bread off the loaf and sopped up Caesar dressing out of his glass bowl. "As I explained to your associate before he met his unexpected misfortune"—he put the bread in his mouth, chewed, then continued, mouth still full— "we have certain overhead costs that already soak up that money. It is ours, and it will stay ours. Don't get brilliant with me."

Pratt jumped to his feet. "Who do you think you're dealing with?" He motioned around the room, as if for an audience. "Huh?" He leaned forward and slammed his hand on the table. "I am not one of my father's lackeys, Catalano. I will *not* be jerked with."

The thugs around the room tensed up, ready for action. Bones held up his hands, "Boys, boys," he said to no one in particular, "we are all friends here. No need to get tense."

He leaned over to Fat Cat, who was returning Pratt's glare, whispered in the old man's ear, "We kill him, his father will just give up once and for all. Then it's all ours."

Fat Cat, breathing through his nose, nodded once, and Bones gave a signal to his man by the door. With three quick steps he reached Pratt, shoved a gun in his back. Before Pratt's man could react, he was clobbered from behind.

Pratt looked for his opening to bolt, but all his options were blocked. Fat Cat's men were coming out of the wallpaper.

As the thugs led Pratt to his execution, dragging the extra man behind, Fat Cat smiled to Bones. "He shouldn't have tried to get brilliant." He offered Bones a Cuban. "Have a cigar. They're my only quote–unquote weakness."

– 109 –

Griggs was barreling down the interstate. Had stopped off at an exit for gas and caffeine and gotten back on the highway.

He heard chatter on the police band, saw a black car on the side of the interstate pulled off at an awkward angle, like someone had run it off the road. The doors were flopped open like someone had fled or been dragged out.

Griggs debated a second about stopping, saw the flashing lights of black-and-whites arriving at the scene, and decided it was already handled. Kept going.

It never occurred to him to think that federal agents had been left bleeding in the woods.

⌐ 110 ⌐

Carla lit the candles by the altar. During the process, lighting ten, fifteen candles around the area, she heard Solo stomping around in back, upstairs, all over the building. If she hadn't heard his brusque search of the little church, it would never have occurred to her it had so many square feet.

They had started out looking for a light switch, but apparently the place didn't have electricity. Or bulbs. Or phones. Maybe the state had closed the place down, maybe it was abandoned.

She had found matches in a drawer in a room off to the side of the altar, as waning sunlight streamed through the windows. By the time the sun was headed below the horizon, she had lit a good many candles. The effect was creepy, but at least they would still be able to see after the sun had gone down.

By the time he gave up his search of the perimeter, she was sitting on the steps leading to the altar. He sighed and sat next to her, a step higher. He was slouching. She hadn't seen him like that. Like something inside of him had broken.

She thought she would reach out, make a connection. "Who was she?"

"Hmm?" He returned from some far-off place, remembered she was sitting there, shivering as the temperature continued to drop. "Maybe nobody," he said at last, looking away, candlelight bouncing off his glazing eyes. "Maybe my mother."

She wasn't sure what to make of that. "How can you not know?"

"What do you mean?"

"You spend all this time going through the cemetery out there," she nodded toward the front, sticking hands in pockets—it was really getting cold now—"and you don't even know who it was you were looking for out there? Like maybe it was your mom, maybe not? How could you not know?"

"I left home a long time ago," he said in a flat voice. "I never saw her since. This person I was looking for may have been her, with a different name."

He shut his eyes tightly, mumbling to himself. Was he praying?

~ 111 ~

Kansas City, Missouri. The station, abuzz with the news that one of their own had turned traitor, that a cop's wife had been kidnapped and taken across the state line, that Griggs had slipped out on "unofficial business." Calls were being made, orders barked. Detective Robert Utley, head of homicide division, sat at his desk considering the events of the afternoon. He and Griggs had a history—make no mistake, they hated each other's guts—but even he wouldn't have wished the likes of this on Griggs.

A uniformed officer came into Utley's office, had a report in hand. "Detective Utley, sir."

"Yeah?"

"We just got a call about a coin-op laundry downtown. You'll never believe what they saw."

~ 112 ~

Slumping on the steps to the altar, Solo didn't know what to think. Where to go. He had never expected to be at this place, to have the nerve to come this far, but here he was, sitting in a house of God and looking for evidence of a woman who might be his mother.

He remembered the woman sitting next to him, tried to fill the silence. "You ever needed to make something right?"

She blinked at him, unsure of the question. "I don't know."

He glanced up at the candles, flickering, making the shadows dance in the growing darkness. "Like maybe you were so full of...full of *wrong*...that you wanted to find that one good thing that could make it right?"

He looked over at her and saw her staring in the distance. "I don't know how qualified I am to answer that," she whispered. "I mean, I'm sitting here, wondering what happened to my marriage, wondering whether my husband is even going to come, and all I can think is something Hemingway wrote, *Don't we pay for what we do?*"

He watched her feel around her pockets. She stopped, laughing to herself. "Right, I don't have the cell phone."

Solo was mulling over something she'd said.

Something she'd said.

She turned to him, "You think we should walk into town or what?"

He rubbed his head, looking down at his shoes. "What's your hurry?"

"I want to get back to the motel," Carla said innocently. "See whether my husband has tried to call us there."

"Why do you think he might—" He whirled and grabbed her wrist suddenly, dead eyes looking in hers. "What did you do?"

"I called my husband," she said, wishing now she hadn't brought it up. "I called him from the motel. When you were unconscious, sleeping off the bullet wound and all."

"You talked to *him*?" Solo asked, leaning in. "You talked to *only* him? Or did you leave a message?"

She tried a fake smile on him, finally realizing he was trouble in a can. Was this man crazy? Who was this man that she thought she could have trusted him? "I talked to his partner," she said.

He let go of her wrist as suddenly as he'd grabbed it, cursed as he jumped up, pacing down the length of the aisle between pews.

"Why?" Fright rising in her voice. "What's wrong with calling my husband?" He was pacing more furiously now, she was trying desperately to take control of the situation. "He's my husband. He would have been worried, us suddenly leaving like that, leaving behind the house all shot up like that." He seemed to be ignoring her. "Blood on the walls."

He suddenly whirled and came back to her, grabbed her by the shoulders, gripped her tightly. "Listen to me," he said through gritted teeth, "we are in real trouble here."

She nodded nervously. "Okay."

"They will be coming. Here. They will be coming *here*." He stood and looked more cold than she could ever have imagined. "We've got to leave."

They could hear a noise outside, the noise of a car. Out here, this far from the nearest house or store or rest stop. She saw him rush to the window and look out. He looked back at her. "Too late."

~ 113 ~

Albert Holland and Todd Sallis were sitting at the E–Z Laundry, sitting in those uncomfortable molded plastic chairs fastened to little tables. Holland was engrossed in his paperback, the cover rolled up in one hand. He was humming another show tune.

Sallis had already gone through three cigarettes, mostly out of boredom. "Whatcha readin'?"

Holland held the cover out to show him. "That Japanese guy I mentioned, Haruki Murakami. *A Wild Sheep Chase*."

Sallis nodded, didn't really care. "Huh." Glanced at the rows of dryers, wondered how their project was doing. He crushed his cigarette in the ashtray before it was finished, just for something to do, pulled out another and lit it.

He checked his watch. How long had their project been spinning, thumping, spinning in the hot dryer? Holland had shoved a lot of quarters into the slot. Sallis motioned with his head toward the dryer. "You sure this will work?"

Holland looked up from his Murakami, shrugged. "Seems plausible. The heat accelerates cellular decay. Should give the lab guys a false time of death."

Sallis nodded, unsure. Checked his watch. The late crowd would be showing up anytime. "We're taking off soon, right?"

"Sure, sure." Holland had his nose back in his book.

Sallis fumbled with his cigarette again, stopped himself from stubbing it out. Checked his watch again. Glanced again at the dryer. How much longer? "You ever read Shakespeare?"

"I prefer it onstage, but yeah, I like Shakespeare."

"Which kind?"

"What do you mean, which kind?"

"The tragedies, the comedies, what?"

Holland sighed, thinking. "I like the histories, I guess. What was *King Lear?*"

"I think it was a tragedy."

"You know, I was always fascinated with the fact that one of the characters disappeared without explanation."

"When was that?"

"This character, he's all over the first half of the play or so, and then suddenly in the second half he's gone. No explanation. Nobody even mentions him again."

"Sounds like the chauffeur in *The Big Sleep.*"

"Yeah, except there the author literally forgot all about the character."

"Huh."

Sallis heard the doors open and turned, sure he was going to have to tell somebody to scram—a drunk looking for a place to sleep, some battered housewife with a basket of soiled laundry, whatever—and was shocked to see an assortment of cops and plainclothes detectives rushing in, guns poised. One of them shouted, "Freeze!"

The two gunmen jumped, dropping their smoke and book respectively, hands raised. One of the cops in suits, gun in both hands, inched forward. "Don't move, fellas."

Holland mumbled to Sallis, "Got a piece handy?"

Sallis nodded. His heart jumped. His partner couldn't possibly have anything crazy in mind. But Holland smiled grimly and nodded. "You know what Chekhov says."

Sallis, mouth dry, nodded back. Holding his breath, hands up, he glanced at the cops, their guns pointed at his heart.

Out of the corner of his eye, he saw Holland reaching for his gun. Sallis couldn't believe he was doing the same.

The two got off only a couple wild shots before they were cut down in a hail of gunfire.

As the two men lay in a pool of blood, Detective Robert Utley and a second man went to the dryer, popped open the door. A wicked stench rolling out in a hot blast of air. The drum slowing to a stop. While the second detective ran to vomit, Utley made a face and turned to the uniformed officers. "Well, now we know what happened to Colin Pratt."

~ 114 ~

Griggs squinted in the dark, had taken the exit, had stopped in at the motel. Had talked with the person behind the counter, an older woman, who had no information for him. He had flashed a badge, but she didn't know which room to point him toward. He showed her the slip of paper, she said it was certainly the number for one of their rooms there.

In fact, yes, this phone number would connect directly with that particular room. Here's the key, Officer, I don't want trouble.

Griggs had impatiently stridden across the parking lot, across the sidewalk, counting rooms until he found the right place. Knocked loudly, yelled for Carla, had pulled his gun, gripped it firmly in one hand, had carefully tried the key in the lock. Had entered the room, found it dark, found it empty. He flipped on every light he could find, pulled open all the drawers, looked for evidence his wife had been there, evidence to discover the identity of her companion.

He sat on the corner of one bed—fell was more like it—had to think. Where would she be? Why wouldn't she be here at the room?

Had they gone on, gotten back on the interstate? Headed south maybe, Florida, Mexico, South America?

Where are you, Carla? He was still boiling, surprised to find he still held onto his anger toward her. Still clung tightly to unforgiveness. This was not about saving her for her sake, this was about proving a point.

— 115 —

The room was dark, the air thick with danger. Dr. Bones in the chair, sitting in a halo of light in the garage. Waiting. Men standing around, impending doom. A man was ushered in from the outside, Bones heard the bell at the door, heard ordered footsteps approach, saw Chicago boss Joey Pratt step out of the shadows and into the circle of light.

Pratt calmly took the chair across from Bones, thugs and killers circling, arms folded. Pratt sat back in the chair, crossed his legs. "So, Earl," he began, adjusting his moustache, "maybe you and me should have a heart-to-heart."

Bones sucked in a breath, licked his lips. This was going to have to be the story of his life.

— 116 —

Solo had found the pews harder to turn over than expected. Must have been bolted to the floor. As it was, one of the wooden pews now stretched across the main doors, hopefully blocking them, but he didn't know how sturdily.

It had been a bear trying to kick over the pew. Even after several kicks, after he finally heard the wood split at the base where it was bolted, he had to wobble it, rock it, until it finally went over. Dragging it to the back of the sanctuary was more trouble.

Behind him, the woman was in a side room digging through drawers for sharp objects. Was instructed to slink into the farthest corner with her sharp objects and wait out the fire and brimstone.

He looked at the one, lone pew blocking the doors. He had to think of something, quick. Because it only took one look out the window to know what kind of men were exiting that car.

This would be like shooting fish in a barrel. And Solo was the fish.

— 117 —

Fix, Lugo, Nardo, Duncan, Ritchie. Exiting the car, guns in hand. They had seen the flicker of light in the little church as Lugo had pulled up. Had seen Holland's Lumina parked off to the side.

Lugo leaned against the car door, thumbing toward the church up the muddy hill, asking Ritchie, "What do you think?"

"Ah, it'll be easy," Ritchie answered, gleam in his eye, fiddling with shells in his coat pocket. "Like those Feds back there."

"*Callate,*" Nardo said in a harsh whisper. "Killing is never an easy thing."

As they pulled weapons from the trunk, they heard a racket from inside, someone banging around. But no one was shooting at them, they couldn't see any heads in the windows, so they confidently marched toward the little church, pumping shotguns.

– 118 –

Solo felt a shudder go through him. That preacher man had done a number on him back in Kansas City, had turned his whole life, his whole career, upside down.

Now there were five or six men coming to kill him and the woman. Normally, the odds would be deadly but doable. But "normally" meant Solo could still plunge a screwdriver into a man's eye and not think twice about it.

But now, Solo felt the pistol in his hand, felt his hands shake. These were the worst odds of all. A killer who can't kill.

But he had to. Had to.

He heard a cannon outside and then the doors splintering, shards of wood and glass flying through the sanctuary. He couldn't see it from his vantage point, didn't know how many were coming in. Maybe they were surrounding the place. Of course, they probably didn't expect much of a fight, six against two, out here in the middle of a cow patch like this. Maybe they were all at the main doors.

He heard several footsteps on the wood, overlapping so he couldn't make a count. He suddenly became aware of his musky odor. He tried to ignore the thought that he hadn't showered in too long.

He heard one of them say, "Check the pews. I'll check up front."

Solo took that as his cue to slip out the side door.

— 119 —

Griggs had gotten directions from someone at the truck stop, which led him to a store in the tiny town. It was a hole in the ground, really, what Griggs' dad would have called "a one-horse town where the horse had died." At the store, the man at the counter expressed surprise when he had asked about Carla and the man she was with, when Griggs had presented a photo.

The man had pulled off his cap and scratched his head. "They were here not more than an hour, couple of hours ago," he said. "Were asking about some woman who used to live around here. I sent them up to the old church."

Griggs nodded, trying to stay calm, professional, look official. "Did the woman seem all right to you?"

"I don't know what—"

Griggs cut him off. "Did she seem to be in any sort of distress? As if she were worried, perhaps upset?"

The man stared at the counter a second, then shook his head as he looked up. "Not as I can remember. They in trouble or something?"

Griggs wasn't sure the best way to answer that. "Not necessarily—"

"Because you're the second to ask me about them since they came through."

Griggs heart stopped, but he kept going. A group of men had just been by not a few minutes earlier and asked about them. The man had also pointed them in the direction of the old church.

The man didn't know who the others had been, had not been presented with any ID. There was never any trouble in Priest Pointe, so it never occurred to him there might be a problem.

The man had given Griggs the same directions. Griggs knew his cell wasn't working this far out in the sticks, so he gave the man instructions to call the Kansas City field office of the FBI and ask for Special Agent O'Malley.

As Griggs sped down the lonely road, he tried to hold onto the hope that the men who had asked about Carla were the FBI agents O'Malley had mentioned.

Please be the Feds, please be the Feds.

━ 120 ━

From outside the building, Solo peeked in the window, saw two of them, a Hispanic and a scary guy with an eye patch. Eye-patch guy was looking up toward the balcony, looking for stairs or a ladder. The Hispanic, moving slowly, headed toward the podium at the front.

Solo crouched and held his breath, listening. Not hearing anyone nearby, he stealthed around the corner, headed for the car they had stolen back in Missouri. If it belonged to a made guy, it probably had supplies in the trunk. Solo mentally kicked himself for not having checked sooner.

Reaching the car, he stayed low, peeking from all angles to make sure no one could see him in the moonlight, then went around to the passenger side. Fortunately, he had left his window down. The woman had been cold, had griped, but this meant he could enter the car without tripping the inside light.

He crawled in, cursing his wound as he twisted through the window, then he clung deep to the seats, the awkward features of the cockpit stabbing him. He reached around the steering wheel, found the keys, and pulled them out. Then, twisting to sit slouched in his passenger seat, he waited again, holding his breath.

He couldn't hear anybody, so he risked opening the door. He was sure crawling through again would kill him.

The interior light burst on. He ducked out of the car and slammed the door harder than he meant. He heard shouting and footsteps crunching snow in his direction.

Stupid, Solo, stupid, stupid, stupid.

— — —

Joe Fix saw the light, heard the door, ran for it shouting for Lugo, the Hungarian. He had his shotgun out, pumped and ready to fire, had seen the silvery moonlit outline of somebody ducking toward the back, was circling around the rear of the car.

This was going to be a turkey shoot. Fix nearly chuckled with glee, popping Sudafeds, when he heard something behind him and turned to speak to Lugo.

It wasn't Lugo.

The night was alive with fire, BLAM, BLAM, BLAM. Fix dropped his shotgun and collapsed to the ground.

— — —

Inside, the tall one with the eye patch, Duncan, had climbed to the top of the stairs, the balcony. He was sweeping the perimeter with his shotgun when he heard shouting outside, heard shots. His first instinct was to run to the window or to run outside and see what had happened, but he stopped himself.

Knew that was how simpler men died, rushing to do the first thing that came to mind.

Downstairs, Lugo yelled up, "Hey! I'll check that out!"

Let the man check, Duncan thought, *I'm not making any sudden moves.* In this sacred place, under the sign of the cross, the shadows seemed alive.

— — —

Griggs, driving up the empty road, heard the gunfire ahead and cut the headlights, attempting to follow the line by moonlight. He could make out the little building, white on the top of the hill. He stopped the car and, without bothering to switch it off, tumbled out the driver's side door, a pistol in each hand.

— — —

Solo, watching the front corner of the church again, back to the wall, had a clear shot at the two guys dallying by the body of the guy he'd shot. But in the dark, Solo wasn't sure how well-stocked he was at this point. He had grabbed the man's shotgun but couldn't tell in this light whether it was locked and loaded.

After the two guys had conferred a moment, backed away, then turned toward the church, Solo risked going back to open the trunk of the car.

— — —

Griggs saw movement in the flickering light from the windows of the church. It looked like they were moving about by candlelight. He had no idea who or what was out here, couldn't just start shooting away. The terrain was slick and muddy, although it was hardening in the cold. Griggs kept his pace low, slow, methodical.

— — —

Ritchie stepped down the stairs into what looked like a cellar. In the dim light, he had no idea whether he was stepping into a storm cellar, a wine cellar, or what he thought they called a "ruckus" room.

Testing each step before he took the next, he reached the bottom and tried feeling about for a light switch. No good. He didn't know whether the man and woman they were hunting had shut off the power or blown the fuses or what.

He stopped and held his breath. All he could hear was a dripping, off somewhere down here. He was afraid to step farther into the blackness, so he turned for the stairs to get a candle.

He had reached the third step from the bottom when there was a sudden, sharp pain in his ankles. He yelped and fell back. He tumbled over some object at the bottom of the stairs and dropped the shotgun, which clattered off into nothingness.

He struggled to regain his bearings. Squinting, he saw a slight figure racing up the stairs. He yelled as he saw the door close, heard a lock sliding. He was trapped in pitch black.

— — —

On the way back to the car, Solo dropped the keys. He picked the jumble off the ground, couldn't figure out in the moonlight which would open the trunk. He cursed under his breath and decided he would make do with what he had left.

He looked around again, saw a figure to his left moving in shadow, so he slunk down beside the car and waited for it to pass. Then he went toward the opposite side of the church, ducked by a window.

— — —

Griggs crept past one of the cars parked at the bottom of the hill, saw one man dead on the ground, had no way of knowing how he fit into this. Careful to avoid the patrol circling the church, he reached the tree in front and leaned hard into it, hoping it hid him from whoever was out here.

— — —

Duncan was done checking from the balcony, there wasn't much to see. He knelt by the railing overlooking the sanctuary and propped his shotgun against the wood. He remembered deer-hunting with his uncle, waiting up in the tree for hours on end, barely breathing, barely moving, until the unsuspecting prey had nonchalantly walked into the sights of his rifle.

Duncan knew this would be his perch. He could wait. Let the others circle, do their noise and their tromping.

He would wait.

— — —

Lugo re-entered the church, was going to resume checking the sanctuary. "Hey, Mr. Patches!" he called, didn't know the man's actual name, never bothered to learn it, but there was no answer. *Fine,* Lugo thought, *I'll do the man's job and check this place.*

After what had happened outside, Lugo had his shotgun ready, kept light on his feet, ready to turn, ready to jump, whatever it took to stay alive and make the other guy dead.

Then he heard a crash at the window behind him and whirled and before he could fire, the barrels of a shotgun were already there, BLAM, got him dead in the chest.

~ ~ ~

Outside, Manzano heard the noise and thought to run in, but decided to think through his options. Dark, lonely place, somebody running around with a gun, hiding in the shadows.

Maybe hiding in the shadows right here—

A stone voice said, "Don't move." He felt the barrel of a gun tap the back of his head.

If this guy wasn't going to kill him dead, he wasn't going to be a problem. Manzano whirled, bringing the shotgun up—

He heard the pop and then he was gone.

~ 121 ~

Ritchie. In the darkness, groping for his shotgun. The concrete floor felt cold and damp. He crawled slowly, meticulously. Careful for sharp corners at eye level. Mulling over ways he was gonna hurt whoever stabbed his ankle and left him locked down here, flashes of hate driving him, making him squeeze his eyes shut until he saw spots floating in the dark.

As he crawled, slowly, he tested his left ankle, twisted it around. It hurt, but it still seemed to work. Whatever the little ferret had stabbed him with, it must have broken skin. His sock felt damp—blood?

He sat in the black and tried to fold his legs Indian style. Felt around for his ankle.

Yes, the sock was wet. Hurt to touch. He felt around tenderly, couldn't find any foreign object sticking in him.

Ritchie sucked in his breath, anger welling up again, and set about finding his shotgun in the darkness.

He was going to enjoy killing whoever'd stabbed him.

— — —

Carla. Huddled in the darkest corner of the kitchen, panicking, afraid she was breathing too loud. Clutching the bloody scissors to her chest, she worked at slowing her breathing down…softly, more softly.

She felt dizzy now. She shut her eyes tightly, seeing stars. *Breathe, Carla, breathe.*

— — —

Solo. After risking the shotgun blast through the window, he had ducked back into darkness outside the church. He had heard a dull thump, had not waited to see whether his man was winged or dead. If he had stuck around with his face in the glass, the window frame would have provided a perfect set of crosshairs for some trigger-happy thug.

Right after he had let loose with both barrels and ducked, he heard more shooting from around front. Sounded like a pistol.

But the killers were all packing shotguns. Was it the woman? Had she found a pistol in one of the kitchen cabinets? Solo had his doubts.

In the moonlight, he popped in two more shells, taken off the dead guy. He had five left. Once he was sure he was in the clear, he crept along the side of the building. He found a narrow hole under the back porch and crawled in.

～ ～ ～

Griggs. On the front porch, back to the wall, to the left of the damaged front doors. He still had two pistols, one in each hand. One man dead a few yards away, one man presumed dead down the hill by the car. How many more were there? What was really going on here?

When were those Feds coming?

～ ～ ～

Duncan. Balcony, shotgun propped by his side, against the railing. Waiting.

～ ～ ～

Ritchie, shotgun in hand, had stumbled his way to the top of the stairs. Pressed hard against the door, didn't think he could get the leverage to really whump against it without losing his balance and falling back down the stairs.

He braced himself, right foot on the top step, left foot a few steps lower, leaning forward, took the shotgun and smashed the butt against the door, testing in the dark for a knob or latch. He heaved against it three times before he heard the sound of splintering—one more and the door swung open. Dim candlelight blew in, feeding his hungry eyes like happy sunlight.

He grinned and stepped into the kitchen. Now to kill somebody.

— — —

Carla had crawled, crouched, slouched, sneaked from doorway to doorway, moving target, had ended up in what looked like an office, books lining shadowy walls. Moonlight struck through the window, hit a desk covered with a blotter.

She briefly wondered who had been here, why the place had been locked up. Was this still a working church? Would someone come by in the morning and find the evidence of the fight here?

Would someone come in the morning and find her body?

— — —

Solo had found a trapdoor, had pushed through and found himself behind the podium area. Stinking of rotting leaves and compost, he ducked through a door off to the side and found himself in a hall. He heard noises to the left, muffled noises of thumping, smashing, before he heard metal and wood break and a door slam open against a wall. He was still in the hall, a sitting duck if someone should come in here.

Sitting on his heels, his back against the wall, saw a door with a men's room sign on it, reached up for the knob and opened it. Snuck inside.

— — —

Griggs, focusing a moment on controlled breathing, mentally counted to three and then whirled and faced the door, both guns held out in true cowboy style. *I'm the law around here, boys, don't want none of your cattle rustling around here.*

There was the sound of a smashing, a thumping, in a room out of sight. Griggs' eyes locked on a hallway up by the front. Someone was up there, wreaking havoc.

— — —

Solo, cursing mentally because the floor was sticky. Crouching in the dark, he had lost his balance, touched his hand to the floor. Had dropped the shotgun.

Hoping nobody had heard.

— — —

Ritchie, rage coursing through him, burst through the kitchen and into the hallway. He thought he heard something out here. If it was that ferret with the knife, he would—

What was that? A noise? Inside that door, halfway down the hall. A sign on it labeled MEN'S ROOM.

— ⁓ —

Duncan, sitting forward, watching down through wooden slats. Hand on the shotgun. Someone was making a ruckus up front.

Fine, he told himself. He had the time.

— ⁓ —

Griggs saw a figure, a shadow moving, had ducked behind the door to peek as a man brandishing a shotgun moved from a room off the side of the podium and slipped into the hallway.

— ⁓ —

Ritchie stomped down the hall, hornets buzzing in his mind.

He was done jim-dawdling. He walked right up to that men's room door, yanked it open, swinging the shotgun around and catching the man on the floor off guard. Narrowed his eyes and growled, "Don't even think it."

Long, breathless moments passed before Ritchie motioned with his shotgun for the man to stand up. The man raised his hands.

Ritchie didn't want just one of them, he wanted both of them. He stepped back and nodded his head toward the sanctuary, down the hall. "Walk slow."

∼ ∼ ∼

Griggs held his breath, heard a man barking down the hall, heard footsteps coming toward the sanctuary. A hostage?

Carla?

He flexed his grip on the guns. *Keep it together, Tom. Stay focused.*

∼ ∼ ∼

Solo, hands on head, mentally kicking himself for getting caught like that. Lucky he hadn't gotten his head blown clean off. Wasn't sure why he hadn't.

He had left the shotgun in the bathroom back there. But this greasy doodle didn't know Solo had an ace in his coat pocket.

He reached the sanctuary, the doodle tromping behind him, clearing his voice, preparing to announce something, when a new figure jumped from the front doorway, two-fisted justice, "Stop right there!"

Solo leaped forward, hitting the floor as the doodle bellowed and brought his shotgun round, even got off a wild blast but got ONE, TWO, THREE, FOUR shots square in the chest and crumpled over the front pew.

Solo, on the floor, fumbling in his pockets, *no, that isn't the gun,* got his hand on the pistol, pulled it out. Saw a shadow moving above, beyond the newcomer, in the balcony, pulled his gun around—

— — —

Griggs saw the two strangers, one with a face in the shadows, hands on his head, another one, Ritchie Catalano, clearing his throat like he was about to announce something. Griggs jumped in the door, holding both weapons out. "Stop right there!"

The first man dove for the floor, Ritchie bellowed and brought his shotgun around firing wild, but not before Griggs let fly with two-fisted justice, BLAM, BLAM, BLAM, BLAM, and Ritchie Catalano fell over a pew.

Griggs let out a breath, lowered the guns wearily, started walking over to the man on the floor. Trying to think what to say. Suddenly realized the man was drawing a weapon, turning right toward him, aiming up toward his head, firing off a round and Griggs flinched, fired twice into the man, BLAM, BLAM, and the man dropped the gun to the floor.

Griggs heard a noise behind him, high, turned and looked up and realized there had been a man up in the balcony. A man who now dropped his shotgun over the wooden rail and followed, hitting the wooden floor below with a dead thump.

The stranger wasn't aiming at me. He was saving my life.

— — —

Carla, huddled in the office, rocking, holding her knees close, crying silently. A series of crashes and explosions, a man yelling. *Was that Tom?*

— — —

Griggs knelt by the man, cradled his head, wiped blood off the man's lip. "I-I'm sorry," he whispered hoarsely, "I didn't know."

The man was groggy, moving slowly, reaching into his coat pocket, fumbling around for something. He pulled something out, a book. *A man is dying and he wants his book?*

Griggs was dimly aware of the sound of sirens approaching from the distance.

The dying man locked eyes with him, eyes that were clouding, locked his gaze on Griggs and pressed the book into Griggs' hand. He worked his lips a bit before he croaked out in a harsh whisper, "I...forgive you."

And then the man slumped. And he was gone.

The sirens were close.

⁓ 122 ⁓

Late morning in Kansas City, Missouri, Frank Catalano and Judge Hapsburg Reynolds talking in the penthouse office, Catalano encircled by his best and most trusted men. Catalano was saying, "I don't get how this could happen." Reynolds was saying, "You made your choices, Frank. You set these things in motion."

The men surrounding Catalano, his inner circle, holding an emergency meeting to try and stabilize the operation. Catalano pulled a cigar from his coat pocket and bit it nervously. He didn't have time for this. He had a campaign to wage.

Frankie had tried to go to the cops and got whacked. Nobody knew where Ritchie had gone. Lousy kids, he had trusted his own sons, his own flesh and blood with the family business, and in a matter of days the whole operation was falling apart, two sons dead and one missing, shooting in the streets, kidnapping, out-of-towners making a scene at the bus depot of all places, a lot of sloppy business.

Catalano shifted from left to right foot in the center of the circle, turning, looking from eye to eye, Judge Reynolds, Earl "Dr. Bones" Havoc, the others. These were the men he should have trusted. "Boys, you been with us a long time," he smiled a weary smile, lighting the cigar and taking some starter puffs. "Some guys out there have tried to get brilliant," he said. "But we can rebuild this."

"Sure, Frank," Bones was saying, "whatever you say."

There was a commotion out in the hall, someone barging past the men guarding by the elevator. All eyes turned toward the door, but only Catalano was surprised to see boss Joey Pratt stroll in, here all the way from Chicago, flanked by a couple of his guys. From this angle, Catalano couldn't see his own guards out in the hall, slumped to the floor.

Catalano chuckled, hiding nervousness, "Hey, Mr. Pratt, welcome." Puff on the cigar. *Cool, keep it cool.* "All the way from Chicago." Another puff, then holding arms wide. "To what do we owe the quote–unquote treasure?"

Judge Reynolds rolled his eyes. How could he have ever thrown in with this idiot?

Pratt didn't mince words. "I'm disappointed, Fat Cat." As Catalano bit his tongue, Pratt casually strolled across the room to Catalano's desk, swiveled the captain's chair and sat. "Very disappointed."

Catalano licked his lips. "You'll have to come back later, Joey," he said, drawing confidence from his superior position. Here in his own den, surrounded by his trusted lions. And this out-of-towner pulls this stuff here? "We're in the middle of something."

"No, I think you're done." Boss Pratt leaned back and propped his feet on Catalano's desk.

Catalano growled as he stepped toward the desk, "Where do you get the—"

He stopped, a sharp pain in his back. He instinctively reached back, brought back his hand with blood on it. He looked up, realized he was encircled with stone faces, men he knew and trusted, had known for years, wearing stone faces and clutching knives. Who carries knives anymore?

Catalano whirled. Saw blood drizzling off the knife in Bones' grip. "Earl," Catalano rasped, mouth dry, "you of all people?"

He heard a low, dark laugh coming from his desk. He heard Pratt say, "Finish it."

Catalano fell to the floor, the weight of betrayal crashing in on him, sharp pains in his arms, back, shoulders. He tasted blood but could not find the strength to scream before he slumped completely to the floor.

And then everything went black.

He couldn't make out what the others were saying, congregating over his body, his life slipping away, he couldn't hear the Feds rushing in and arresting the lot for murder, his life slipping away, he wasn't aware when the paramedics arrived, too late to stop the bleeding, his life slipping away.

And then Frank Catalano was gone.

~ Two Weeks Later ~

"Hate cannot drive out hate; only love can do that."
—MARTIN LUTHER KING JR.

~ ~ ~

"Let him that would move the world,
first move himself."
—SOCRATES

~ 123 ~

"I'm not sure about this." Jordan, flashing a nervous smile.

"C'mon, it'll be fine." Charlie, a little wobbly on his feet, but improving. Leading her up the sidewalk, reaching for the handle on the glass door. "You'll love it."

He held the door, motioned like an usher for her to enter before him, always the gentleman. She laughed, a cute little laugh that made Charlie's heart melt. Like it was the best laugh in the world.

Following her inside, Charlie made a grand gesture. "Well, here it is."

She looked around them, smiling tentatively. So this was a comic-book store.

~ 124 ~

The Griggs home. Windows boarded up. Strands of yellow police tape blocking off sections of the house and yard that needed repair.

Carla answering the door, thinking it's sweet he rang the bell first.

Tom, box in hand, meeting her eyes with a sheepish grin.

The two of them entering their home together.

A start.

Turn your eyes upon Jesus;
Look full in His wonderful face;
And the things of earth will grow strangely dim
In the light of His glory and grace.

An award-winning writer and editor, **Chris Well** has spent the past twenty years as editor and writer for a variety of magazines and newspapers. He wrote the radio-drama series *Mammoth City Messengers* and serves as managing editor of *Homecoming* magazine and contributing editor to *CCM* magazine. *Forgiving Solomon Long* is his first novel.

THE CHAMBERS OF JUSTICE SERIES
by Craig Parshall

The Resurrection File

When Reverend Angus MacCameron asks attorney Will Chambers to defend him against accusations that could discredit the Gospels, Will's unbelieving heart says "run." But conspiracy and intrigue—and the presence of MacCameron's lovely and successful daughter, Fiona—draw him deep into the case toward a destination he could never have imagined.

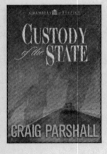

Custody of the State

Attorney Will Chambers reluctantly agrees to defend a young mother from Georgia and her farmer husband, suspected of committing the unthinkable against their own child. Encountering small-town secrets, big-time corruption, and a government system that's destroying the little family, Chambers himself is thrown into the custody of the state.

The Accused

Enjoying a Cancún honeymoon with his wife, Fiona, attorney Will Chambers is ambushed by two unexpected events: a terrorist kidnapping of a U.S. official...and the news that a link has been found to the previously unidentified murderer of Will's first wife. The kidnapping pulls him into the case of Marine colonel Caleb Marlowe. When treachery drags both Will and his client toward vengeance, they must ask—*Is forgiveness real?*

Missing Witness

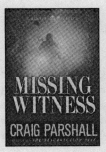

A relaxing North Carolina vacation for attorney Will Chambers? Not likely. When Will investigates a local inheritance case, the long arm of the law reaches out of the distant past to cast a shadow over his client's life and the life of his own family. As the attorney's legal battle uncovers corruption, piracy, the deadly grip of greed, and the haunting sins of a man's past, the true question must be faced—*Can a person ever really run away from God?*

The Last Judgment

Happily married and with a young son, the last thing attorney Will Chambers wants on his hands is a religious apocalypse. But his client, self-styled prophet Gilead Amahn, is accused of having incited a terrorist cult to bomb the top of Jerusalem's Temple Mount into rubble. Now the lawyer must uncover both the evidence and the key truth about his client's "mission." And further, Will must also make a final judgment about his role as a husband, a father...and a man.

THE MILLION DOLLAR MYSTERIES
Mindy Starns Clark

Attorney Callie Webber investigates nonprofit organizations for the J.O.S.H.U.A. Foundation, giving the best of them grants ranging up to a million dollars. In each book, Callie comes across a mystery she must solve using her skills as a former private investigator. A young widow, Callie finds strength in her faith in God and joy in her relationship with her employer, Tom.

A Penny for Your Thoughts

Just like that, Callie finds herself looking into the sudden death of an old family friend of her employer. But it seems the family has some secrets they would rather not have uncovered. Almost immediately Callie realizes she has put herself in serious danger. Her only hope is that God will use her investigative skills to discover the identity of the killer before she becomes the next victim.

Don't Take Any Wooden Nickels

Just like that, Callie finds herself helping a young woman coming out of drug rehab and into the workforce who's suddenly charged with murder. What appears to be routine, though, explodes into international intrigue and deadly deception. A series of heartpounding evens lands her disastrously in the hands of the killer, where Callie finds she has less than a moment for a whispered prayer. Will help arrive in time to save her?

A Dime a Dozen

Just like that, Callie finds herself involved in the life of a young wife and mother whose husband has disappeared. But in the search for him, a body is discovered, which puts Callie's job on hold and her new romance with her mysterious boss in peril. Trusting in God, she forges steadily ahead through a mire of clues that lead her deeper and deeper into danger.

A Quarter for a Kiss

Just like that, Callie finds herself on her way to the beautiful Virgin Islands. Her friend and mentor, Eli Gold, has been shot. This unusual—and very dangerous—assignment sends Callie and her boss, Tom, on an adventure together to solve the mystery surrounding the shooting. Though Callie's faith in God is sure, will her faith in Tom survive their visit to the island of St. John?

The Buck Stops Here

Just like that, Callie finds herself in the middle of an intense investigation of a millionaire philanthropist and NSA agent—Tom Bennett, her boss and the man she hopes to marry. When Callie overhears a conversation in which her boss implicates himself in her late husband's fatal accident, Tom's association with the NSA prevents him from answering her questions. But she must have answers. With God's help she embarks on an investigation that leads to a conclusion beyond her wildest dreams.

Harvest House Publishers
Fiction for Every Taste and Interest

Phil Callaway
Growing Up on the Edge of
the World

Linda Chaikin
Desert Rose
Desert Star

Mindy Starns Clark
THE MILLION DOLLAR
MYSTERIES SERIES
A Penny for Your Thoughts
Don't Take Any Wooden Nickels
A Dime a Dozen
A Quarter for a Kiss
The Buck Stops Here

Roxanne Henke
COMING HOME TO
BREWSTER SERIES
After Anne
Finding Ruth
Becoming Olivia
Always Jan

Melanie Jeschke
Inklings
Expectations

Sally John
THE OTHER WAY HOME SERIES
A Journey by Chance
After All These Years
Just to See You Smile
The Winding Road Home

IN A HEARTBEAT SERIES
In a Heartbeat
Flash Point
Moment of Truth

Susan Meissner
Why the Sky Is Blue
A Window to the World

Craig Parshall
CHAMBERS OF JUSTICE SERIES
The Resurrection File
Custody of the State
The Accused
Missing Witness
The Last Judgement

Raymond Reid
The Gate Seldom Found

Debra White Smith
THE AUSTEN SERIES
First Impressions
Reason and Romance

Lori Wick
THE TUDOR MILLS TRILOGY
Moonlight on the Millpond

THE ENGLISH GARDEN SERIES
The Proposal   The Visitor
The Rescue   The Pursuit

THE YELLOW ROSE TRILOGY
Every Little Thing About You
A Texas Sky
City Girl

CONTEMPORARY FICTION
Bamboo & Lace
Beyond the Picket Fence
Every Storm
Pretense
The Princess
Sophie's Heart